Also by Langdon Pierce

Heaven Bend Down

Pillars of Heaven

Hope of Heaven

Moultrie

The Salt Horses

The Benteen Brand

Weapon of Choice

Mrs. Dennison

Sam Dollar and the Santa Rita Rose

The LONG WAY HOME

a novel by
LANGDON PIERCE

This is a work of fiction. Names, characters, places and incidents are either the product of the author's imagination or are used fictitiously.

Copyright © 2018 Langdon Pierce

All rights reserved. No part of this book may be reproduced or used in any manner without written permission of the copyright owner except for the use of quotations in a book review.

Book Design by Emy Peterson

ISBN: 978-1-7287-4564-0

Published by Red Canyon Press

"And Ruth said, Entreat me not to leave thee,

or to return from following after thee:

for whither thou goest, I will go;

and where thou lodgest, I will lodge:

thy people shall be my people,

And thy God my God"

King James Version (KJV)

Prologue

S TEPPING DOWN FROM THE TRAIN, a thickset man halted and looked about him. He was six foot tall with gray starting at the temples of his thick brown hair. Whether it was his clothing, not quite of the style of the times or the way he held his head upright, as if sniffing the tenor of the place, he caught the eye of more than one woman as she walked by. Yet, none stopped or spoke as they bustled to the station with the crowd, but he continued to linger.

About him, the small Midwestern city looked like many others. White clapboard walls greeted the eye as far as one could see. Over the roof tops, elm trees lined streets while horse drawn buggies and wagons filled the area before the station. A steeple pointed skyward at the end of the street to his left, and another at the end of the street to his right. Satisfied with what he saw, he turned and walked toward the town.

As he walked past a group of men standing outside the building smoking their cigars, one of them looked up and nudged another. He narrowed his eyes as he watched the man stride by them, nodded, then turned and walked rapidly down the street.

A bell chimed as he walked into the Sheriff's office.

"Hello, Hopkins," Sheriff Wynn Tucker greeted him. His gaze slid to the closing door. "Who's been chasing you?" The man had been considered handsome in his younger years, but was grown heavy in his office, his beard hiding a sagging jawline.

Though his tone was sarcastic, Hopkins paid no attention. "Frank

Pascoe is in town."

The words brought Tucker's attention back on him.

"The hell you say," the sheriff got up from his chair and walked to the window. "I thought he was dead."

"So did we all."

Tucker looked up and down the street.

"You think he'll head to Cecilia's? I mean, Mrs. Sinclair's?"

"Why else do you think he's in town?"

Hopkins had followed him to the window, then moved to the door and put his hand on the knob.

"I don't know why. But, I know I don't like it."

Tucker glanced dourly at the other man. "You don't have anything to worry about. His wife didn't marry you!"

"Nor you!" Hopkins jerked open the door. "My wife sets store by Cecilia. I wouldn't want anything to happen to her."

The sheriff nodded and added softly, "And, my daughter sets store by Cecilia's son." He frowned. "You're sure it was Pascoe?"

"Older, grayer." Hopkins assured him. "Bartram pointed him out, first."

Tucker nodded. "Keep me posted."

Walking into the Springfield Mercantile and Grocer, Frank slipped off his hat and looked around. Though proprietor Mr. Tam Osgood's name was on the sign outside, it was apparent that he merely oversaw the other clerks from the comfort of his rocker, toward which he was heading.

II *Langdon Pierce*

"Hello, Mr. Osgood," Frank said, softly.

Osgood was beginning to sit down, but stiffened in surprise. "Frank! Frank Pascoe!" He walked forward, his hand outstretched. "It's been a few years, but you haven't changed!"

Frank's lips stretched into a slight smile as he shook it. "Neither have you."

The shopkeeper glanced at the chair behind him. "I'd like to think so, but my rheumatism tells me different." He waved to the rocking chair beside his. "Have a seat! Tell me how you been!"

"I'd like to, Mr. Osgood," but he hesitated.

"Tam," was the reply. "You're old enough now to call me by my first name." He looked Frank up and down. "I always thought they mistreated you. Gave you a hard way to go."

"That's all over and done with." Frank assured him. "I'm just lookin' for Cecilia. I thought she might be at her mother's."

Osgood shook his head, frowning. "No. No, she isn't there." He gripped the arms of the rocker. "Once Marge Mansbach felt like she'd done all the damage she could do, she passed on."

"Are you alright, Father?" A young woman came up to him, a curious gaze on Frank. "We can hear you all over the store."

"Annabelle, this is Frank Pascoe, a past resident here. Springfield treated him shamefully, shamefully, I say. Did everything but run him out of town!" He slapped the arms of the rocker.

"Father! You must be quiet!"

Frank nodded to her. "A pleasure to meet you, ma'am."

The young woman looked down, coloring a little. "I'm a miss. And, the pleasure is all mine, I'm sure." Her gaze locked with her father's. "Quiet please, Father!"

Osgood waved her off, then motioned to Frank. "You sowed your oats when you were young. Like the rest of us. But, when you married Cecilia, you settled into harness like you'd always been there." He shook his head. "They just wouldn't leave you alone."

Standing before him, Frank smiled his small smile. "I've nothing against Springfield. What's done is done." He bent forward to put his hand on the man's frail arm. "Where is Cecilia?"

Osgood looked up at him and sighed. "Number twelve. Pleasant Street."

When Frank didn't move immediately, he raised his head. "She thought you dead, thanks to that no-good mother of hers!" Then, he quickly added, "God rest her soul!"

Frank smiled a little. "Indeed. Mrs. Mansbach had a soul. Heard about it all the time."

The older man's eyes clouded. "She's married again, Frank. Cecilia. To Gerard Sinclair."

For a moment, all was silent. As if the clerks and the customers all happened to pause at the same time. From the street, there was no sound.

Then, Frank nodded. "Thank you, Mr. Osgood." He patted the man's arm again, then slowly turned to walk out of the store.

"I'm sorry!" Osgood called to his departing back. "By dam', I'm sorry," and he pounded his fist on the arm of the rocker for emphasis.

Perhaps Pascoe's feet moved a little slower with the realization that his wife had thought him dead and remarried. If so, none seemed to note it. With his shoulders back and his chin up, like they had once been at Vicksburg marching with Grant, he made his way to Pleasant Street. Number Twelve.

The house was two storied, painted white like most of the others.

Wooden siding ran up the sides, clear to the eaves. A circular room capped with a metal turreted roof, complete with a flag on top, jutted onto the front porch. Almost the whole front of the house was lined with windows, even the turret.

Frank walked across the porch, noting its cleanliness, and knocked on the front door. When he turned, waiting for an answer, he noted the man on the sidewalk who hurried past. Had he seen him at the train station as well?

He might have spoken, but was halted by the door behind him opening. As it swung wide, he noted the burnished floors, heavy, brocade curtains at the windows, and the smell of dinner cooking. It was with some surprise that he realized he had to look down to meet his greeter.

"Hello," said the young girl. "Can I help you?"

Frank swept off his hat. "I was hoping to speak to your mother."

"Who are you?" The girl had Cecilia's direct way about her, as well as blue eyes that hid her thoughts.

"My name is Frank Pascoe."

"Who is it, Abigail? A woman's voice came from the interior of the house.

Frank gave a slight smile in response. "Would you ask her?"

Before the little girl could turn around, her mother had come up to the door. She stopped, stunned for a moment.

"Hello, Cecilia."

Her hand went to her throat and she stared at him. "Frank!"

"Who is he, Mama?" Abigail asked.

The woman continued to stare and only when her daughter tugged on her apron did she come to the present.

"Go," said her mother. "Go. Go help Ida in the kitchen." Cecilia gave her daughter a little push in the direction of the kitchen. When her daughter hesitated, she said, "Now, Abigail! Your father will be here at any moment!"

Reluctantly, the young girl moved away.

"You're as beautiful as ever," Frank said, softly.

And, she was. A vision of perfectly smooth white skin, light blue eyes and blonde hair piled on top of her head, only a little darker than in her youth. The pale blue fabric of her dress was cut in the latest style, showing off her small waist. Undoubtedly, the color was chosen to accent her eyes, for Cecilia did nothing in terms of dress that was not deliberate.

It was a thought he would not have had twenty years ago and the gladness he felt at seeing her again was brought up short. He felt an inward pulling back, as if he'd just reined in his horse.

"I thought you were dead, Frank." Her lips thought about smiling but then she frowned and there was a warning note in her voice.

"Yeah. I keep hearing that." His eyes met hers. "Why is that?"

"You. You went west. I never heard from you again!"

"I wrote."

Cecilia shook her head. "I never got a letter." At his intent look, she put a hand to her throat. "No letters at all." Something about his presence gave her concern.

"But, you got my money."

"No. No. Nothing." She looked down. "I can't believe this!" Her body shook with agitation as she tried to get her breath. "Why did you just write? Why didn't you come back?"

Frank nodded. "I should have." He looked at her bowed head. "I've thought of that many a time, since. But. I was young. Prideful. Wanted to come back to you with pockets full of gold." He stepped forward, taking her arms. "But, I'm here now."

Cecilia looked up at him, her eyes staring. "You can't!" She pulled away. "You must go!"

"You loved me once."

"I thought I did!" Her eyes were wide as she took a step backward. "But Mother, Mother told me. I was just – under your spell!"

Frank shook his head. "I was under your spell."

"I don't love you, Frank. I – I have a new life. A husband who is here every day and every night." She emphasized the last word. "You must go."

There was a call from inside the house, a male voice. Cecilia stiffened, her eyes wide. "Go, Frank. You must."

She tried to push him away, but he stood firm, interested in who had called to her.

"Who is it, Mother?" A young man appeared behind her and stepped forward. He was as tall as Frank, with light green eyes and thick brown hair streaked with blonde.

"It's a man I used to know." Cecilia said the words deliberately.

Frank held out his hand. "I'm Frank Pascoe."

The young man shook hands with him and his palm was as firm as the older man's. "I'm Shelby Tarrant."

Cecilia gave him a nudge.

"Sinclair," he added.

Frank's gaze locked with Cecilia, who stared at him defiantly.

"It's good to meet a friend of my mother's," Shelby went on. "She

The LONG WAY HOME   *VII*

doesn't speak much of her past."

"Your father will be home soon," she reminded him. "You'll need to wash up and clean up. You've been out with the horses again!"

Shelby laughed a little. "I'm always with the horses, Mama! They make more sense than people do!" He nodded to Frank. "It was nice to meet you, sir."

"Likewise," was the reply as he watched him leave. "You've taught him well."

"No thanks to you!"

"How old is he?"

"Twen." She stopped mid-word and stared at him. "None of your business."

Twenty?" Frank smiled a little. "That would make him -."

"Stop it, Frank! He's not your son!" But, she hesitated for a moment and laid a hand on her heart. "You never raised him! You've had nothing to do with him!"

"Yet, you gave him my middle name."

"Frank." There was steel in her voice and her hands were fists by her sides.

He looked at her.

"Would you move aside? My husband is here."

Frank did as she asked and watched as a man a few years older than him came walking up the steps.

"Cecilia, my love! What a pleasant surprise! Greeted at the door!"

She held out her hands and he took them, then brought her close to kiss her cheek. Coming from the brightness of the day to the shadowed porch, it took a moment for him to be aware that Frank

VIII *Langdon Pierce*

stood nearby.

Before he could react, Cecilia spoke up. "Here's an old friend of mine, dear!"

The man turned to face Frank, his hand out. "Gerard Sinclair."

"Frank Pascoe," was the reply as they shook.

"An old friend of my wife's? Would you like to come to dinner?" Hunsaker motioned to the interior of the home.

"No thanks, Reverend," Frank replied, having noticed the collar around the man's neck. "I just stopped by for a minute. I'm headed west on the next train."

Cecilia's body relaxed for a moment.

"There are plenty of trains," smiled Sinclair. "Come join us."

She glared at Frank.

"Another time, Reverend," was his reply. "Though I appreciate the offer."

Sinclair looked at his wife. "I'm sure Cecilia is disappointed, as am I."

"I'm sorry I can't."

The man stood in the door for a moment. "Well, it's been a pleasure, Mr. Pascoe."

"Yes sir. Likewise."

"I'll see you in a few minutes, my dear," Sinclair kissed the top of Cecilia's head, then walked into the house.

"You always hated it when I did that," Frank spoke up once the man was out of earshot.

"You aren't Gerard," was her pert reply.

"No. I reckon not."

"And, your speech, Frank. You've gotten careless with it."

"Ain't so important in the West." He deliberately used the slang word.

Cecilia stiffened again.

"You're my wife," he reminded her. "Because if you thought me dead, you didn't divorce me." Taking her hand, he lifted it to his lips.

"I will now!"

"How will you explain it to the Reverend? Living in sin all this time?"

His words and his presence were a surprise to her and she bowed her head, thinking. Then, after a moment, her chin came up. "I'll tell him. We have no secrets between us."

"None?" Though he knew he was leaving, never to return, he couldn't resist needling her a little, if just to see her reaction. "What about the boy? Shelby?"

"He knows Shelby's father is dead."

"Not anymore." Frank reminded her, because if the boy was twenty, he was certainly the father. Or was he?" He put the thought aside and glanced into the house. "It's nice that he likes horses. I tend to agree with him. Horses are easier to figure out than people."

"You stay away from him!" She hissed at him. "He's got prospects here. He's going to the college and he's going to be a lawyer."

Frank smiled. "We all make our own hells."

She lifted her chin. "This isn't h-h-hell, Frank." She looked around them. "This is heaven. I've never been happier." The look on her face dared him to deny it.

Their eyes met once again.

"Good-bye, Cecilia." He put on his hat and touched the brim. "I hope you have a good life."

Langdon Pierce

"Good-by, Frank," she replied. "I hope the same for you as well."

Turning, he walked across the porch and down the steps.

She watched him go, a fist to her mouth and a hand over her heart. At a call from inside the house, she quickly wiped her eyes. Putting a smile on her face, she walked inside and closed the door behind her.

Evening found Frank, not on a train as he had planned, since there had been a storm somewhere to the east that had delayed it, but in a billiard hall. The gentle click of the balls, the smell of cigars and tobacco, along with the mild taste of sour mash whisky gave him a sense of peace.

It wasn't as if he had thought she would wait for him all these many years. It was a shock to add them up and realize it had been twenty. But, he wanted to know, to make sure, before he went back to the west. The surprise was to learn that she had thought him dead. Why or in what matter he had supposedly died, he did not know. The thought inserted itself that perhaps Cecilia's mother, Marge Mansbach, had suggested it and even, fomented it. She had never liked her daughter's choice of husband. He couldn't say that he cared much for his mother-in-law either. If asked at the time, he would have said that her dislike and continual disparaging of him was one of the reasons he had left Springfield. But now he knew, he only had to look in the mirror to know why he had left.

Frank thought back to the last time he had come to Springfield, about ten years ago, though Cecilia had not known of it. He finally had a going concern, a little ranch in Texas, with a cabin he'd built with his own hands. As he worked the place, it was in his mind to go back to Springfield, swoop up Cecilia and take her back with him. And, like any other time he considered an action, he followed through on it.

The train pulled into Springfield and he stood up, feeling mighty shaky inside and his heart pounding. He didn't know what kind of greeting he would get from Cecilia, but he had hope that she would agree to his plan.

Opposite his seat, there was a woman traveling with three small children trying to take care of her offspring and get the bags and boxes she traveled with. Noticing her lack of success, Frank helped to get her bags situated then tipped a porter to carry some of them. The train gave a jolt and he looked up to see Cecilia outside facing the train, her face alight, expectant. He could hardly believe that she would have that kind of welcome for him. His heart leapt up and his knees were like water. This was too good to be true! After all those years of unanswered letters!

Yet, as he watched, a tall man in a fine suit stepped down from the train and greeted Cecilia. It was only then that Frank noticed the slim boy beside her because the man acknowledged him as well. The boy shrank back, but not too far.

Then, a shrill voice caught his attention and Frank saw Mrs. Herbert Mansbach greet the man effusively. It didn't surprise him to note the surreptitious looks the woman gave the crowd at the station, as if making sure everyone saw who they welcomed.

Frank stood there, stunned, as if he was only a shell with his insides having disappeared. He noticed the glow of happiness on Cecilia's face as she looked at the man and Mrs. Mansbach's nod of approval. It was more than he had ever gotten from her.

He moved out of the aisle to let others pass by and watched the little group walk into the station. Then, the train jerked again and began moving. Frank sank into a seat, aware that though it was sunny outside the car, all about him darkness had already fallen.

In the billiard hall, someone bumped into him as they passed by and brought him forward to the present. There were faces and voices around him, but they were a blur. The bartender said something and he took the offered drink, the whisky seeming to have no taste, just a dull burn.

Why had he gone to Springfield those many years ago, when he had received no word from Cecilia? In the hopes that they could start over and begin a life together in Texas, was what he told himself. That sounded logical. Why hadn't he gotten off the train and made himself known? There was something in her face and her eyes as she looked at the man he now knew was Gerard Sinclair and he was stopped. She was happy and he could not ask for more.

But, why had he come back now?

Was it to make her choose between the Reverend and himself? To see the boy? No, he thought to himself. Cecilia was the reason he was in Springfield. There was more than a ranch, now. There was money. Would it make a difference if she knew?

Somehow, he didn't think so, though it might have if her mother was still alive. In the intervening years, he'd had plenty of time to go over the days, months and years of his marriage. And, he'd realized just how much Marge Mansbach had influenced her daughter. Not only that, his mother-in-law had taken every opportunity to compare him to Cecilia's former suitors, with them always coming out the better. Especially she focused on the fortunes of Wynn Tucker who was being groomed to take over his father's position at the bank. He wondered if it had come to pass; then realized it didn't matter; he was headed west on the next train.

He shrugged his shoulders in his jacket, as if to fill them out that much more.

"It's your shot, Pascoe!" A voice broke through his reverie.

"What's done is done," he murmured to himself, then bent over to make his shot. The white ball hit a yellow one and spun it just enough to knock another yellow ball sideways.

Along the wall, bystanders stood, their gazes intent on watching both balls roll to their respective corners, hesitate, then drop in. Immediately, there was shouting, back slapping and calls for more liquor.

"I've seen some good play, but that one takes the cake." A broad, burly farmer dropped a coin on the felt. "You're a good 'un."

"Luck," Frank assured him. "And, I have to admit, I'd rather be lucky than good."

"Game's not over, yet," came the sharp reminder from G.W. Muir, his opponent. The man was big, his vest hanging open and revealing shirt buttons straining to hold together.

"You're right," Frank viewed what were left of the balls on the table. He made two more shots, the last of which had a bit of bad luck and rolled to a stop along the side rail.

Muir immediately grabbed his cue stick and from the sound of his boots on the wooden floor, stomped to the other side of the table. He made a shot, a red ball dropping smartly into the pocket. With an abrupt motion, he leaned over and sent another red ball bouncing off the side rail then into the opposite pocket.

Silence again reigned in the room.

"Side pocket." Muir tapped the intended target and sent the ball into it.

Now, the last two red balls were grouped with three yellow balls, the lone black one in the center. All he could do was break them apart and hope that one would drop into a pocket, but none did, except the yellow ball Frank had hit previously which had teetered near a side pocket.

There were murmurs of sympathy from the onlookers.

Frank surveyed the table. He took his time eyeing the angles and lining up his shot. With a sharp, decisive move, the white ball hit a yellow one, spinning it into an end pocket.

"Six, five," one of the onlookers murmured the score.

Frank bent low again, intent on his shot, when someone walking behind him knocked his cue stick that had just struck the white ball. It spun off into a pocket of its own.

"Foul!" Cried some of the onlookers.

"I didn't see it!" Muir announced.

But, the bystanders were adamant and Frank was allowed to shoot again. Upon contact, the last yellow ball rolled the length of the table and into a corner pocket.

The immediate clapping and cheering became subdued at Muir's glare at them.

Frank walked around the table, noting that the approach to the black ball was blocked by two red ones. He shot the white ball, which hit a long rail and a short rail before rolling aimlessly to a stop.

It was G. W. Muir's turn. He sent a red ball into a side pocket, then brushed the last red ball just enough to drop it into a pocket.

There was some cheering, but noticeably less in volume.

Muir tapped a corner pocket, indicating where the last ball would land then lined up behind the cue ball. He struck it sharply and all watched as it rolled into the black one, which began moving. Slowly, so slowly it made its way to the designated pocket, seemed to take a breath, then dropped in. But, not before the cue ball rolled into the one opposite.

Immediately, bedlam broke out, with men shouting and pounding one another on the back, while Muir stepped back from the table in shock. He was big and men made way for him while he backed up until the bar stopped him. The cue dropped from his grip, while all around him men were celebrating.

Frank took the money that was pressed into his hands, for many had bet on him and were giving him tips. Then, he put the cue away and walked to the door, checking his pocket watch. Surely the train would be there by now.

As he pushed open the door to leave the parlor, he almost collided with a young man coming in. It was Shelby Tarrant Sinclair. Frank stepped aside to let him pass, but Shelby stopped to face him.

"I thought you'd be gone by now."

"Train was delayed."

Shelby glanced into the parlor. "Are you any good?"

"Ask him," Frank jerked his head back at Muir.

"I've got money. I'll play you."

Frank looked again at his watch. "I've a train to catch."

"I'm pretty good. I beat G.W. all the time."

Slowly, Frank looked him up and down. "There are better things to be good at."

"Are you saying you won't play me?"

A train whistle broke through the evening air and Frank looked up.

"It was nice meeting you. Say good-bye to your mother for me, will you?" Frank turned and began to walk away, but a hand on his shoulder turned him around.

He stopped and looked in the young man's eyes. "I must go." The words were said quietly, mildly.

There was something behind the statement, an edge that the younger man had never encountered before. Quickly, Shelby stepped back to let him pass just as a young man of about his own age came to the door of the billiard parlor and greeted him.

"C'mon, Shelby! Let's have a drink, then a game!"

Shelby hesitated, as if undecided.

A few feet away on the boardwalk, Frank turned around and looked back at him. "You know your mother would rather you wouldn't."

Shelby waved his friend away, then watched Frank cross the street to the train station.

"Wynn will be glad to see him go."

Turning, Shelby saw Hop Hopkins beside him, his deputy sheriff star shining dully in the dim light under the awning.

"Why?"

"That's Frank Pascoe."

"I know."

"He was a hell raiser from way back."

"Not doin' too much, now," Shelby noted.

"We thought he was dead."

"Why?"

Hopkins glanced at the young man. "Him and your Ma were married once."

Shelby stared at him. "What? Mother? And him?"

Across the way, through a gap in the buildings, they could see people getting on a train.

"Didn't she tell you?"

Shelby's attention was on the train. "I don't believe it! Not Mother! To a – a . . "

A small smile crossed Hopkins' lips. "We was all young once."

After a call from the conductor, the train began to slowly leave the station.

"Wonder why he come to town? Didn't see anyone but Cecilia, that is, Mrs. Sinclair."

"Yes," said the young man. "That's where I met him."

Hopkins lost his interest in the train. "What did she say?"

Shelby shrugged his shoulders. "I don't know. Not much. He wasn't there but a minute or two. Father invited him to dinner."

"To dinner!"

"Yes, yes of course. Father is always inviting people to dinner."

Hopkins nodded. "Well, I guess I'll amble down to the Sheriff's office. Wynn was wanting to know when Pascoe was leavin'." With a nod to Shelby, he walked in that direction.

Behind him, Shelby put a hand to his forehead. Though his eyes followed Hopkins, his mind raced with a thousand thoughts.

It was nearing dusk when Sheriff Wynn Tucker made his rounds. As usual, he tried the doors to the bank to make sure they were locked. Each time, he grasped the knobs, he was taken back in time to the night twenty years ago when they hadn't been secured.

Blaine Tucker, his father, not feeling well, had left the closing up of the bank to him and Fred Hinkleman. Being young men, their minds were more focused on the dance that night, rather than on the business at hand. Somehow, the doors were not locked. And, somehow, someone knew of it. Or perhaps it was just a chance thing. Regardless, a robber or robbers entered the bank, blew open the safe, and stole the money.

The bank lost so much of its funds, it had to close. Almost everyone in the area was effected by it, some losing their farms and others, their life's savings. Of course there was a trial, which his father claimed was a waste of money since nothing was decided. Wynn spent his time glaring at Frank Pascoe in the jury box, believing that he had something to do with it.

Regardless, days afterward, Frank and Cecilia announced their engagement and were married soon after. Wynn's father, ruined by the robbery and feeling responsible for the loss of the money, died months later.

Blaine Tucker left enough money for his wife to be comfortable, but Wynn immediately began searching for a job. Sheriff Hank McGlone, whose deputy was planning on moving back to Pittsburg for his wife's sake, accepted the young man as his replacement.

Though Wynn kept an eye on Frank, as the community said, he fit into the harness of marriage like he was born to it. The man worked for his mother-in-law, doing nothing untoward. Yet, Wynn had his suspicions then and he had them now. As for the money, neither it nor the robber ever turned up.

And now, after a twenty year absence, Frank was back. Interesting that the very thing he suspected Frank of in the past had become a reality after he moved west. The sheriff wondered if he had come back to get the money from the bank robbery. Surely it wasn't just to see Cecilia, though he had to admit, the woman was still worth looking at.

His thoughts were elsewhere when he looked up, feeling like someone was watching him. Glancing to the side, he saw a man's silhouette in an alley, one that he knew very well.

"Hello, Wynn," the voice was conversational.

"Hello, Frank," Tucker tried to match the lightness of his tone. For some reason, his tongue wanted to cling to the roof of his mouth and he swallowed. "I thought you were on the train."

"Something broke," was the reply, as he continued walking toward Tucker. "I went for a walk."

From the direction he had come, the sheriff knew he had to have gone to his office.

"What are you doin' in town?" It was a question his office could ask anyone.

"Came to see the place. People."

"But, you're leavin'?" His voice sounded weaker, tighter than he'd like.

Finally, Frank came forward enough to be out of the shadow and onto the street. Tucker's eyes went immediately to his right side, but the man's coat was too long to see if he wore a gun.

"You look well," the sheriff swallowed, surprised at his own observation.

"For an eight year stint in prison, you mean?" He walked up to the sheriff and looked him over. "You've not missed many meals yourself."

Tucker's gaze went over the man again. If ever breaking rock agreed with someone; that person was Frank Pascoe. The man looked strong and well muscled. And, he looked healthy, Tucker told himself. He wasn't used to a prisoner looking that damned healthy.

A train whistle blew, alerting the passengers that it was getting ready to leave.

"That's your train."

"It is," Frank agreed, but he didn't move. His eyes had a glint, a hardness to them and Tucker felt he was cutting through to his soul.

"It was your sayso that put me in prison, Tucker."

The sheriff swallowed hard. He was wearing a gun, but everyone knew how fast Frank was. He'd seen him draw and shoot before. The man was quick, damned quick. "I don't know what you're talking about."

"I saw you in the gallery."

"I was there on other business."

"Why didn't you tell them who I was?" Bitterness filled the words.

"I didn't know but what you'd taken up a new name." Tucker raised his hands to show his innocence. "Like I said, I was there on other business. Just stopped in to see the show."

It was true; trials were a type of entertainment when there was nothing else.

Frank nodded then said softly, "You always were a terrible liar."

And there it was, hanging between them, a challenge waiting to be refuted with gunfire.

"I'm not going to shoot you," Tucker told him, hating the way his voice wavered.

"I'm not going to shoot you, either," was the mild reply. And with the words, Frank opened his coat to show that he wore no weapon. "This is the East, Wynn. It's supposed to be civilized."

With that, the man walked by him as if he had no care in the world. As if there hadn't been a standoff right there on the street of Springfield, Ohio.

It was only when Frank had disappeared into the station that Tucker drew a deep breath. Then another. After that encounter, he needed a drink. He looked around. The closest place was Bill's Saloon. The usual patrons were drunks and laborers; none of his friends or anyone he knew frequented the place, men who would question his presence there.

Slipping the badge into his vest pocket, he walked into the bar. It wasn't to hide his identity, just to show that he was off duty. At least, that was what he told himself as he took the offered glass of whisky.

When the final train whistle blew, signaling departure from Springfield, Tucker raised his glass in salute.

It was perhaps an hour later when he left the saloon, well fortified against what the rest of the night might bring. He almost felt like singing, life felt that rich to him.

Continuing on his rounds, he walked and checked doors until he reached Red's Billiard Hall. He knew that the family men would have left and a younger, more rowdy crowd would be there. As yet, it was still quiet, so much so that he almost walked by Shelby Sinclair who sat on the window ledge outside.

"What are you doing out here?" Tucker asked, with a grin. He felt like smiling at everyone. "Everyone else is inside."

Shelby raised his head and looked at him. "Why did you want to know Frank Pascoe's whereabouts?"

The older man glanced up the street at his office where Hop Hopkins sat whittling, then looked at Shelby. "He was once a pretty dangerous man."

"Why did you think he was dead?"

Tucker looked at him. "Maybe because he never came back to Cecilia. Maybe because there was talk he was a bandit and the crowd he ran with were killed."

"A bandit?"

Tucker nodded. "I think I have a wanted poster of his in my office."

"Wanted poster?" Shelby sat up and looked at the sheriff. "Why didn't you arrest him?"

Tucker looked at the young man, stung by the question. Was he accusing him of dereliction of duty? "That was quite a few years ago. Probably not valid anymore."

"I'd like to see it."

The sheriff nodded. As a matter of fact, he'd like to see it, too. To make sure that he was right, that he'd done the right thing, all those years ago.

XXII   *Langdon Pierce*

With a glance around the now empty street, Tucker turned his steps toward the office. "Things seem pretty quiet. I guess I can spare the time."

Together they walked to the sheriff's office. As they entered, Shelby noted that Hopkins sat in a corner, knife and stick in his hands, curls of shavings on the floor at his feet and his head resting on the wall, asleep.

Tucker opened the middle drawer to his desk and pulled out a yellowed reward poster. "Here it is." With a flick of his wrist, he spun it to land facing toward Shelby.

"Jack Davis," Shelby read aloud. "Omaha Train Robber." His eyes met Tucker's from across the desk. "That's not Frank Pascoe."

"Lookit the picture."

In looking at it, Shelby had to admit that the sketched face of Frank Pascoe looked back at him. "What does that mean? He's not Jack Davis."

"If you were a train robber, would you use your real name? What if you had a wife and ch- family back here? Would you want them to know you were a bandit?" Tucker scoffed. "Lots of men went west to disappear."

Shelby shook his head slowly, his gaze still on the poster. "Omaha Train Robbers. Sam Bass and other outlaws. Jack Davis. 5 feet 11 inches high, some say 6 feet. 180 pounds, 30 years old. Broad shouldered. Green eyes, dark hair. Beard, moustache. Talks, drinks a great deal. Rode a dunn colored horse with a glass eye."

"Well, I can attest that Frank Pascoe drinks a great deal!" Tucker laughed.

Shelby glanced up at him. "He didn't drink at the billiard hall."

"Or did." The sheriff corrected.

"What did they rob?"

"Did you ever hear of the Sam Bass gang train robbery? Some called 'em the Black Hills Bandits. They stopped the Union Pacific train in Big Springs, Nebraska. Rode away with sixty thousand dollars in gold coin and some change."

"But, Sam Bass is dead. A long time ago."

"Ten years," said the sheriff. "Of the six robbers, two got away. Jack Davis and Tom Nixon. Less than half of the money was recovered."

Shelby looked down at the paper again. "Reward. Ten thousand dollars."

"That's a lot of money."

"Contact the nearest office of the Texas Rangers," he continued to read. Once finished, he handed the paper back to the sheriff.

"Are you headed to Texas?" Tucker's tone was half-joking.

Shelby turned to leave.

As he reached the door, Tucker spoke up. "Ten thousand dollars. That's a lot of money."

The young man hesitated and the sheriff added, "I have a friend in the Texas Rangers. I could see if it is still open."

Shelby stopped and turned to him. "No, thank you, sir." His eyes surveyed the street before him. "This is home. No traipsing to Texas for me. My Mother has lost enough family to the West."

The door shut behind him.

From the corner, Hopkins sat up. "You'd sic the pup on his father?"

"Doesn't sound like Cecilia has confided in the boy." Tucker sat down in his chair and put his feet up. "And yes. For what Pascoe did..." Or perhaps, he thought, had just done. He wanted to stretch, to get the fright out of his body, but Hopkins was watching. "I most certainly would send his boy on a wild goose chase."

"I thought your daughter had her heart set on Shelby?"

Tucker shook his head. "I found out at dinner, she's changed her mind. Seth Brady's boy is more to her likin'."

Chapter
ONE

THE QUICK FLIT of the hummingbird caught her attention as it went to the rose bushes along the front porch. From the porch roses, it moved on to the rose bush tangled over the arbor, then into the shade of the oak tree.

On the porch, Nancy Cyrus sat with a bowl of just snapped green beans in her lap. She looked up to watch the bird and then, just beyond, the tall grass in the fenced cemetery rippling in the increasing breeze. Across the valley, a cow called to her calf, her bell ringing as she went in search of it. The drone of bees busy among the flowers and the nearby garden made her eyelids grow heavy.

"Sure is hot, ain't it, Mama? A girl of about ten years old came around the corner of the cabin, a stick in her hand. She was slim, almost thin, and her hair loosened from its braid was a blond halo in the sunlight. Light blue eyes sought her mother's, pools of blue in a tan face. Anywhere her dress, almost a shift, did not hide it her skin was tanned and freckled. A bonnet hung down her back by the strings, pushed away because of its restriction.

"Yes it is, Evie," replied the woman. "It's close, too." She glanced up at the towering clouds above. "It's gonna rain, that's certain."

"More rain, Mama?" A small girl around four years old and just beginning to lose the plumpness of babyhood, followed her older sister. She was a smaller and rounder version of Evie.

Nancy Cyrus looked down at her daughters. "I'm afraid so, Stella." Unlike her daughters, her hair was brown, almost black, and her eyes were brown as well. With full lips and high cheekbones, she reflected what was said of her heritage; that of Cherokee Indian. Whether it was her ancestry or it was something all of her own, she had grace of movement and a quiet way about her. And when she walked to church or to Helton's General Store at The Forks, all would stop to watch. As Birdie said, "as if a queen walked among us."

"Uncle Stone said that if we get much more rain, we're gonna get a flood." Evie sat down on the top step.

Her mother nodded in agreement. "Are your chores done?"

"Yes, ma'am," said the older girl. "And you said, if they was done, we could go swimmin'."

Nancy looked up, noticing the clouds blotting out the sun.

A breeze picked up, snapping the sheets on the clothes line. "Let's wait a bit, Evie. It might rain again. And, the creek's still up, ain't it?"

"Yes, ma'am," Evie sighed, realizing that the cooling

pleasures of the water might be put off. "I was thinkin' of the quarry."

"How about makin' a peach pie?" Her mother smiled.

Evie looked down, her shoulders sagging. "The kitchen's still hot from breakfast."

"And, we'll have a little picnic in the shade," her mother added. "Maybe up on the hill, under the white oak tree, where there's a breeze almost all the time."

Both girls looked up at her and grinned. "A picnic?"

"Yes. And while the pie's bakin', I'll have the green beans on."

"Makin' the house real hot!" Evie put in.

"And, we won't care. Because we'll be outside havin' a picnic."

But when it was time for the picnic, they had it on the porch because it had begun to rain.

"Let's eat outside all the time," Stella looked up, remnants of the pie around her mouth and on her hands. "Too hot in the house."

"It might get a little chilly in the winter," her mother teased.

"All the time, now. When it's hot," the little girl went on.

"Here comes someone," Evie spoke up, her eyes on the road below them. For the most part, the two sandy tracks that made up the road to the Forks followed the creek, sometimes piercing the green pasture. "Looks like Uncle Albert."

"And Birdie," Stella clapped her hands together, then used them to stand up.

"Give me those hands," her mother reached for her and wiped them, now dirty from pressing onto the porch. "I thought one of you swept the porch this morning."

"Yes, ma'am," Evie replied. "That was before the dogs came up from the creek and tracked all over the place."

As if on cue, a pair of dogs, seeming twins in their coloring of tan and white came rushing forward to greet the two men. At first, they barked aggressively, then grinned and wagged their tails as they recognized them.

"Good afternoon, Miss Nancy," Albert Cyrus grinned, revealing even, white teeth and swept off his hat. "And girls." Though all of the children of Abe Cyrus had thick black hair and bright blue eyes, Albert believed himself to be the handsomest. Ollie had been slim with narrow shoulders and had a slanted forehead and a thin high bridged nose, like his mother. Isaac was still too young to notice the ladies and had not yet gotten his height and breadth. Ethan and Lucas had died in the war; which left him, Albert, the pick of the litter. He was broad shouldered and as he liked to think, physically well made, his thick black hair and beard adding to his allure. Blue eyes swept over them, then the house and yard. "It's hot, ain't it?"

"Hod do, Mrs. Cyrus," the man beside him was thin and lanky. His hair and eyes seemed to be of the same color, a light brown. Bending in half, he greeted each dog in turn, his voice and manner mild. "Hush now, Sal," he told the smaller of the two then motioned to the other. "Sit, Sam." The dogs immediately sat down, watching him expectantly. He did not disappoint, but brought out some bread crust that the dogs made disappear.

"Birdie!" Stella, now free from her mother's grasp, went running to the man and hugged his legs, stopping his progress.

But, Albert kept walking up to the porch, resting a boot on the bottom step.

"Hello, Uncle Albert," Evie stood up and seemed to fade into the shadow of the porch post.

"Al," Nancy nodded to him, then greeted the man stopped by child and dogs. "Birdie." Her gaze went to Albert. "It's hot to be traipsin' about this time of day."

"We wuz helpin' Aunt Tildy. She needed some wood cut and stacked." Albert's eyes never wavered from Nancy. "How are you-all doin' up here?"

"We're doin' fine. Thank you, Birdie, for cuttin' wood for us a couple days ago."

Albert threw an irritated glance at the thin man. He had come close to the porch, possibly to be in the shelter of it due to the rain. Yet, his voice grew more intimate in tone, "Anythin' else you be needin'?"

"I don't believe so."

"You can't fool me, Nancy. Brother's been dead more'n five months. About time you found yourself a new husband."

"I've got all I need."

"You miss me," he moved closer to the porch by moving around the steps, putting his elbow on the floor and looking up at her.

"They's a shotgun behind that door," Nancy told him, a nod indicating the house. "I'd hate to use it on my husband's brother."

"There's no need for that," Albert grinned, sure of himself. "Next time, I'll come alone"

"Suit yerself," she told him. "You been warned."

"You need a man," he glanced down at the steps, as if considering leaping up them.

"I've had about enough of men right now," was her curt reply. "If you've no other business, you might as well keep walkin' down the road."

"Are you kickin' me off yer place?" It was hard to tell if he was joking or incredulous.

"Take it as you will," Nancy stood up. "I've work to do."

As she stood up, her dress, due to the humidity, kept its shape around her body. His eyes seemed to bore into her belly.

"You're with child!" There was no disguising his incredulity. In another moment, he had run up the steps to stand beside her, his eyes never leaving her belly. He grabbed her wrist. "Mine!" The word was hissed into her ear.

Nancy pulled away from him. "Ollie's."

"No," he followed her. "He was in no shape to father a child, sick and hurt as he was."

"You don't know that," Nancy stood her ground. "You know nuthin'!"

They stood there, eye to eye, for she was a tall woman and him, well built as he was, was not a tall man.

"You leavin' now, Uncle Albert?" Evie asked from the door of the cabin. "This shotgun is gettin' almighty heavy."

Both Nancy and Albert turned to see the slim young girl holding the shotgun, though she was having trouble keeping it steady. It was worth noting that it wasn't aimed very high.

"Why yes, I am leavin'," he grinned at her, then looked at Nancy. "You're raisin' a spitfire!"

"Remember that, too," Nancy watched him trot jauntily down the steps. "If you're ever this way again."

"I'll be back!" Albert waved his hand in the air and kept walking.

Behind him, Birdie set Stella down on the ground, gave the dogs another pat and followed behind him.

Nancy looked at him, realizing that since his attention been on the child and dogs, it was unlikely he had seen what had gone on between her and Albert. But, the burning glance he gave her along with a nod of good-bye made her think differently. As he followed Albert back to the road, his head was sunk more forward, deep in thought. She shrugged it off. If he thought ill of her for being pregnant, with a husband months dead, well that was up to him.

It was still raining when Birdie came back to the cabin. Though he wore a slicker, it was as if it hung on a frame, so narrow was his body.

"Good evening, friends!" He walked up to the porch and was motioned to come on in.

"Good evening, Birdie." Nancy sat in her rocking chair, the Bible on her lap. On either side of her stood the girls, his arrival having interrupted their daily reading.

He hung his slicker on a peg on the cabin wall and took off his hat. "I wanted to apologize for earlier."

"There's no need. You did nuthin' wrong," Nancy assured him.

"That's the thing. I did nuthin' at all." Long, slim fingers turned his hat brim around and around in his hands. "It just took me by surprise is all." He looked at Evie, then Stella. "I never seen him act that way before."

Nancy nodded. "He's been -," she glanced at Stella, "more plain about his thoughts and intentions since Ollie died."

"Wal, there's no call to be actin' like he does," he stated. "And, if you don't mind, I'm gonna keep a lookout for you."

"Oh no, Birdie. You've got your own place to look after. You can't be spendin' time over here."

"I've decided," he stood tall, his mouth firm. "You need lookin' after and I'm gonna do it."

Seeing that he wouldn't be dissuaded, she nodded. "Thank you, Birdie."

"Will we be seein' more of you?" Stella asked.

Birdie grinned at her. "Yep."

On Sunday, it was still raining, only in fits and starts. The hollows were filled with mist, the mountains rising above them, as if in some dreamland. They would have walked to church as usual, but Birdie insisted that they take the wagon. He harnessed the team and arrived at the front door just as they were walking out. Nancy didn't argue about the horses needing a day of rest as well, but smiled her thanks.

It seemed that many of the congregation had the idea to drive, for the church yard was full of wagons and buggies.

"There's Uncle Albert," Evie's voice was at her ear, her tone low.

Albert Cyrus drove his shiny black buggy with yellow spokes into the church yard. He made a great show of his horse turning this way and that until he made his way to a spot under the trees. Jumping down, his eyes sought hers, but she'd already turned away.

He came hurrying in their direction, but Birdie was the one helping her down from the wagon. She tugged at her dress, getting the shape back to something less revealing of her condition.

As she and the girls walked to the church, Polly Parsley came over to her and took her arm. Birdie was still at the wagon, taking care of the horses and Albert had been detained in conversation with another man.

"I seen you tug at yer dress," Polly said, softly. "Yer in the fam'ly way."

"I am," Nancy did not see fit to speak other than the truth.

"When are you due?"

"September."

Polly nodded. "The last of Ollie's seed."

"It's a Cyrus, alright," Nancy admitted grimly, a hand on the bulge above her waist. "I believe it would leave my womb right now if it could."

The other woman laughed softly. "Though we glory in bearin' chillern, we want 'em gone about as soon as they're in."

Nancy stopped and put a hand over her belly. "I won't be comin' to church no more. Not til .."

"You're not showin' that much, yet."

"I just don't feel well."

Polly looked into her friend's eyes. "You have the look of pain about you." Then, her gaze swept the area about them. "Any of these men givin' you trouble?"

"It's not that. Besides, Birdie's been keepin' watch on the hill behind the house."

"So. There is a man troublin' you."

Nancy took her friend's arm. "Let's not talk about that."

Taking her arm again, Polly walked with her friend. "If I could spare Bobby Lee, I'd let him take a turn watchin' over you." She turned her head here and there, as if able to spot the man giving her trouble. "You'd ought to have taken yer cousin Beck's offer to live with him. That farm's too much for you an' yer little girls. Especially now."

"Ollie built that place," Nancy's voice grew firm. "And we're stayin' til God roots us out."

Polly patted her arm. "It don't do to challenge God, Nan."

"He's the one what took Ollie. Took these girls' father. He can provide another," she stated, then added quickly, "in due time." She lifted her chin. "He'll show me the way."

"You certainly have a tough row to hoe," Polly patted her arm once more, then released it as they walked into the church.

For two hours, singing and preaching filled the hollow where the church sat. When the last Amen was said the people filed out, glad to get outside where, though hot, at least there was a breeze.

After the church emptied, Nancy continued to sit alone, her girls having gone to play with friends.

"It's mine, I know it is." Albert came up the aisle and sat down beside her.

"Go away, Albert."

"You'd ought to marry me. Seein' as how you're carryin' my child."

Nancy put a protective hand over her belly. "This is not your child."

His eyes bored into hers. "I say it is." When her gaze did not waver, he added, "there's no way Ollie was in any shape to . ."

"You speak of things you know nothing about."

"What if I spread it around that it is my child?"

"I'll tell anyone that you lie."

"You're over there, livin' alone. No man around. Who do you think they'll believe?"

"Is that how you'd treat the widow of your brother? A woman clingin' to the last vestige of him? Tellin' tales like that?" She stood up. "Brother! You're not worthy of the name!"

He stood as well and grabbed her elbow. "You'd best be thinkin' of marryin' me. Or you'll get more of the same."

Nancy drew away from his grasp. "I'm just hopin' you remember where that shotgun was pointed." With that, she left the pew.

Birdie stood in the door, holding it open as she passed. For a long moment, he and Albert exchanged glances. Then, he put his hat on his head and followed her to the wagon.

Albert continued to sit in the pew but a sound caught his attention. There seemed to be movement in the window of the church, perhaps sunlight on the head of a bright headed child but when he turned his head to make sure, it was gone.

Night, made blacker by clouds shielding any celestial light, surrounded the cabin. Rain pelted down, a drum roll of sound on the metal roof of the cabin. At the fireplace, Evie cleaned a pistol, her attention on the weapon and not the weather. In the rocker, Nancy sewed, looking up now and again to check the roof. So far, no water leaked into the house.

"More rain, Mama?" Stella asked, standing at the half open window of her home. Drops of water bounced on the sill and sprinkled on her dress. She could scarce be heard over the roar on the roof.

"Seems so, Leelee." Nancy used the nickname the girl's father had given her.

"Lap, Mama?"

Nancy set aside her sewing and helped Stella up. "Are you afraid?"

The little girl looked about, her fist with thumb exposed not far from her mouth. She thought for a moment. "No." Her hand dropped. "Just wantin' lap."

"Is it true, Mama?" Evie asked. "You're in the family way?"

Nancy met her daughter's gaze. "Yes. We should have a new little Cyrus come September."

"Papa's?"

Though rain drummed a crescendo on the roof, quiet settled into the room.

After a long moment, Nancy replied, "Mine." Then she added, "Ours."

"But . ."

"God gave us this child. It is up to us to raise him or her. Our child. Part of our family."

"Not Papa's."

"Ours," Nancy said, firmly.

"I want it to be Papa's." Evie put her head on her mother's shoulder.

"Me, too," said Nancy as she stroked the fine blonde hair. "Me, too."

The only way to tell it was bedtime was by the old clock on the mantel, for it had been dark for several hours, the rain incessant.

"Is it ever gonna stop, Mama? Stella came to stand by her rocker.

"Do you think it's gonna come a big flood?" Evie looked out the window. "Like Noah and the Ark?"

Nancy smiled a little. After a moment, she got up and went to the window as well. Then, she stepped outside onto the porch. Only then did she realize that the roar they'd been hearing was the creek in flood, rather than rain on the roof.

"The rain has let up," she noticed.

"Is it bad, Mama?"

With clouds covering whatever heavenly light they would get in the narrow valley, it was hard to see.

"I don't know," she frowned. "Get me the lantern."

It only took a moment for her to throw on Ollie's slicker, take the lantern, then step out into the wet. She glanced back at the anxious faces of her daughters. "You stay here. Don't leave the porch."

Using the lantern, she made her way down the slope to the water's edge. Was the noise of the rushing water only being magnified in the little valley or was it truly a torrent? In the dark, with only a few feet visible on either side of her, it was hard to tell. Taking a stick she had picked up along the way, she stuck it into the ground. It would help her gauge the rise of the water. Then, she walked back to the cabin.

"How is it, Mama?" Evie asked as she came up on the porch.

"It's over the road," was the calm reply. It wouldn't do to tell the children that the water lapped only a few feet from the porch. Nancy took off the slicker then led them into the cabin. She looked around the main room. "Let's gather a few things together. We may have to move to higher ground."

Evie looked at her. "We're on a hillside, Mama," she said, as if reminding her.

"Yes," was the reply. "I'm guessin' the river is up too and that's why the creek is risin' like it is. That's a lot of water that needs a place to go." She looked at her daughters. "Let's get doin'."

It was quiet in the cabin, the rain barely murmuring on the metal roof, lulling its occupants to sleep. In the rocker, Nancy sat with Stella in her arms, their eyes closed. At the table, Evie leaned across it, her head resting on her arms.

A sudden thudding came at the door. "Miz Cyrus! Miz Cyrus!"

Nancy quickly stood up and put Stella back in the chair, while Evie ran to the door.

"Where's your Mama, missy?" Birdie stood in the opening, his head just as wet as if he hadn't worn the hat in his hand.

"What's the matter, Birdie?" Nancy came to the door.

For answer, Birdie pointed at the creek. "The Creek's a' risin', Miz Cyrus! You gotta git, right now!"

He stood aside so that Nancy could get a clear view of the creek. She didn't have to look far, for the water was almost lapping at the bottom of the steps.

"Thankee for your warning, Birdie."

"Is there anythin' I can do to help?" He looked around, expectantly.

Nancy stood at the door, a hand at her throat. "You think it's still comin' up?" She peered into the darkness, a hand laid protectively across her belly. "We cain't be leavin'. We got nowhere to go." The words were said softly, as if to herself.

Beside her, Birdie put out his hand as if to touch her shoulder, but drew it away. "I know you don't want to leave, Miz Cyrus. All yer mem'ries of Ollie and all. But, d'ya think he'd want you and the chillern quick or daid?"

"Mama?" Evie asked, coming up behind her. "We're leavin' ain't we?"

Straightening her shoulders, Nancy turned to her, "Of course we are."

"Where we goin', Mama?" Stella sat up in the rocker, barely awake.

"We're headed out of here," was the reply. "Let's get our things together. Quickly now."

It helped that they'd already bundled up some things in a quilt and packed the carpetbag.

Still at the door, Birdie held out his hands. "I'll take the little 'un." After buttoning his slicker around Stella and himself, he took up the shotgun as well.

When Evie stepped out onto the porch, she clutched the oilcloth from the table at her throat as protection against the wet. In her hand was the quilt bundle. Glancing at the bottom of the steps, she could see that the water lapped a foot away. Even as she watched, it seemed to gain several inches.

Nancy went about the cabin making sure of things, then followed. She wore Ollie's raincoat and his hat on her head. In one hand was the lantern and in the other, the carpetbag. Lightning flickered as they took the trail around the house and up the hill behind it.

They hadn't gone far before the hem of Nancy's dress was sodden with rain and mud. Putting down the carpetbag, she quickly ripped a good four inches from the bottom of her skirt. Then, she picked up the bag and followed the rest up the hill.

It was hard going because the ground was so wet and they were trying to make their way uphill. They slipped and slid and once, Birdie went to his knees. But, he was able to get up in the next stride, with never a sound from Stella.

As they walked along, there was a sudden crash and crack and the very ground they stood on shook. For a moment it seemed that the creek halted its mad rush down the hill and there was silence except for the rain. The rise of the flood was unmistakable.

"That's what's causin' the crick to rise so fast," Birdie stopped to tell them. "A big rock fall into the crick. They was another one, just below Jimmy Muncy's. Seems like half the hill is gone."

Nancy nodded. "I hope they're alright."

"They'd already left their place. May have lost some cattle, though."

"Where's Sally?" Stella asked from under Birdie's slicker. "Where's Sol?" She referred to their hound dogs.

"They were under the porch last I see 'em," he assured her. "Don't you fret none. Huntin' dogs hunt and they'll be alright."

Nancy felt someone brush against her and looked down to see Evie standing beside her. Her eyes were on the path behind them and she shivered a little. "Will we be comin' back, Mama?"

"Why yes, child. We'll be back. This is home."

"Seems like the whole world is changin'," was her daughter's reply. Then, she moved on to trudge alongside her mother until the trail grew too narrow and then, she followed.

The roar of water grew louder, while their path grew straighter and more level. Then, Birdie walked down the hill and they followed. When he halted, they halted.

"This here's Holdy Branch," he told her. "Never seen it run like that, have you?"

In the dim light, it was hard to see the stream, but they could see the lacy foam that edged the shore. More than that, they could hear its wild tumult.

Nancy stood beside him and shook her head.

Birdie unbuttoned his slicker enough that he could get out of it, yet have Stella remain protected. She looked like a headless man, since it was up over her head.

Before them was a footbridge of logs with a line of single planks nailed onto the log frame and a lone handrail for support.

"I don't know if it holds." Birdie shook the handrail, then stepped one foot onto the bridge

Before she could answer, there came the murmur of voices and out of the dark came a group of people, their slickers shiny in the rain.

"What ho, is that you Birdie? Where's your slicker?"

"The little 'un's got it," was his reply.

"Why hello, Miz Cyrus! What you doin' on this side of the hill?" The speaker came forward and looking them up and down.

"Hello, Shy," said Nancy.

"Burgess," Birdie nodded his greeting.

"It's floodin' on the other side." She went on.

"Like the end times," said Birdie.

"So, you're no better off over on Camp Creek than here?" Shy almost bellowed to be heard over the roar of the creek. "You'd think so, since you're closer to Heaven than us down on the flat!" He laughed at his own wit.

"They's a rock fall just below Jimmy Muncy's," Birdie's mild voice was quite the contrast to Shy Burgess.

"So, that's what brought the water up so quick," Burgess nodded his head in understanding. He turned to the bridge and put his hand on the rail. "If you're a wonderin' about this bridge; my boy Ezra come across it not more'n an hour ago."

"Are you-all flooded out, too?" Nancy asked.

"Yeah, we're headed over to her mother's on Paint Creek," Burgess indicated the group behind him waiting in the shelter of a pine tree. "You're welcome to join us. Plenty of room." Anyone being around Shy Burgess for any length of time could tell that his name did not describe the man. In actuality, it was a nickname bestowed upon him for his very lack of shyness or consideration that his opinion wasn't shared by others.

"If the bridge is safe, we can get to Ferguson Creek, where my cousin Beck lives."

"That's a far piece. And with these two little 'uns. You might as well come along with us. Paint Creek's a bit closer."

"Thankee for the invitation. But, we'll head on to Beck's."

"Wal, good luck to ye." Burgess glanced around them. "I don't reckon we'll see you at church this week, but maybe next!"

"See you then!" Nancy spoke the words, but felt no assurance they were true.

They watched the group walk past with Burgess' booming voice echoing behind them. Only for a little way would they take the trail; then, at Rock House, they would cut across the hill and follow the ridge to Paint Creek.

It immediately felt colder without the warmth of Burgess with his ready smiles and big voice. With a shrug, as if shaking off the feeling, Nancy took hold of the handrail and put her foot on the plank.

"You'd ought to let me go first, Miz Cyrus." Birdie held out his hand, as if to stop her.

Nancy walked out on the bridge holding the lantern high, her body silhouetted in its light. As she continued to walk, she seemed swallowed up by the night and rain. Yet, in moments, she was back, smiling. "It holds!" There was relief in her voice. "It holds!"

Once again buttoned in the slicker with Stella, Birdie grabbed the hand rail and stepped onto the little bridge. Nancy indicated that Evie should go next. Putting the quilt roll over her shoulder, the girl followed after Birdie. Yet, as she reached the middle, a log coming downstream hit the middle support of the bridge. The bridge shook and Evie grabbed for the handrail with both hands as she went to her knees.

Nancy could only watch, her hand at her throat,, then breathe prayer of thanks as her daughter slowly got to her feet.

When Evie was across, Nancy stepped up onto the plank. Anxious faces peered through the gloom, their faces lit by the lantern Birdie carried. Her lips moved, then, holding her head high, she took hold of the handrail and walked to the other side.

"Well, what are you waiting for?" Nancy asked as she joined them. "On to cousin Beck's!" She looked at Evie. "You remember cousin Beck don't you? He's got a white beard down to his belt"

"Down to his belt?" Her oldest daughter grinned up at her. "Let's be doin'!"

With Birdie and Stella leading the way, mother and daughter walked side by side along the path to Ferguson Creek. And when Evie put her hand next to her mother's Nancy took it with a squeeze. So, hand in hand they made their way through the dark and the rain toward the hope of warmth and welcome.

Chapter
TWO

WALKING ALONG THE FOREST TRAIL beneath a leafy tunnel, it was hard to tell if it was still raining or just dripping from the trees around and above them. When the dark closeness ended, Nancy grew aware that they were out of the forest, yet still it dripped. So, it was still raining. Not hard, but still, raining.

Birdie halted and a flash of lightning revealed the reason. A big lake of water lay before them and in the middle was a two story house.

"Cousin Beck's," Nancy recognized the place. Most everyone had a home of logs, whether one story or two story. But, Beck Ferguson had added on to his cabin with white board siding and then put it over the original logs as well.

"No light. No one home," was Birdie's comment.

"Likely," was her reply.

"Now what do ya wanna do?"

"Everyone is tired and wet. All we want to do is get dry and get some sleep." She stated the obvious, but it was to try to spark her fatigued brain into finding an answer.

"Where's Cousin Beck, Mama?" Evie asked her.

"Looks like they left. Like we did."

"Didn't you grow up here?"

Nancy smiled a little. "Yes. I spend many summers here. When my Pa was out gettin' work, I stayed with Cousin Beck and Aunt Gert."

"And you had a pony to ride?" She was too tired to hide the envy in her voice.

"Yes. My sister and I rode Chief. He was a spotted pony. Unusual at the time." Her voice grew distant, as if going back in time.

"I'd like to have a pony," Evie said, softly, knowing her mother was not listening.

Beside them, Birdie shifted his weight, for Stella was asleep and heavy.

"And, didn't you camp out and sleep under the stars?"

Her mother smiled with the memories. "Yes. And, we slept in a cave as well." Even as she spoke, she had a realization and her eyes met Birdie's. "Come on! Let's go!"

"A cave?" Birdie caught on at once. "There's a cave around here?"

When Nancy halted again, it was to pull some weeds and brush that blocked the entrance to the cave.

He held the lantern high so that they could see, then followed her in. Neither the entrance nor the cave was very large. Only in one spot could he stand without bending over. Yet, it was dry and just inside the entrance was a mound of dry wood.

"Thank God!" Nancy breathed the words. She motioned to Evie to start a fire.

"I never knew this was here," Birdie knelt down, helping Stella out of his slicker.

Nancy grinned at him. "Of course not. It was for girl secrets."

Much to the dismay of many women seeking husbands, Cousin Beck had never married, giving as his reason, caring for his mother. Even when she passed away, he ignored any and all who desired to marry him. It was a strange situation to many, since they heeded the Biblical call to be fruitful and multiply. He'd had a year or so of being alone and only lately had taken in his mother's sister, Aunt Gert. Yet, he always welcomed his nieces and nephews to come stay with him.

Near the entrance of the cave was a blackened area where once there had been many fires.

"We've found arrow points in here. And, fire circles. Cousin Beck said Indians must have used it for shelter."

"Just like us!" Evie's eyes gleamed with excitement.

"Just like us," Nancy assured her.

She was thankful she'd made bread the day before and had the food to take with them. Against Birdie's protests that he didn't need a lot, she divided one loaf between them, insisting that he take the major share. After all, he'd carried Stella up hill and down. After eating, it didn't take long for the warmth of the fire to make them drowsy and send the girls to sleep.

Nancy sat upright, her back to the cave wall, almost asleep, with Stella's head in her lap. Beside her, Evie slept on a quilt with her feet toward the fire.

Every little bit, Birdie would leave the cave, but it was still raining and it drove him back inside.

"What is it, Birdie?" She roused at his entrance.

He twisted his hat in his hand. "This ain't seemly, Miz Cyrus."

Nancy looked at him and frowned a little until his meaning seeped into her tired brain.

"You and me. Not hitched."

She regarded him, then spoke. "Do I have anything to fear from you, Birdie McComas?"

"Lordy, Miz Cyrus! What a thing to say!"

"Well, you've nothin' to fear from me. Now go to sleep."

The next morning, daylight showed Cousin Beck's house with water halfway up the first floor windows. Brown water surged around it, seeking its way downstream. Though it wasn't raining at the moment, the sky above was gray, promising more rain.

Evie stood beside her mother as they looked out of the cave together. "Do you think our house has water in it?"

"Our house is lower than this one. I'm sure it does."

Birdie came walking down the hill from above them, still tucking his shirt in his pants. "Do you think this is a flood, like Bible times?" He shook his head and grinned, lightening the subject.

Evie looked up at him, then at her mother. "Do you think so, Mama?"

As if for answer, it began to rain again.

"I'm hungry, Mama," Stella rubbed her eyes.

Leaning in the opening of the cave, Birdie kept his eyes on the creek. "Don't you start nuthin', yet." He straightened his lengthy frame. "I think I'll go for a quick scout around."

"Me, too!" Evie followed him out of the cave before her mother could voice an opinion.

When they came back with handfuls of chicken eggs, Nancy was quick to give thanks.

It seemed that Birdie had seen a chicken coop go floating by which halted in a tangle of vines and brush along the creek. Evie volunteered to crawl through it while Birdie kept it from going further downstream. As they had hoped, there were eggs in the abandoned nests.

"The Lord provides!" Birdie grinned at Nancy.

She looked up at him, as if his words reminded her that the Lord also takes away, but she only nodded and took the eggs from his hands.

Since there were so many eggs, Nancy didn't feel it necessary to slice the bacon very thick, thus saving it for another day. As Birdie said, the only thing that could top off their meal was some nice, fresh milk. But, since no cows came floating by, they made do with tea.

Nancy had packed some coffee, but it was something else to save for another day.

"What now, Mama?" Stella asked, coming to stand beside her at the entrance to the cave. She took hold of her mother's skirt with one hand while the fist of the other hovered near her mouth. Though she'd stopped sucking her thumb before her father died, ever after, whenever she became worried, she would do it again. Nancy told Evie to ignore it; that the habit would go away on its own. She wasn't surprised that the little one had regressed.

Before them, the short grass of the hill opposite seemed to have disappeared, pounded into the ground, revealing the black soil beneath. The cow trails that crisscrossed their slopes had been transformed into a series of waterfalls. In the middle of the brown lake that was the flooded creek stood the log home of Cousin Beck and Nancy marveled that it withstood the onslaught of the water.

Above, the sky was a mass of gray clouds, with a light rain peppering the surface of the flood. It seemed that the world was made of three colors, black, brown and gray.

"Where did all this water come from?" Evie asked with some wonder in her voice. "Won't it take a while to go down?"

Nancy nodded absently.

"What are we gonna do now, Mama?" Stella's voice had grown smaller.

Birdie looked at her. "You got any more people around here?"

"Uncle Albert," Stella spoke up. "Don't he live on Hash Ridge?"

Nancy looked down at her daughter, then back at the flood.

"What about Ike Cyrus?" Birdie mentioned Ollie's uncle's name. Though Abe and Isaac were twins, they weren't much alike. Isaac had narrow shoulders and a triangular face. And whereas his brother liked nothing more than to drink and fight, Isaac loved to sing and read, the same characteristics as Ollie. Perhaps that was why he had been her favorite of all the Cyrus clan.

She shook her head. "They live at the mouth of Emily Creek. They have to be under water, too."

"Cousin Perry?" Evie spoke up. Though she didn't recall ever meeting him, she had heard his name mentioned.

For a long moment, there was silence, then Nancy nodded. "Cousin Perry moved to Mount Joy a couple of years ago."

"Mount Joy?" Birdie asked. "On the river?"

Nancy did not answer as she gazed intently upstream. In her mind's eye, she could see over the hills to their valley. By now, it was flooded and she wondered if the cabin still stood. Tears came to her eyes, but it seemed something pushed her away. Then, she turned her face to the west. Somehow, her heart softened. Taking a deep breath, she said, "Let's go this way."

Evie looked at her mother. "Leave the valley?"

"We need to get dry and warm. I don't think this is the place for it." Nancy turned back to the cave and began getting things packed up.

Birdie patted Evie on the shoulder. "For now," he assured her.

Watching Nancy packing, Stella's eyes grew big. "I'm hungry again, Mama," She tugged on her mother's dress.

"You just ate, honey," Nancy smiled at her. "But, I'll make a sugar tit for you to suck on."

It was the work of a moment to put some sugar in a bit of cloth, twist the end and hand it to the child. The little girl was more acquiescent then and let Birdie boost her onto his back.

"We'll have to keep to the hilltops." Nancy stated as she picked up the carpetbag.

When she straightened, she noticed that Evie had been watching her. "What do you say, little one?"

"I say, we're burnin' daylight," Birdie put in and began walking away.

Yet, Nancy hesitated, waiting for her daughter's reply.

"Let's go!" Evie grinned. "Let's be doin'!"

Two days later, it was a tired group that looked out over a broad expanse of brown river water, with whitecaps whipped up by the wind.

"Reaches from hill to hill," Birdie commented on the width of the river.

It seemed impossible, but it was true. The trees that normally lined the river banks were surrounded by water and island of debris, perhaps half a mile from the newly created shore. Just in back of the trees were buildings scattered here and there, but all had been overtaken by water.

"We sure are in a pickle." Birdie commented.

"Look," Nancy pointed. "There's a town over there. Along the hill."

Because of the wall of rain between their shore and the one opposite, it was dimly visible.

"You're right," his voice grew more excited. "But, it's over there. Across the water."

"Will we be dry again?" Stella asked.

"Why sure, honey," her mother was almost at eye level with her, bundled on Birdie's back like she was.

"Look, Mama," Evie pointed almost directly below them.

On the high ground, there was a train track and beside it a road. Buildings filled the open space around it, using every bit of ground available.

"They've been flooded before," Birdie noted the location of the buildings.

As they watched, groups of people came from both directions down the road, some on horseback, others in wagons, but mostly afoot. They carried what things they thought important in their hands, lashed across their backs or held on their heads.

It didn't seem to matter if they were hill people or farmers or travelers; it was a stream of people seeking shelter and perhaps, like them, a way across the river.

"This is a depot," he went on. "They take stuff off the train and ferry it across the river."

Nancy looked at him.

As if caught out, Birdie shrugged and grinned. "I leave the hills sometimes."

"Look, Mama!" Evie pointed up river.

As they watched, a shed came floating down the river, chickens perched on the part that rode highest in the water. A rooster crowed, his neck outstretched, while nearby boats tried to get close to it. Apparently a chicken dinner was on everyone's minds. Yet, the shed avoided the boars and kept floating downriver, the rooster announcing their progress to all and sundry.

"Someone's belongings," Nancy murmured. Even as it floated down the river, one could see that it had been painted red with cream colored trim. "Someone's put time and effort into it."

"And chickens!" Stella added from beside her.

"It's just like you to worry about other people's troubles, 'stead of yer own," Birdie said, his voice unsteady.

"Says the man who faced flood and storm to warn us of the crick risin'," she replied.

It seemed that he blushed and silence punctuated by big fat raindrops hitting the ground followed her words.

Nancy took Evie's hand. "Well, let's go join them and see what's doin'."

They soon found out Birdie was right. Lester's Landing was a depot, used to take goods from one side of the river to the other, since there was no bridge within a hundred miles and it downstream.

On the other side of the river, Mount Joy was a town built on a bluff, having been flooded out a few times in the past. It was indeed a town, with six streets, five avenues and saloons, hotels and such. But, between Lester's Landing and Mount Joy a vast river of brown water flowed.

There was a ferry, but what with the current and the waves, the ferryman was reluctant to cross, regardless of the large amounts of money offered him.

Once down on the road, the little group from Camp Creek joined the throng headed for the buildings. One of them seemed to be something resembling a general store and they made for it.

Birdie shook his head. "Where's all these people goin'? They ain't enough room for 'em here." He looked at the bluff above them, towering over the railroad track and the cluster of buildings.

"Look!" Evie pointed toward the riverbank. In between the trees, they could see a flotilla of various kinds of boats, waiting to take passengers across the river.

Apparently, there were other men that would take passengers over to yonder town, for a price.

"Looks a little risky," Birdie murmured, looking out across the broad expanse of the river. Not too far out from shore, whitecaps topped the waves and large trees, their roots protruding menacingly from the water, bobbed by.

"I have a cousin Perry across the river," Nancy spoke up. "He and his wife live on a farm just outside of Mount Joy."

"Do you think they're under water?" It was a question to ask, since it seemed that all of the bottom land on both sides of the river had disappeared.

"I don't think so. In the letter he wrote when he bought it, he said they were on high ground."

As they walked among the buildings, it was to see men standing about in the shelter of the warehouses, some sitting on bags of grain, smoking their pipes and cigars as they watched them pass. A steady stream of people headed to the general store and they followed the crowd to it.

"You want to cross the river?" Birdie held the door for her and the girls then followed them into the store. It was packed full of people trying to escape the rain. An overpowering stench of sweat and wet wool filled the place, but she tried not to notice.

Nancy hesitated and looked into his eyes. "We have to." Then, she walked into the store.

Before he could follow, a cluster of people pushed their way into the store, blocking Birdie from entering. "I'll meet you back here when I get us passage," he called to her, not sure if she heard. The store was busy and people shouted their questions over the drum of the rain on the roof. With a glance at her, he turned away to see what he could find.

As they made their way into the store, Nancy noted a large man sitting on a stack of crates, a shotgun in his hand. Whenever anyone left, he would accost them, glance at one of the clerks to make certain they'd paid for their merchandise, then let them pass.

"I'm hungry, Mama," Stella tugged on her sleeve as they passed the candy case.

"Not now, honey," was her mother's reply. Her gaze swept the crowded room filled with bags of flour, sugar and coffee, crates and fabric as well as pelts and trapping supplies. "Evie, take your sister over there," she nodded to a corner that seemed fairly empty. A pile of bags that had tipped over made a little corral, blocking the corner from the main part of the store. "Don't move til I come for you."

Taking her little sister's hand, Evie did as she was told.

Looking about the corner, she could tell that sacks of flour had been stacked there, but either through getting brushed by passersby or pushed over by a disgruntled customer, they had toppled. The hills and valleys made by the sacks were just the sort Stella liked to play in and Evie let her loose to do just that. She even played hide and seek with her until a couple of men sat down nearby.

They were rough looking with their beards, long hair and mud splattered clothing. But, perhaps they'd been flooded out as well and had no way to clean up. Evie signaled to Stella to stop crawling through the bags and come sit beside her.

"What's your name, little girl?" One of the men held a peppermint stick in his hand, and offered it to Stella.

"Never you mind," Evie told him.

"Then, what's your name?"

She ignored him and stood up to look around for her mother.

"Hey now, I didn't mean anythin'," said the man. "No need to get riled. It's just that she reminds me of my baby girl."

"You have a baby girl?" Stella was keen on anything that was a baby.

"I did," was his reply. His lips tightened. "Until the Yanks come along."

With the mention of Yanks, Evie relaxed her guard a little. After all, hadn't her father and his brothers fought on the side of the Confederates?

"Would you come and sit on my lap?" He asked, offering the candy stick. "Like my little girl used to do?" He smiled.

Stella hesitated.

Evie looked about for her mother, unsure of what to do. Meanwhile, her sister approached him shyly, which was not her usual wont.

"And be your little girl?" She asked.

"Yep. You can call me Uncle Harry." He held up the peppermint stick. "And you can have this."

Stella looked at the candy. "Me hungry." She didn't even look at the man as he swung her up onto his lap, her eyes on the striped stick.

"Here you go," he handed the candy to her then turned to Evie, nodding in her direction. "And, Uncle Sid has one for you, too."

Evie was suddenly aware of another man standing beside her, a peppermint stick in his hand. He offered it to her, but she ignored the temptation. Standing on her tiptoes, she looked for her mother in the crowd of people. Sid moved to where he stood before her, blocking her view.

Stella suddenly cried out and Evie turned to see Harry walking hurriedly away, the little girl in his arms. Before she could move or shout, another man put his hand on Harry's shoulder and turned him around. His head jerked back as a fist hit his jaw. Rather than fight, Harry tucked Stella under his arm and tried to run. Again, the newcomer spun him around and hit him. Twice, three times! The blows staggered Harry who dropped Stella. Quickly the little girl crawled under a nearby counter.

Meanwhile, Evie felt a strong arm around her chest and under her arms. Immediately she fought, so that he couldn't pick her up, but he dragged her away. Kicking did no good and trying to elbow him was to no avail. She kicked and flailed her legs, then reached down and bit the man's arm. He cursed and threw her from him, even as the newcomer reached out and spun him around. Solid blows rained on his body, even as he cried out for help from the crowd. Staggering back against a counter, he raised a hand to wipe his bloody mouth and looked around for a way out.

Meanwhile, the newcomer wheeled about, his fists up, ready to take on anyone else. But, the area had cleared of men. While his attention was on the crowd in the store, Harry and Sid got up and ran.

"What's going on?" One of the clerks came forward, a thick club in his hand.

The crowd quickly dispersed while the newcomer talked to the clerk, telling him what had transpired.

"They'd better keep clear of the store!" The man raised the club and shook it. Then, he turned back to his counter, while the newcomer approached the girls, concern in his eyes.

"Are you alright?" The newcomer came over to Evie and helped her up. "Where's your Pa?"

"I am, thank you, sir," Evie replied. "My Papa's passed on, raisin' hell in heaven, my Mama says." She kept looking at him and blinking, as if she couldn't quite see him or get her eyes to focus. Though he was dressed like the other men, somehow, he looked different. Perhaps, it was because he didn't have a beard, but a goatee.

"Is your Mama around?" He walked over to the counter where Stella was hiding then turned to face Evie.

"She's lookin' for passage across the river." Her eyes slid over him, noting his thickset frame and light blue eyes. She got the feeling he was like a human rock, very solid and strong.

He nodded. "Would you happen to know where your sister is? I saw her around here somewhere."

Evie stared at him, then realized he was teasing. It was a surprise to know that rocks had a sense of humor. She glanced down at her sister who was hiding on the shelf under the counter, nearly hidden by the man's legs. "She does a good job of hidin'," the girl went along with the game. "I don't know where she is."

"Here I am!" Stella crawled out from her hiding place and stood up. Once upright and seeing the crush of people, her lip began to tremble. "Where's Mama?"

"It's alright," Evie reassured her. "She'll be back in a minute." She glanced at their corner. "We better get back over there before she misses us."

Kneeling, the man looked from one to the other of the girls. "If that ever happens again, you need to scream," he told Stella, then met Evie's gaze. "And you, too."

Stella regarded him with big eyes. "Don't you let someone offer you candy, either."

"Yes, sir," she told him.

The man stood up and looked around. Something or someone coming in the front door caught his attention. "I- I have to go. But, I want you girls to promise me something. Stay away from strange men."

"Yes sir," was said in unison.

"Now go. Go back to your corner." His words were rushed and his attention on the front door. With that, he started to walk away.

Evie watched him and noticed that his path led along the candy counter. As if on cue, her stomach growled. She glanced at the floor where both peppermint sticks lay crushed into pieces.

When she looked up, the man was back. He knelt before them and held up two peppermint sticks. "This is for being brave girls." One was pressed into the hand of each, then he stood up and disappeared into the throng.

Evie looked up, trying to find where he was, then at the front door to see what had concerned their benefactor. Her attention was drawn to a young man pressing through the crowd, struggling to get by. He seemed in a rush. "Let me through! Let me through!" Yet, no one seemed in a hurry to let that happen. "Official business! Official business!" He held up a badge yet even with that authority, people were slow to move aside.

She looked in the direction their rescuer had gone and then, briefly, saw him at the back door. Even in the shadows, she could see that he gave her a wink.

The gesture decided her and Evie motioned for Stella to join her as she sat down on the floor. When the young man came rushing through, he stopped when he saw the girls in his path.

"Move! Move!" He motioned for them to get out of his way. For a moment, his hand hovered near his vest pocket, as if to bring out the badge, but he hesitated, his attention on the door at the back of the building.

Evie paid no attention to him, handing her peppermint stick to Stella to hold, while she tied a boot for her that did not need tying.

"Could you hurry that up?" Frustration was in the young man's voice. He slapped the counter beside him, which held bolts of cloth but the sound of his hand smacking the fabric was not as satisfying as the wood would have been. Cursing under his breath, he wheeled about and took another route through the throngs on his way to the back door.

Evie stood up to watch him finally make it to the door and leave. As she turned back to her sister, she was aware of two things. First, that a strange man had saved her and her sister from being kidnapped. He had then offered them candy, even while warning them of strange men offering children candy. The other was the young man. When she had looked up into his pale face with high cheekbones, dark blonde hair and intense light blue eyes, it was as if her heart did a flip. Lightning, she told herself. The feeling was like lightning striking her.

Somehow, the world was not the same. There was a tug on her sleeve.

"Can we?" Stella held up the peppermint stick. "I'm hungry."

Evie helped her sister to her feet, then nodded. They looked at one another, then the candy in their hands. Together they took a long lick of their stick. Slowly, they walked back to the corner to enjoy the candy.

When their mother found them, their faces and hands were sticky. Stella tried to tell her what had happened, but the store was too noisy. Besides, Nancy had found them passage across the river and was anxious to get started.

Once outside, they could see that though the brief downpour had passed, the sky was growing dark again and more rain threatened.

"Hurry, girls!" Nancy encouraged her daughters as they walked quickly out of the store and then, down the path to the shore where many boats waited. Though she looked around for Birdie, he was nowhere to be seen.

"Where's Birdie?" Evie voiced her mother's concern.

"I don't know," was the reply. "And, we must hurry."

There were throngs of people at the river's edge, as well as a variety of boats large and small jockeying for position that would allow for passengers to wade to them.

"There!" Nancy pointed toward a older man in a boat that looked like it had been a lifeboat, perhaps off an ocean going ship. She hurried her girls down to the river's edge.

"Here I be!" Birdie's familiar voice called to them.

Looking up, she saw him standing knee deep in water next to a boat fifty feet further upriver. For a moment, she hesitated, wondering whether to go in the boat she had hired or in the one Birdie had rented.

"There's Birdie!" Stella cried out and ran toward him.

"Stella!" Nancy's voice was drowned out in the scream of a train whistle coming into the station. "Wait!" She told the boatman, then gathered her skirts and ran after her youngest daughter while Evie followed.

When she made her way around the crowd, it was to find Stella in the arms of Birdie, both of them grinning delightedly at one another. Nancy glanced back at the boat she had rented to find two men getting into it.

"Mr. Kyper, wait! That's my boat!" She did not realize she had spoken her thought until she felt Birdie looking at her.

"You – you rented a boat?" He seemed taken aback, as if he had lost his footing.

"Yes," was her reply. "I couldn't find you, so I hired my own."

Birdie frowned, but said nothing.

"If'n you don't want this boat, I kin sure rent it to them fellers!" Called the man at the oars of the boat Birdie had rented. He nodded to a group of men waiting anxiously at the water's edge.

"We want it!" Nancy took Evie's hand and held up her skirt, ready to wade into the water.

"No," said the boatman. "I don't take chillern."

Nancy stared at him.

"Hit's a risky proposition, ma'am, crossin' this here river in flood, an' I'll not take responsibility for any but growed persons." He shook his head with finality.

Meanwhile, Nancy's attention was taken by the boat she had rented, already well on its way across the river. "That man has my shotgun."

Birdie looked at her. "I wondered where you got the money."

"Well, it's heavy and I thought to get a pistol or somethin' a little easier to heft."

"What now, Mama?" Evie asked from beside her.

"Do we have to cross the river?" Stella's voice was plaintive in its tiredness.

Birdie waded to the boatman and took back his money. Turning, he walked ashore then scooped the little girl into his arms. "We sure do," he told her. "That's where Cousin Perry lives!"

Softly, gently, it began to rain. Stella held out her hand. "Will we ever be dry again?

When her mother did not answer, Evie spoke up. "Of course we will! This is just a little wet. We musta been plenty dirty, for God to send us this much rain!"

Beside her, Nancy looked up and down the river bank. As many people as were being rowed across the river, it seemed just as many walked to the shore, looking for a ride across.

"Perhaps we can find shelter on this side of the river," she murmured. After all, it was late afternoon and with the overcast, dark would come early. "Isn't that a farmhouse?"

Everyone looked in the direction she was pointing. As they watched, a two story farmhouse came floating down the river, like some new kind of ship. Yet, as it continued its course, it began to sink, riding lower and lower in the water. In the middle of the river, the boatmen fought to avoid it, but the current seemed bent on steering it into them. Finally, the house floated on by, with the boats still upright and continuing their slanted course to the opposite shore.

Nancy turned her face to the sky. "We could sure use a miracle about now."

Beside her, Birdie said, "Amen."

Suddenly, Evie pointed upstream and shouted, "Look, Mama! Here come the Harmon boys!"

Nancy and Birdie looked up the river to see a large raft once used for ferrying, bearing down on the group. In order to stay out of the strongest current, they were keeping close to the shore. Though there were men at the tiller and sweep, it was still hard to handle, yet they were managing.

"Where you headed?" Cried out one of the men standing nearby. "Mount Joy is that way!" And he pointed across the river. All around him, people laughed.

As they watched, a man with thick, long black hair and beard called to the men on either side of the raft. Though neither were as dark as the first, it was clear to see that they were brothers. The sons of Josiah Harmon were well known for their powerful physiques, which their shirts open at the neck and rolled up sleeves revealed. At his signal, they brought the ferry to the shore, where it stopped abruptly.

"We're headed for Mount Joy, boys! If you've the fare, come aboard!" The leader called out with a wide grin.

Birdie waved his arms to get his attention, then nodded to point out Nancy standing beside him.

Sweeping off his hat, Homer Harmon bowed to her. "Welcome, Miz Cyrus! Can I give you a ride to the other shore?" It was notable that he did not say 'we'.

"Yes, Mr. Harmon. I believe we would all like to get to the other side."

With a grandiose gesture, Homer bowed and motioned to the ferry. "Come aboard, m'lady, come aboard!"

Already the available space was being filled as the Harmon brothers took fares and motioned to an open space.

Homer held out a hand to Nancy to help her aboard. But Birdie quickly handed Stella to Hiram Harmon, then turned to help Nancy. She gave him a grateful smile.

"Where did ye find a craft such as this, Homer?" Birdie asked.

"It come floatin' up to me like a lost Ark," he informed him. "An' it's gonna make me some drinkin' money tonight!" He glanced at Nancy. "Beggin' yer pardon, Miz Cyrus!" The grin accompanying his comment made forgiveness immediate. After all, he was unmarried with no one to answer to but himself.

Nancy moved further into the ferry, her daughters beside her. There was a railing above the sides of the craft and she held onto it because the waves were choppy as they came into the shore.

Beside her, another woman grasped the railing as well. "This might be an Ark," she confided, a flat tone to her voice, "but I have my doubts about reachin' yon shore."

Though the woman was not confident in the ferry, Nancy took some comfort in hearing the familiar dialect of the hills.

"All aboard!" Homer called out in a booming voice. It was clear he was enjoying his role as captain.

"Looka thar," the woman nodded toward the back of the craft. It was so heavily loaded, it did not want to respond to the sweep that two of the Harmon boys were pushing, trying to maneuver the ferry.

Finally, it obeyed and they set out across the river. It was a bumpy ride and the craft continually wanted to turn in a circle around the sweep. They could feel the current grow stronger as they neared the middle of the river. To add to their discomfort, the white capped waves grew in height and frequency. The passengers began to look about worriedly.

Yet, the ferry breasted them, though the impact as they hit the waves jolted many off their feet.

Nancy held on as best she could, but it was hard. Thankfully, Birdie held Stella in his arms and still managed to stay on his feet. Evie faced forward, her eyes bright with the thrill of the adventure.

"Homer! Homer Harmon!" The woman beside Nancy called out. At the sound of her strident voice, Nancy suddenly recognized her. She was Mrs. Polly Maynard, wife of Si Maynard and schoolteacher at the Forks. "Look here!" She pointed down.

Standing at the rail, his eyes to the far shore, Homer was unaware of what might be happening behind him. Yet, hearing her voice, even now, many years removed from school, he turned immediately to see what needed his attention.

Nancy followed Mrs. Maynard's pointing finger. It was clear to see that the craft had been built in two pieces then bonded together by logs nailed to the perimeter. The constant pound of the waves had broken some of the bonding logs and the craft was separating into its two original pieces.

Since the sweep and the tiller were on the back half, their weight sank their end, tilting the other end into the air. People and parcels began sliding toward the back, furthering its rapid descent. It was strange to watch it happen and even more so, to note how quietly.

Evie was glad to see that once rid of its load, the back section bobbed on the water, ready to be held onto and many were doing just that. Other people were being picked up by the many boats that were in the area, among them, Hiram and Hosea Harmon.

As yet, the front half of the ferry was still afloat and Homer Harmon stood with one foot on the railing, his fists on his hips, as before. But as they watched, the floor boards began to part revealing the logs that made up the underneath of the craft. The raft gave a lurch as a large tree struck it, roots first. Homer lost his balance and fell backward into the river. In moments, his brothers were beside him in the boat that had picked them up and they had commandeered.

"Mama!" Evie pointed at the town that seemed further away than ever.

The tree that had impaled itself on the raft was taking them further from the shore. Even as they made their way toward the main current, the boards and logs of the ferry continued to loosen and fall away into the river.

Looking about, Nancy could see that her little family and Birdie were all that remained on what was left of the ferry. Cold water washed over her shoes and she knew that they would soon be in the water. With a quick glance skyward, she called out, "Lord! I've been keepin' my faith an' my patience. But, I have to know, why did ye bring us this far if . ."

She wasn't able to finish her statement for she had to grab onto the railing for balance. Apparently, the same current that had impaled the tree onto their craft released it and they were free to head toward shore. Yet, they had nothing with which to guide or propel the raft.

Another log with its attached boards broke free and began floating downstream.

"I know how to swim, Mama!" Evie's voice was tight with excitement.

"Me, too!" Stella chimed in.

"Thanks be to your father for that!" She looked at her daughters and gauged the distance to the shore.

"Miz Cyrus?"

Nancy turned to see that the section of railing that Birdie had been holding onto had broken free. The logs rolled and he was dunked into the water, but came up almost immediately. Yet, even that quickly, they were separated from him. There was no way he could catch up to them. She wanted to wave to him, but would it be good-bye?

A sudden lurch and she grabbed onto the railing, holding it tight with one hand, her other trying to shelter her daughters. She looked down. Water poured over the remaining boards. "To Thee O Lord, we commend our spirits," Nancy let go of the railing, closed her eyes and held each of her girls close.

But, Evie stiffened and pulled away from her. "Look Mama!" She pointed upstream.

Nancy turned to see that a small riverboat was almost upon them. It had to have been commandeered, for no sane riverboat captain would have allowed it on the flood with all of its dangers.

At the front stood a man in a slicker, one hand on a post for balance and the other free, ready to be of assistance. Behind him were gathered a group of people already rescued from the river. As the boat came alongside, it pushed water onto the raft and Nancy could feel the river up to her knees.

"O please sir, do ye have room for two more?" Her eyes sought the face of the young man who knelt on the deck.

Even without his answer, Evie had picked up Stella to hand her to him. It was the work of an instant to pull the young girl up and almost toss her behind him then stretch out his hand once more.

The raft was rapidly sinking and the young man lay down on his stomach in order to reach Evie who Nancy pushed upward toward him. He grasped her wrist, then slowly pulled her up to the deck.

Nancy's skirts were heavy, pulling her down, trapping her legs. It was alright, she thought. The girls were safe.

But then, the young man again stretched out his hand to her. "No!" He said. "We've room for three!"

Something in his eyes made her reach for his hand, even as the last bit of the raft disappeared from under her feet. But both of their hands were wet and their grasp slipped. He put his other hand around her wrist and pulled. For a moment, she dangled half out of the water, only a couple of feet away from the deck and for a moment she had hope of rescue. But, the current tugged harder and she could feel herself being dragged under the boat.

It was no use. He had tried and that would have to be enough. Nancy looked into his eyes, grateful that her girls were safe and then she let go.

Yet, she didn't sink into the water. Someone had grabbed the waistband of her skirt and she was lifted as if light as a feather, onto the deck. The moment her feet touched, she looked up to see who was her other benefactor. A man was backing away into the crowd but as their eyes met, he tipped his hat to her, revealing wrists that were shackled.

"Mama, Mama!" Stella wrapped her arms around her legs. "You're safe! I'se so scared!"

"I'm alright, baby," she assured her daughters, for Evie held her

Langdon Pierce

tightly as well. In looking down at them, Nancy was aware that her wet dress clung to her gently swelling belly. She put a protective arm around it, then looked at the young man. "Thank ye, thank ye."

"He's a sheriff," Evie recognized him from the general store hours.

"Yes, yes, I am," he doffed his hat. "I'm Shelby Sinclair, late of Springfield, Ohio. Glad to make your acquaintance."

"I'm Mrs. Oliver Cyrus," Nancy replied. "My daughters, Evelyn and Stella. Thank you so much for saving us."

"It was my pleasure," he smiled. "Let me get you some blankets."

"Did you happen to pick up a thin fella, too?" Nancy asked, but he had already hurried away.

"I seen a boat pick Birdie up, Mama," Evie murmured, her eyes on the direction that Shelby had gone.

"Thank you, Lord," Nancy softly breathed the words. "An' forgive my lack of faith."

Beside her, Stella tugged on her hand, pointing at the man in the shadows. "And, he saved us, too!"

She looked at him, "And thank you as well."

With a sardonic smile, he nodded to her, accepting her gratitude.

Evie started to speak, to explain what Stella meant, but was distracted by Shelby coming up to them with blankets.

"We're headed to shore, now. We'll have you warm and dry in two shakes." He handed a blanket to Nancy who wrapped Stella up in it. She was already starting to shiver. When he offered one to Evie, she drew away.

"What's got into you, girl?" Nancy asked. "Take it and wrap up."

With that, Evie shyly took the blanket and did as she was told.

Chapter THREE

WHERE MOUNT JOY WAS SITUATED, the river made its way close to the bluffs of Lester's Landing, leaving a wide, level space for the town on the opposite shore. However, it hadn't taken long for the townspeople to realize it was a flood plain and they moved the town to the higher ground. They were grateful there was a gentle rise up to the bluffs and the town was planted on it. Though there was no canal for which it was named, Canal Street stretched along the length of the town, closest to the river. The equally descriptive Hill Street was the main thoroughfare up the bluff, while Main Street paralleled Canal Street at the top of the hill. Church Street was the next street over with two churches, one Catholic, one Methodist and a Wesleyan church, planned. Elm Street connected the two on the west end of town and Sycamore Street ran between them on the east end.

Due to the rain, the streets were thick with mud. And, because of it clinging to boots and shoes, the wooden sidewalks were equally muddy. Nancy found an unused stall at the livery stable and changed her clothes as well as the girls. In the carpetbag was her one other change of clothes that was not her Sunday best. Quickly she put on her 'next best', though she knew the dress would get dirty and stained. She wanted to look her best now that she was in town.

"Where's Birdie, Mama?" Stella asked, leaning on the stall wall.

Nancy knew she was tired; they were all tired. But, there was more to be done. "He found some friends of his," she answered. "They needed him to help them with somethin'."

"Will we see him again?"

Nancy smiled. "Yes, I'm sure we will." She ran her hands over her hair and hoped that she was presentable. It was hard to tell without a mirror.

"I hope so, Mama. He smells like home."

"Yes, he does. But, we're gonna make a new home, now."

"A new one?" Evie's head appeared around the open stall door. "Here? In Mount Joy?"

"Where the Lord leads us," her mother assured them and put a hand over her heart. "There's a place that will feel right to us. And, that will be home."

"How will we know?" Stella frowned.

Nancy smiled. "We will just know."

At the stall door, Evie turned away to face the aisle. She bowed her head, put a hand over her heart and said to herself. "I already know where my home is."

As they were leaving the barn, Nancy overheard Mr. Ainsley, the owner of the Ainsley's Livery, telling his wife that the pianist for their church was ill and they were looking for someone to take his place.

After ascertaining which church it was, Nancy took each of her daughter's hands and started up Hill Street.

It took some time to make their way to Church Street and even with trying to be careful mud trimmed the hems of her dress. Nancy shook it off as best she could, bade Evie to stay with Stella, and walked into Mount Joy Methodist Church.

Outside, Evie and Stella amused themselves by counting the pickets of the fence surrounding the churchyard. When a wagon or buggy would pass by, Evie would make up stories about where it might have been and where it was going.

They could hear when the piano began to play and Evie sang along with Stella trying to follow the words as best she could. In between songs, Stella would sit down, her arm over her stomach. "I'm hungry, Evie."

"We'll be eatin' soon," her sister assured her. She was hungry, too. All in all, it had been a trying day and both girls were tired.

Yet when Nancy came out of the church smiling, their flagging spirits were raised.

"Well, it's a Methodist church, not a Baptist one. But, they need someone to play the piano and I can do it."

They hugged, then Evie looked at Stella. "She's mighty hungry, Mama."

"And that's just what we're gonna do. Going," she corrected herself. "We're going to get something to eat." She focused on saying each word like a flatlander. "Elder Deering has invited us to his home for a meal." Taking each child's hand, she began walking down the street, singing, just loud enough for them to hear, "Praise God from Whom all Blessings Flow."

The sun peeked through the clouds as they walked along Church Street, then turned back toward the river on Sycamore Street. Their eyes were big with wonder as they looked at the large homes lining the street. On the corner of Sycamore and Main Street was the biggest one of all.

Evie looked at it, noting the porches and turrets and many windows. "Is he rich?"

"It would seem so," Nancy opened the gate and followed her daughters up the walk.

Inside, the house seemed to echo what was going on outside. It was dark and gloomy except for the many lamps lit in the dining room. And, on the table was dish after dish and platter after platter of things to eat. Rolls glistened in heaps in baskets. The smell made their knees weak and mouths water.

Elder Deering was above average in height and above average in looks, as far as he was concerned. He wore his clothes and robes well and kept his long slender fingers clean and the nails filed. If anything detracted, it was the fact that he had gone bald early in life and had to affect a combover to keep his head concealed. His voice was rich in tone and when he commanded his flock, they knew they had been commanded. He also had thick eyebrows roofing big, dark eyes, which he could use to great effect. Indeed, God had known what He was doing when He had called Kimberly Deering to minister.

When he walked into the dining room, it was with his shoulders back and head up, a move guaranteed to garner attention.

"Thank you for coming to my humble home," he stood by the chair at the head of the table. He motioned to the one at his right. "Mrs. Cyrus?" He helped seat her.

To his left stood a twelve year old boy, clearly resentful of the guests.

"May I present my son, John Wesley?"

Evie and Stella both gave a curtsy while John Wesley mumbled, "Pleased to meet ya" and sat down in his chair.

"Speak up, son, speak up!" With a slight frown, Deering motioned that he should seat Evie.

But, the boy's head was down and he continued to sit in his chair.

Evie and Stella seated themselves, their eyes never leaving the food on the table. It was hard not to lick their lips, everything looked so delicious.

"It's a pleasure having a woman in the house again, isn't it, John Wesley?" Deering asked, smiling at Nancy.

But, his son continued to ignore him and continued to stare at the table.

Deering began to reach for the meat platter, but Nancy interrupted him by saying, "Bow your heads, girls." She clasped her hands together and bowed her head, her daughters' actions almost in unison.

The minister quickly retracted his hand and bowed his head. "Heavenly Father, we give thanks for what we are about to receive."

Before he could go on, John Wesley broke in with a flat, "Amen."

Nancy and her daughters repeated, "Amen."

Immediately, the boy pulled the bowl of potatoes to his plate and began emptying it.

"John Wesley," his father reprimanded him. "Our guests."

The boy looked up to see Stella staring at the mound of food on his plate. Glancing at Evie, he noted that she looked away.

"We ain't et much but stale cornpone fer two days," Stella said, in plain honesty.

Nancy gave her a look and a little smile. "We thank you for your hospitality. She's right though. With the flood takin' – taking – over our home, we didn't have a chance to grab much in the way of foodstuffs."

"Here," John Wesley spooned some of the potatoes onto Stella's plate. "Foodstuffs! Who says that?" He looked at Nancy critically. "You're not goin' to try to marry her are you, Pa?"

"I'm not sure what put that in your head, son." He looked at Nancy. "I apologize for him, Mrs. Cyrus. He's been without a mother's influence for some time." Deering passed the platter of roasted chicken to her.

"Since then, there's been no other woman in the house."

John Wesley seemed to have trouble swallowing a mouthful of food, but worked mightily at it after a drink of water.

Nancy smiled at the boy. "I'm sure your father has plenty of chances of matrimony, John Wesley." Then, she looked at his father. "I thank you for giving me a chance to work."

The minister smiled and nodded, then paid attention to his food. Nancy noted that he used a knife and fork in cutting the chicken from the bone and only allowed a certain portion of food on his fork at a time. It wasn't something seen in the hills and valleys where she was from. Evie noted it, too, but apparently, John Wesley had no such compunction. He scooped food into his mouth, as much as he could get, before closing it and attempting to chew.

Yet, the food was good and filled all the nooks and crannies, as Evie said later, reflecting on the meal.

"If you don't mind me asking, where will you be staying?" Deering looked at the faces around his table, then at the plates. Everyone's was empty except for John Wesley. What he hadn't eaten, he had made mounds of and trailed gravy between them.

"I've a few friends here in town and a cousin, too. We'll have a bed tonight, I'm sure."

Deering nodded as he leaned back in his chair. "Well, I do have a cottage that I rent out. The Reverend Mr. Boley stays there when he is in town."

"He's a circuit riding preacher," John Wesley put in, then burped.

Before his father could reprimand him, he said, "Excuse me," and put a hand over his mouth. Stella laughed before Nancy gave her a look.

"We know Preacher Boley."

"I give him a flower every time he comes round," Stella added, then yawned.

"That's nice," Deering turned to Nancy. "Would you like to see the cottage?"

She smiled a little. "We have taken advantage of your hospitality long enough. We should get on down the road to my cousin Perry's house."

"It's no trouble at all," he protested. "I'd be glad to show it to you." Tapping his napkin to his lips, he put it down and spoke to his son. "John Wesley, why don't you show the girls your pigeons?" Turning to Nancy, he added, "He sends messages to friends of his in Memphis and they to him."

"I'll be right back," Nancy assured her daughters.

Evie looked at her mother, nodded, then took Stella's hand. Quietly, they followed John Wesley to the rear of the house and up the back stairs to the pigeon roost.

"Those of the birds that do not perform well end up in the pot," Deering gave a small laugh as he led the way out of the dining room. "John Wesley doesn't know the difference and they still have done a service."

The cottage was next door to the large home, almost unnoticeable behind an orchard that filled its front yard.

"This is it," Deering motioned with his hand.

Nancy stopped on the walk and looked, a hand to her throat, aware that tears threatened. Was it the sight of the board and batten home with lace curtains in the windows or the smell from the roses climbing the trellis at one end of the porch that touched her so? Her gaze went to the two rockers sitting side by side, moving slightly in the breeze as if with invisible occupants.

The scene was like a dream come to life. If only Ollie would have lived and been able to build the larger home he had promised. They'd talked about it many times, even when he was ill. Most telling of all was the rose bush at the end of the porch, just as they'd planned. She swallowed. "It looks . . . precious."

Deering seemed pleased with her pronouncement. "Let's take a look inside."

At his suggestion, Nancy walked into the cottage and stopped immediately. Polished floors gleamed around the hooked rug on the floor. A settee sat to one side and across from it, two chairs that matched. She blinked hard. This was too much; too like the dream she and Ollie had created.

"What do you think?" Deering's voice seemed overloud in the quiet of the room. "Two bedrooms. A pump in the kitchen. No walking outside to a well." He was extremely proud of the last fact.

Nancy shook her head, still stunned. "It's too much." Then, she added a reason he would understand. "I cannot afford this."

It seemed that these were the words he was waiting for, because he came close to her, very close. "I'm sure we could work something out." His voice dropped to a low tone. "Did I tell you that my wife passed away two years ago?"

Perhaps because of his nearness or maybe she wanted to see more of the house, Nancy moved away. Deering followed.

"And you, having been married, knows that a man has needs." He stood behind her, close enough that she could feel the heat of his body.

Turning around, she looked at him, surprised by the sudden change in his demeanor and the light in his eyes. "What are you saying, Elder Deering?"

"I'm saying that we could . . . work out payment."

Her hand crept across her belly, as if protecting it. "You know that I am with child."

"It doesn't have to be a deterrent," he motioned with his hand, as if waving it away. "We could get a wet nurse for him."

She took a step backward, as if to get her balance. "I thank you for your hospitality, Elder Deering, but I -."

"Your children would never go hungry," he stepped toward her, leaning forward, as if to kiss her. "And you'd have the finest clothes to wear."

"Thank you, Elder Deering."

"Call me Kim," he broke in.

"But, I can't accept." Nancy stepped backward, but it was only so that she could get around the table with the lamp, since he prevented her from walking forward.

"You won't make it out of here without my say-so."

"I believe this is a free country." She kept walking to the door.

"I can make it hard for you to get work. People are suspicious of hill folk anyway."

At the door, Nancy turned and looked at him, suddenly aware that he was much closer than she had anticipated. "You will do what you must. And, I will as well." Gathering her skirts, she opened the door and stepped outside. "Good-bye, Elder Deering."

He hastened after her and at the garden gate, reached for her elbow, as if to keep her from leaving.

Yet, before he could follow through with his action, he became aware that two men were walking up Main Street toward them. One was fairly young and the other older and thickset. In a few strides, they would be upon them and even now could likely hear any interaction between Nancy and himself.

   On the street beside him, a wagon came rolling by and the driver called out to the men.

"I see that they've got you trussed like a turkey, Frank! They gonna roast you, too?"

From beside the driver, a woman slapped her thigh. "Pascoe with his hands bound! Never thought to see it!" Her voice was heavy with insinuation and she laughed uproariously.

Because the two men had their attention on the wagon and its occupants, they nearly walked into Nancy and Deering who stood, hesitating, at the garden gate.

"Watch what you're doing!" Shelby looked up in time to narrowly avoid walking into Deering.

"I beg your pardon, young man! It's you who should be watching!" Deering struck the walk with his cane.

Meanwhile, Frank stood before Nancy, a slight smile on his face. With his shackled hands, he lifted them to his hat and tipped it to her. "Ma'am," he said, just as Shelby pulled him off the sidewalk.

"What does he mean, bringing a criminal up this street?" Deering demanded, again tapping the walk with his cane. "The jail is on Canal Street!"

"I believe that is the Sheriff's office yonder," she said softly, watching as the two men crossed the street and entered the sheriff's domain.

But, Deering wasn't listening. "He didn't bother you, did he? It's a good thing he's in shackles. Who knows what might have happened otherwise!"

Nancy brought her gaze back to the minister and lifted an eyebrow. "Indeed." The word was said with irony lost on the man. Her gaze caught a glimpse of a moving curtain in the upper story of Deering's house and she wondered if the face that moved away had been one of her girls or John Wesley.

It was quiet and dark in the barn loft, with only one lantern glowing. Nancy sat with her back against the barn wall and watched as Stella crawled into her lap. Outside came the sound of a gentle rain, while below, a horse stamped in its stall. The smell of the hay and the horse were familiar and comforting.

"I like barn," the little girl said, leaning against her mother. Her eyes drooped sleepily.

"I do, too." Nancy stroked her daughter's hair. With her other hand, she patted the floor next to her.

Evie moved to sit beside her mother. "It's nice that cousin Perry is letting us stay here, ain't it?"

For a moment, Nancy wondered about correcting her daughter, but everyone was tired, so she let it pass. "Very nice of him." She glanced down at Stella, who was already asleep. Gently, she adjusted her so that only her head was on her lap, the rest of her on the floor.

"It's nice to be dry," Evie commented.

"Yes, it is."

Quiet settled over them. Then, Evie stirred. "Why is that man in shackles?"

"What brought that up?"

"Saw him when I looked out of the pigeon roost," was the laconic reply. "You're not going to marry him, are you?"

Nancy looked at her. "Who?"

"Elder Deering."

"Why would you think that?"

"John Wesley said you would. He said his father told him he was going to have you, even if he had to marry you."

"Well, it's a little early to be talking about marrying again," Nancy said, thoughtfully. "But no, Evie, I am not going to marry him." She gave her a little smile. "Now, settle down and let's get some sleep."

Her daughter sank down into a mound of hay and made herself comfortable. Beside her, Nancy reached up for the lantern, blew out the flame, then put it on a board just over her head.

"Mama?"

"What, Evelyn?" She didn't often use her daughter's full name and when she did, Evie knew she meant business.

"You don't have that job, do you? Playin' piano."

"No, I do not."

"What are we gonna do?"

Nancy thought for a moment. "We're gonna trust. We're gonna trust that everything will turn out alright. Good night, Evie."

"Night, Mama," she murmured, her voice barely audible.

Beside her, Nancy rested her head against the barn wall and looked up into the darkness, her lips moving.

The next morning found her walking briskly along Main Street, her head held high to stave off disappointment. She had just left Hudson's Mercantile who had more offers of help than they needed. At the corner was a tavern, where the clink of glass and the murmur of voices attracted her attention. For a moment, she hesitated, as if debating whether she would go in. But then, she noticed the pair of men she'd seen the day before walking toward her.

Apparently the young sheriff was taking his prisoner to the jail, for they were headed down the hill. As they passed her, the prisoner tipped his hat to her, using both hands as before and she was surprised to note the humor in his eyes. But, the gesture had done its work.

"I'm going to have to practice what I preach," Nancy told herself then smiled as she realized what she had said. There were some preachers who did not, as she well knew. "I'm gonna have to have faith that the Lord knows what we need and He will provide it." With her chin up and decision made, she turned from the saloon and walked back up the hill to the main part of town.

At the top of the hill, she glanced back at the river, still big and wide, the flood not having abated. As before, logs and debris floated downstream, but there were no whitecaps, just the bulge of the flood. Across the water were the bluffs and beyond them, the hills where she had been born and raised. Where Ollie and the children had been born and raised as well, she corrected herself.

A tall, thin man broke loose from the crowd of people moving along the sidewalk, some headed down to the dock and some up the hill. She wondered if it was Birdie and then wondered that she hadn't thought about him since the day before.

"The world sure has turned different," she murmured to herself. Glancing once more at the hills, she considered whether it would ever be the same again. "At least, I ain't in jail," she looked down at the squat building down on Canal Street. Then, her gaze went to the river. "But, it's sure got us hemmed in."

Taking a deep breath, she squared her shoulders and began walking with purpose along Hill Street. Her Cousin Perry's farm was a good five miles from town and she needed to get going. Besides, it looked like it might rain again.

"What are you gonna do?" Celitha Perry sat in a rocker in the parlor of her home cuddling her baby, yet with concern in her voice and eyes for Nancy. She was in her early twenties and just now nursing her first baby. The young woman basked in the knowledge that she had finally joined the ranks of motherhood, though her infant was cranky and would rather cry than latch onto her breast. "Nobody's hirin' for nuthin' right now. At least not til the water goes down." She continued to offer the nipple and finally, the baby seemed to notice. When he was sucking, she sat back, satisfied.

Nancy looked around the parlor. Though small, it was well appointed with fairly new furniture, unlike her own home. "It seems so," she agreed. "I hate to keep takin' advantage of your hospitality."

"Think nuthin' of it! It's our pleasure!" She adjusted herself so that the baby could take advantage of the other breast. "Ain't it funny that your girls wanted to sleep out in the barn? You know, they's a bed in the back room you could use!"

"It's all I can do to keep Evie in the house, back at the Forks," Nancy smiled. "Besides, you have enough to do already."

The baby stirred and Celitha gave it her full attention. When he was once more nursing, she turned to look pointedly at Nancy's belly. "You'll have enough to do shortly, yourself! How much longer?"

Nancy put a hand over her stomach. "September," was the quiet reply.

"You hardly look that far along!" Celitha exclaimed, though quietly, so as not to disturb her baby. "It must mean suthin' to you, to be carryin' Ollie's last born."

Nancy nodded. "Yes. It means a lot to be carryin' this child."

"Boy or girl?"

She shook her head.

"You don't know? You don't have a feelin'?"

"I do."

Without waiting for her further reply, the young woman went on. "I allus thought I'd be havin' a boy. Everyone around me thought it was a girl, all but me and Miz Hooser, the midwife. We thought it would be a boy and it was!" She beamed at Nancy. "We just had to have a boy! You know. The firstborn had ought to be a boy."

Nancy nodded her agreement.

"Except of course, when you have a girl," Celitha added quickly, looking

The LONG WAY HOME

to see if she had offended her guest. Then, her baby fussed and silence hung in the room while she tended to her child. When she could speak again, she went on, "I'm surprised none of those boys at the Forks has proposed, yet. Ollie's been gone how long?"

"Havin' three children scares 'em off, I think."

"What about Albert? He's got that fine farm on Hash Ridge. He allus was sweet on you. Mama always said he was as shocked as the rest of 'em when you married Ollie."

Before she could answer, Celitha went on. "Or Birdie. He's a hard worker and he's always had his eye on you."

"Birdie's been a big help," Nancy admitted.

"He's been around here twicet, lookin' to speak to you."

There was a tap at the door and Celitha sat the baby up and began pulling her shirt down. "I wouldn't be surprised if that was him now."

"I'll get it," Nancy stood up and walked to the front door. Somehow she was not surprised to see Birdie standing there, hat in hand.

"Hello, Miz Nancy!" He looked at her hopefully. "That's alright if I call you that, ain't it?"

"Yes, Birdie," she gave him a little smile. "Please come in."

After wiping his boots once more, he stepped into the parlor. "Hi-dee, Miz Perry."

By this time, Celitha was completely covered up. "Hello, Birdie. I'm going to put Junior to bed. Make yourself to home."

"Thankee, ma'am. Thankee." Birdie stepped forward onto the rug and turned his attention back to Nancy. "We shore have had a time of it." The hat went round and round in his hands.

"Yes, we have. And we, the children and me, wouldn't have made it this far without you."

"I don't know about thet. Almost lost yu to the river."

"Might have lost us up on the Forks, but for you." She stepped forward and put a hand on his forearm. "Thank you, Birdie."

He swallowed and looked away, as if to hide his blush. "I been tryin' to ketch you to home," he turned to look at her again. "That's whut I wanted to talk to you about."

Nancy waited.

"I don't know whut yer plans are, but you cain't go back to yer place on Camp Creek."

She looked at him, frowning, waiting for an explanation.

"They ain't nuthin' to go back to. The water took ever' thin'." He dug in his pocket. "Seen Fletcher Holbrook. He said, to give this to you. He's the one what said nuthin' was left." He handed her a small item.

It was a miniature of herself and Ollie standing in front of the cabin, him barely twenty and her sixteen, proud as punch. She had wound a ribbon through the frame, but it was old and faded.

"Thankee, Birdie." A lump was in her throat, for the photograph had taken her back in time to a lovely spring day where life and love was theirs for the taking. They expected to be tested and tried by the land and by circumstance, that's just the way life was in the mountains. What they hadn't expected was for war to be declared the next month and to spend the next several years with him fighting Yanks and her trying to make a go of the farm. It had been hard, almost overwhelming, trying to eke out a living. Hardly anything could be kept for herself, for what the Yanks didn't buy, they stole. And, at the Forks, Old Man Preece wouldn't take Yankee money or Confederate scrip. Gold or silver were his choices and both were hard to come by.

She shook her head, coming back to the present, for Birdie was speaking.

"They's another thing. He said if'n you weren't goin' back to the Forks, he'd take yer property."

Nancy looked at him, not understanding.

"He's offered a good price, if I say so m'self." He hooked his thumbs under his suspenders. "Of course, I'm the one thet said you'd not take nuthin' less. That is, if yer sellin'."

Though she looked at him, she wasn't seeing him. Reaching behind her, she pulled a chair up and sat down in it, her legs suddenly weak. It seemed that the world had taken on a tilt and she knew it would never be the same.

"Why, Birdie?" She whispered, but sought no answer. "Why would I sell?"

"With the house gone, they ain't nuthin' left fer you an' the girls," he said simply. "But, I'm a' thinkin' that regardless of what yu do, yer gonna need a man."

She looked at him. "What?"

"Wal, you got nuthin' but the land now. If yu sell it, you'd have enough to live comfortable until you get a new place built. Maybe buy a few acres from yer Cousin Beck or Miz Tackett. You could live with 'em while yu get a place built."

Nancy shook her head. Things weren't making sense. "I have to think about this, Birdie."

When the moments stretched long, Birdie shifted his feet. "I seen yer brother-in-law, Albert, in town."

Nancy looked up at him, her arm protective around her belly.

"He ast me about you. How you were. Where you were."

"Did you tell him?" The question came quick.

"He ain't niver done me no favors," Birdie shrugged.

"Thank you, Birdie," she smiled with relief. "You've been a good friend to us through the years. While Ollie was with me and now, when he's not."

Silence filled the parlor once more.

"What should I tell Fletcher? He's goin' back across the river tomorry. He'll let yer cousin Beck know yer comin'."

Nancy looked at him, her thoughts still racing. Slowly, she shook her head.

"Yer not goin' back, are ye?" It wasn't really a question. His shoulders sagged toward one another.

"No," she replied. "You said it yourself. There's nuthin' to go back to." She looked down at her hands that stretched over her belly. "All this time here, I've been wonderin', what if we don't go back? What if we go West?" Her eyes lifted to his. "Ollie an' me, we talked about it, after the war. Why don't we go West and start a new life?" She looked down at the floor, still wrestling with her thoughts. "But then, his Pap died and he had to help with the farm. Then, Miz Cyrus divided up the farm an' give all the boys their own places. After that, it seemed like there was no reason to leave."

Her eyes met his. "But now. Now there's no reason to go back."

This time, Birdie took some time to swallow, straighten his shoulders and then, finally, to speak. "Yu could start over, Miz Nancy." Was it disappointment that made his voice tremble? "'Bout everyone will be startin' over."

She shook her head. "No. I'm startin' over somewhere else. Out there." And she motioned to the west.

"Alone? You goin' alone?"

"With the girls," she said with a smile.

"That's pretty much alone."

Nancy smiled. "The Lord will be with me. With us." She looked down at the miniature in her hands. "He's been with us right along. He will show me the way."

"I wisht you'd let me go with you," he said, softly.

Again she shook her head. "You've got a life back there, at the Forks. A good farm. A cabin a little further up the hill, probably didn't get a bit of water in it."

She looked up into his face and smiled a little.

"This isn't how I wanted it to be, Miz Nancy."

She patted his hand that hung near. "I know."

He swallowed and then took a deep breath. "Wal, Miz Nancy, yer about the bravest woman I ever did see. I thought it durin' the war and I think it more now."

"We were all brave durin' the war."

He shook his head. "You done without, you gave to others, you held off the dam' Yanks that tried to burn yer place. But now, the water has done what the Yanks didn't do."

"I hold no malice, Birdie," she reminded him. "War is war. And God has His reasons for the flood."

He turned as if to leave, then halted and looked at her. "Well, Miz Nancy, if you ever do go back. If the hills calls to you like they does to me, you'll find me there. Waitin'."

Nancy looked up at him, a hurting for him look on her face. "Don't wait for me, Birdie." She stood up and put a hand on his sleeve. "You deserve a woman who hasn't loved no one but you."

He swallowed and it was clear it would take strength to leave the house.

"Thank you for bringing me the news. About the cabin. And this." She held up the miniature. "I'll keep it for the girls."

Yet, he continued standing at the door. Then, he took a breath like a drowning man and started to turn around to face her, but she held up her hand.

"No, Birdie." Her voice was soft. "I know what you're thinkin'. But, I cannot accept."

He nodded and bowed a little, a knight to his queen. "You'll always love Ollie, I guess."

"I've got his girls to raise."

"I could help!" The words burst out of him.

"You've helped me a great deal already. I can never repay you."

He opened his mouth to speak, but she shook her head.

"Thank you, Birdie." It was said with finality.

The air seemed let out of him and he turned back to the door.

"Good-bye, Birdie. And Godspeed," she smiled a little, "back to the hills where you belong."

But, at the door, he turned, unwilling to leave. "I guess I'll tell Fletcher yer sellin' yer place." His voice tightened. "If I had the cash money, I'd buy it!"

Nancy stood at the door, her hand on the knob, a clear hint that he should leave. "I know you would. Tell Fletcher the place is his. We'll settle up tomorrow."

And with that, he finally stepped through and she shut the door behind him.

Chapter
FOUR

Outside, the rain had stopped and the moon was playing peekaboo behind the clouds as they moved through the night sky. When clouds scudded past and the moon was revealed, the loft was well lit, but when clouds blocked it, the area was plunged into darkness.

Leaning against the wall of the barn, Nancy smoothed Stella's soft hair as she lay with her head on her mother's lap. Beside her, Evie lay, once more curled up in a mound of hay.

Below them, horses moved in their stalls and a chicken flew up to a beam to roost.

"Well, Lord, You took care of us at the house and You more than did Your share at the River, and I thank You." Nancy looked down at her daughters, lying on either side of her. "You know we cain't go back to the Forks since the house is gone. And, yes, we could go to Cousin Beck's. Or Uncle Fred's probably got room for us. An' there's half a dozen men what's been after me to marry 'em since Ollie died. But, none of it felt right. None of it but the thought of not goin' back."

Her voice dropped to a whisper. "I don't know where we're goin' or what we're a' doin', but with Fletcher buyin' the place, we've got the funds to get there." She sat back, satisfied. "I await your guidance." Slowly, tiredly, her eyes closed.

Perhaps it was the lack of rain pounding on the metal roof that made her sleep fitful and so quick to startle when she heard a noise downstairs. It didn't sound like an animal. She sat upright and listened. No, she thought, it sounds like a man. Careful not to disturb Stella, she slipped her hand into the carpetbag and brought out a pistol.

There was another sound and the barn went dark as a cloud blocked the moon. It seemed that she could hear someone fumbling at the loft ladder.

Gently slipping out from under Stella, Nancy moved away from her children and brought the pistol to bear on the opening to the loft.

A dark form crawled through the door.

"Halt, whoever you are! I'm well armed!" And the click of the pistol hammer being drawn back was loud in the darkness.

"Don't shoot, please!"

The moon broke free of the clouds and the loft quickly lightened, revealing a man standing before her, his hands up. "And keep your voice down!"

"Who are you?" She demanded. The long barrel of the pistol gleamed in the dim light, pointed unwaveringly at him.

Though he kept his hands up, he didn't seem too concerned about the pistol. "Who are you?"

"I'm Mrs. Oliver Cyrus and my cousin Titus Perry owns this place!"

"Frank Pascoe," he started to lower his hands, but a flick of the pistol had him reaching skyward once more. "I believe we met on the riverboat when I pulled you out of the water."

Nancy looked at him, realizing that he did look familiar. "What are you doing here?" She lowered her voice when Stella stirred.

He noticed her glance at the children. "Leaving town."

"You're a criminal."

"Some would say so."

"Will there be a reward for yer capture?"

"Young master Sinclair thinks so." He was tired of holding up his hands.

"How did you get here?" The last time she'd seen him, he'd been in shackles.

"Long story." And though she still held the pistol on him, he lowered his hands.

Nancy was tired. The long walk to Lester's Landing and nearly drowning in the river had caught up to her. Added to that was the emotional up and down of getting a job as a pianist for the church and then losing it when Deering made advances toward her.

She made herself think. Of course, the right thing to do was to turn him over to the Law. A glance out the hay loft door revealed no light showing in the house. It would be a shame to wake Titus when he might be getting a good night's sleep, what with the baby and all.

It was a long way til morning and she knew she couldn't stay awake and keep her pistol on him. "Well, why don't you go sit over there? With your back to that post?"

Frank glanced at the post, then back at her. "It's a long story, he repeated, then added, "I could tell it to you."

For answer, she motioned with the pistol. In the semi-darkness, she looked pretty business-like, so he obeyed. When he turned to go to the support post, she picked up some rope she'd seen earlier and approached him.

"Hands behind your back."

"Anything I could say that would make you let me go?" Yet he obeyed as he spoke.

"You're a crim'nal, Mr. Pascoe. I doubt I'd believe anything you'd say." Her voice was almost at his ear, since she had to get close to him to tie his hands.

"I thought you might say that." He looked at the children. "Are you gonna be alright? You and your girls?" Since he'd intervened in saving them a couple of times, he felt he had the right to ask.

"Yes, we are," she assured him.

"Goin' back to the hills?"

Nancy was busy securing his hands with the rope, only half paying attention to his words. "No."

"Headed west?" He was loud in his eagerness.

"Hssst! Quiet!" She looked at her daughters and Evie stirred a little.

"They're gonna see me in the morning," he reminded her matter of factly. When she moved away from him, he tested his bonds. She knew what she was doing, that was for sure.

Nancy picked up the pistol and knelt close enough to talk, but not within reach of hands or feet. "Why did you come here?"

"Lookin' for a place to hide for a bit." His voice was relaxed and to her thinking, honest. "Let me go and I'll be gone in the morning."

"Where were you goin'?"

"Headed west." After all, it didn't hurt to tell her. It didn't seem like he was going to get away this time.

"Why?"

"I like it out there. Blue skies. Fresh air. Lots of space."

Nancy leaned forward with interest. "Is it all they say it is?"

"That much and more."

But, she mistrusted his eagerness and settled back against the wall.

"It's my kind of country," he went on. "Big. And sunsets you wouldn't believe. Beauty you have to see with your own eyes." When she was silent, he added, "But, it isn't green. Not like here."

Sitting propped up, Nancy realized just how tired she was. It was an effort to stay awake. "Where was the boy takin' you?"

"Shelby?" Frank asked, surprised at her question. "To Texas."

"Where were you headed?"

"Texas."

Nancy frowned. "Why didn't you just go along with him to Texas?"

The barn loft was dark again while the moon fled behind the clouds.

Frank gave a small laugh. "I prefer to go under my own power, makin' my own way."

"Hain't been very promisin' so far," was her observation.

"Just unfortunate," was his reply. "It's alright. I'll make it to Texas, one way or the other."

She didn't know how many moments passed just that she came awake when he spoke again.

"What about you? Where are you headed? If you're not going back to the hills."

It wouldn't hurt to tell him since he was going back to jail. "We're headed west."

"Anywhere in particular?"

"Not Texas!" She had the thought he wanted to tag along. In the long silence, her eyes closed.

She jolted awake when he spoke again.

"You know what you need?" He paused. "You need a man."

Laughter came to her lips, but she was too tired to let it out. She'd heard that sentiment two times before that day.

"If you had a man along, you'd have someone to share the work. You wouldn't have to worry about getting taken advantage of. Keep people away. The kind of people you want away."

"Listen to him, Mama!" Evie spoke from her place on the floor.

"I could be that man. I've got a need to go west. And well, they wouldn't expect me to have a woman and children along."

"He could help us, Mama!"

Nancy was silent.

"And, if you don't want to stop in Texas, well, at least I could help you get that far."

"Mama!" Evie's eyes and face were pleading.

Nancy crossed her arms across her chest, the pistol clearly visible in the moonlight. "Go to sleep, Evie. And Mister, if you wanna live to see daylight, you'd best be quiet."

And quiet it was in the hayloft until dawn began to gray the skies.

Dogs barked and bayed in the distance and seemingly in the next moment, swirled about the barn, as men and horses filled the space between it and the house. They called to the owner of the farmstead, while Nancy opened her eyes to meet those of Frank.

"It's up to you, little lady." His voice was soft, full of meaning, but no pleading. Behind him, his bound hands lifted for emphasis.

Nancy had meant to pray about it last night or early this morning, but here it was. Time to make a choice.

Beside her, Evie tugged on her arm. "He saved your life, Mama." She glanced at Frank, then back to her mother. "And has never said a word about it."

"And he gave us candy," Stella added.

Evie motioned for her to shush.

"What's that?" Nancy asked, looking from one to the other.

"After he saved us from those men packing us off." Evie hadn't told her mother. At the time, there was the necessity of getting across the river, and later, it hadn't seemed important.

Nancy stared at her daughter, frowning. "What men?"

"Harry and Sid," Stella spoke up again, frowning. "They weren't our uncles!"

"Mornin' Nancy!" A voice called up from below. "Are you up, yet?"

"I am now," she replied. "What's all the noise?"

"They's some men trailin' after an escaped prisoner. The dogs say he's here." Cousin Perry stood below the loft so that he could be heard.

Though he couldn't see her, Nancy slowly shook her head, her eyes on Frank. "You can believe me when I say, they ain't no man here."

Below them, Perry laughed. "I told 'em they was wrong. Them dogs ain't from the hills and don't know a man trail from a snail trail!" He laughed again, then went outside to inform the posse they were following the wrong scent.

Outside, the tracker was as emphatic that Perry was wrong. "These are the best dogs there are and there's none better! In the hills or anywhere else!" Dogs barked and whined as the pack milled about him. "If they say the man's here, he's here!"

Perry's voice broke in as he commanded, "Don't get down until you're invited!"

"Maybe he's right. I'll circle around and pick up his trail." Another man spoke up, his voice younger but firm.

From her mound of hay, Evie mouthed the name, "Shelby!" The lightning man.

In the road, horses stamped and jingled their bits.

"My cousin is a Perry and if she says there's no man in the barn, there's no man in the barn," Perry went on.

Stella had moved to sit beside her mother, Evie following. When the little girl heard this, she opened her mouth to speak, but her sister put a hand over it and Nancy motioned her to silence.

"Alright men," Shelby spoke up. "Let's go. We'll pick up his trail on the other side."

All was still in the loft as they heard the riders and dogs leave. Then, there was a step downstairs.

"I was sorry to wake you, Nancy." Perry called up to them.

"I'm glad you did," she replied. "Because it will help us get an early start."

"Are you leavin'? Celitha didn't tell me that."

"Yes," there was sadness and decision in her voice. "I think it's about time. But, I shore thank you for your hospitality."

"Well, come on down and have some of Celitha's good cookin' afore you go."

"Yes sir!" Evie answered him, eagerly. This stay at the Perry farm had been satisfactory as far as she was concerned. There was pie to be had at every meal!

"We'll be down shortly," her mother assured him then reached for the carpetbag and pulled out a brush.

As was their usual morning routine, each of the girls sat before their mother and got their hair brushed and braided in their turn. Stella pointed at Frank and said, "Mama. If there's no man in the barn, what is that?"

The man with his hands behind his back seemed equally interested in her answer.

"Well, you've seen him in shackles. What would you call him?"

"A crim'nal," was the reply.

Frank winced. "Not proved in a court of law!" But, he grinned and winked at her when he said it.

Evie decided that he didn't seem much like a rock when he smiled, and it was a nice smile.

"Well, that's what he is," Nancy patted the butt of the pistol in her waistband. "Who had best be quiet or get plucked outa here by Mr. Sinclair."

All eyes were on Frank, who seemed nonplussed by her comment.

"But, Mama," Evie added, "Wasn't Papa in shackles, too? At Libby Prison?"

Nancy drew her breath in sharply. "We don't talk about the war," was the firm reminder.

After breakfast, Cousin Perry took Nancy to Mount Joy to meet with Fletcher Holbrook. The girls stayed in the house, helping Celitha with various chores and playing with the baby.

In town, she was glad for Perry's presence, for it seemed the streets teemed with men of various sorts and varying ages. For some reason, they seemed more threatening than they had the day before.

She sold the property to Fletcher who had the ready money. He and his boys did a good business of bringing logs downriver in the spring, so he was flush with cash. Holbrook planned to work the farm in shares with his youngest son, letting him earn it.

The transaction was made at the sheriff's office and she was proud that she could sign her name to the document. It was more than Fletcher could do, who made a rough X.

Afterwards, she bought a light wagon with a square frame over the bed and a canvas cover with curtains that could be rolled up or let down. There were a few other things she purchased, along with a Winchester rifle. Being from the hills, she had an appreciation for a good rifle and this one was supposed to be very reliable, with bullets that would fit both it and a pistol.

Then she thought, Evie could use a rifle of her own, and she bought another as well.

Though the team was a matched pair of bays, she was cautioned that only one could be ridden. The other, which could only be told apart if one brushed the thick forelock from its face to reveal a small spot of white, would turn around and bite the legs of whoever was on its back. Added to that, the rider would be hard put to get it out of a walk. But, the horse would pull like an ox.

Satisfied with her purchases, Nancy drove her team up Hill Street, headed out of town. But at the top of the bluff, she halted and looked down. As far as she could see, the river continued to stretch from hill to hill. Across the brown, white capped river, a train engine puffed beside a warehouse at Lester's Landing, still thronged with people who had lost their homes to the flood. She raised her eyes to the hills that led to the mountains that had once been her home. For a long moment, she looked, as if she could see whatever remained of the cabin on Camp Creek.

"Good-bye, Ollie," she said, simply. And, if she wondered at the lack of feeling she had at the parting, she would lay it to the fact that she had spent so much emotion, praying and begging for his life, that there was nothing left.

Picking up the reins, she clucked to the horses, ready to head to the farm. As the wagon rolled down the street, she noted Elder Deering walking along, a woman at his side, her arm looped through his.

At the sound of the wagon, he glanced her way, then equally quickly looked back and patted the woman's hand, as if to assure himself she was there.

"He's not lettin' any grass grow under his feet," she noted and mentally wished him well.

The woman looked up at Deering, laughing a little too loud and long at whatever he had said.

With a smile to herself, Nancy clucked to the team and hastened her way westward to the Perry farm.

"Now you know you don't have to go," Celitha looked up at Nancy sitting on the wagon seat. She gently bounced the babe in her arms to keep him from fussing.

"You had ought to stay, Cousin," Perry added. "We've plenty of room here, if you don't want to go back to the Forks."

The wagon's canvas sides were rolled up so that Evie and Stella looked out from either side of their mother. They were grinning, filled with excitement.

"Thankee for the offer," Nancy replied. "But I feel like the Lord has plans for us in the West."

"You allus were a prayin' people, you Perry's from the Forks. Prayin' for this and that, this person and the other." She glanced at her husband. "Not that we don't pray."

He grinned at her. "The Perry womenfolk do enough for all of us." Walking up to the wagon, he handed each girl a little sack of candy.

"I got it in town," he explained. "My little one is too young, yet." To Nancy he said, "I wisht there was more we could do for ye."

"You've done a lot already," she told him. "Gettin' this wagon an' team at a price I could afford..."

"That's what family is for!" He put a hand on the rump of the off horse. "Remember, the man said this horse ain't rideable!"

"But he pulls like an ox!" Evie repeated and laughed.

"I don't know why we'd be ridin', anyway," was her mother's reply.

Stepping closer, Celitha told them, "You write, now, you hear? My brother Pat went west years ago and we've none of us heard from him since!"

"I'll write," Evie volunteered and they all laughed.

Only a little while later, Nancy drove out of the farmyard headed west, with her cousin and his wife calling to them out of sight, as if they were still on Camp Creek. A tight knot sealed her throat and for a moment, tears seared her eyes. But then, the sun broke through the clouds, showering the green canopied roadway in a golden light.

"Look, Mama!" Evie tapped on her shoulder and pointed to the side. "A rainbow!"

Nancy smiled. "God's Promise," she told them, and called to the horses to try a little harder.

Behind her, Evie settled back on the quilt they'd spread on the thin mattress Perry had given them and began to sing. "I've got a home in glory land that outshines the sun!"

With the next verse, both Nancy and Stella joined in and they drove westward with a song on their lips and light hearts.

But only a mile or so down the road, Nancy stopped singing and turned to her daughters. "Now. Tell me about Harry and Sid."

In the barn loft, Frank shifted, his hands still bound behind him. It was full dark, the moon mostly hidden by the clouds that had moved in after sunset. Outside in the Perry farmyard nothing stirred and the house was dark.

There was a sound downstairs, perhaps only a horse changing position, but he straightened anyway, his attention on the trap door.

He had just relaxed when he realized that the dark form emerging from the floor was a woman. Silently, she ran to his side.

"Damn, you took long enough!"

Kneeling beside him, she began to untie his bonds.

"You'd ought to be grateful," her voice was low, "seein' yer in a barn and not a jail!"

"Just cut it!" He grew impatient with her struggle to free him.

"Not my rope," she reminded him.

Then he was free and he spent a few moments rubbing his hands and wrists. When he stood up, he had to hold onto the post to keep his balance.

Nancy stood before him, pistol drawn, and watched as he got circulation back into his legs.

"We'd best be going." Suiting words to action, she disappeared down the ladder.

Frank followed her into the dark depths of the barn and wouldn't have known where she had gone, but she opened the back door and was briefly silhouetted against the moonlight. Darting through the door, he nearly ran into her, bent over, an arm across her abdomen.

"Are you alright?"

She straightened, her face to the sky, tried to nod, but bent over again.

"The babe?" His words told her that he'd noticed. "Not now," he told her, as if it was something under her control.

Nancy nodded, agreeing with him, but she didn't move.

There came the stamp of a horse and glancing toward the tree-lined creek, he saw a horse standing there, waiting.

"I just need to – catch my breath." She sank to her knees.

In the distance, a dog began to bark.

Nancy heard it and tried to straighten, to take a few steps, but she had to stop.

His attention was elsewhere, scanning the road. "They're not gettin' me again." There was a warning note in his voice. He edged away from her, to see around the barn.

Another dog joined the first and Frank looked about, increasingly tense.

"Go," she said, bent over once more. "You saved my life. The girls. Go."

Yet he continued to stand there, in his mind, already running to the creek to throw off the scent of the dogs. He wouldn't look at the horse standing in the trees; it was too tempting.

"Thanks," he told her and then he was gone.

Nancy didn't blame him for going, and it allowed her to focus on the pain in her abdomen. Finally, it seemed to ease and she straightened.

"Aw hell," Frank reappeared holding the horse's bridle. "In for a penny, in for a pound." And he maneuvered the animal close to a tall rock so that Nancy could climb aboard. Then, he led them into the darkness of the forest.

Chapter
FIVE

Opening his eyes, Frank noticed a small pouch of some kind moving over his chest. It reminded him of a pocket watch at the end of a chain, but this one seemed to be made of buckskin with beading sewn onto it. He frowned, then followed the leather thong to see Stella at the end of it. "Good morning!" He smiled at her.

"You stink," she replied.

"Stella!" Her mother came into the camp from her ablutions at the creek, her hair still braided from nighttime. "What a thing to say! Tell him you're sorry and remember your manners!"

"You say, tell the truth. Well, he stinks, Mama," the little girl repeated and held up the thong to reveal the pouch.

Nancy hesitated, looking from the man to the girl, hard put not to laugh.

"We make him plague bag."

At her words, Frank rolled to the side, trying to get away from the bag.

Nancy had to laugh at his scrambling to stand, but hid her smile behind her hand. "There's no plague in it."

"It's to ward off the plague," Evie walked into the camp, having been at the creek watering the team.

"Neither one seems friendly," he commented.

"Papa always had one," Evie went on. "Had dried flower petals in it. Made him smell good." She sniffed the air, as if she could still smell it. "Always kept a bullet in it, too, in case he was captured by Indians."

"Or Yanks," Stella added.

"That way, all he needed was a pistol and he could get away," Evie sat down on a rock across the campfire.

"We put good things in it," the youngest girl assured him, opening it to take a deep sniff.

Regardless, Frank was glad to see the pouch leave and shook his head when Stella offered to let him smell it.

"We're packed up and ready to leave," Nancy informed him. "We let you sleep, to enjoy lying prone."

"Thanks for that," Frank said, wryly, looking about for a coffee pot.

Evie held up a biscuit with bacon trailing out of it. "We've had our breakfast."

Beside her, Stella held up another, but it may have been dropped at least once before.

Frank accepted Evie's biscuit and hoped it would fill his stomach enough that he could ignore Stella's. "Coffee?"

"I've never cared for it," Nancy informed him as she handed him a cup of liquid. "Tea is much easier to come by."

It was the work of moments to polish off the biscuit and the tea. He looked up to see Evie and Stella regarding him. His eyes met theirs, then traveled behind them to the team that was already hitched to the wagon, waiting. It was obvious that they were anxious to get on the road.

"Is there a place where a man can . . ?"

Nancy glanced down at the trees lining the creek. From the debris lining the fields around it, the water had already gone down quite a bit. "We washed up down there," she nodded toward the creek.

Only then did he noticed that everyone looked neat and clean, with the mud that collected on dress hems having been brushed off. The girls' hair had already been braided and even as he watched, Nancy pulled her braid around her head and tucked the end of it back in itself. From a pocket in her skirt, she brought out some pins and secured it.

Nancy noticed him watching her. "If you don't mind, we'd like to get on the road."

"I'll be quick," he said as he pulled on his boots. Walking to the creek, he had a few choice words for the fact that jail prisoners weren't allowed razors. He'd have given a lot for a shave that morning.

On the road, Nancy handled the reins. Frank sat beside her and in the wagon bed, Evie played with a stick horse she'd made while Stella drowsed beside her.

"You were in shackles," Nancy spoke up after a long period of quiet. "Why?"

"There's some that believe I was involved in a train robbery." His gaze traveled to the land beside them. It was beginning to flatten out, with hills not quite so tall or numerous.

"Were you?"

Frank glanced at her. "Does it matter? We're headed west, in a mutual endeavor but different goals."

"I'd like to know what sort of man is travelin' with me and my daughters." She slid the rein in her right hand to her left and patted the butt of the pistol in her waistband.

"I should think that my actions back at Lester's Landing would give you reference enough."

Nancy looked at him. "This is what I know about men. "Few of 'em are as straightforward as they'd have you believe."

"I have done some things outside the law." He admitted. "There's probably no man alive who hasn't done the same."

"Is that an excuse for sayin' I can trust you, when you aren't trustworthy?"

Frank inwardly winced at her candor. But, he went on, "I killed a man in self defense, once. And, I served in the Union Army during the late war."

Beside him, Nancy shrunk from him as if the tilt of the wagon seat caused it. In the back of the wagon, Stella opened her eyes and mouthed, "Yank," to her sister.

"What about you?" Frank noticed that Nancy put a hand to her abdomen and took the reins from her with no protest. "Killed anyone?"

"No," she liked talking, because it kept her attention away from her belly. "Yes."

Frank looked at her.

"No," Nancy smiled. "I have killed no one." Her gaze went to the road straight ahead and her eyes took on a faraway look. "Except in my heart. I killed him in my heart."

Frank frowned. "But, he's still walkin' around upright on this Earth."

She took a breath, then bowed her head. "It's a sin to kill a man."

"And the law don't like it much, either."

Behind them in the wagon bed, both girls lay curled into one another, their eyes closed.

A little further down the road, Nancy spoke again. "You never answered my question. Did you ever steal somethin'?"

"Other than the money I'm supposed to have taken in the Omaha train robbery?" Frank's tone was sarcastic. He slapped the rein on Tonmy's rump. Tonmy was the horse that couldn't be ridden, wasn't he? Or was it his partner, Tony?"

"Yeah. I have stolen something."

"What?"

"Food. I have stolen to eat," he admitted and seemed fine with the fact.

Frank looked at her, noting the pain around her eyes and arm across her belly. Talking seemed to take her mind off of it, so he continued. "During the war, I was wounded. Bad. They thought I was gonna die. We were in Texas at the time and I ended up staying there, recovering. Once I was well, I went back to Springfield, got married. Tried to make it work." He shook his head. "But, I kept thinkin' about the West and how free you are."

At his mention of the west, her eyes glowed and she leaned forward with interest. "What happened then?

"Oh, I stuck it out for a few years and then I told my wife, I am going west. You can come with me or stay, it makes no never mind to me."

"That was heartless!" Nancy frowned at him.

"Well, my job wasn't much, worked for my mother-in-law. Tried farming, a place that Cecilia had inherited from her grandfather. By the time I got hold of it, it was worn out. And when I saw that there was nothin' I could do to bring it around, that's went I told her I was goin' west." He slapped the rein on Tommy's rump again. The horse seemed content to let his partner do most of the work.

"I'd had enough of bein' too worn out to get out of my own way, day after day. My wife had some ideas on what our farm should be, what our house should look like and all that I could do for her." He shook his head. "I was done with it. Kicked over the traces." He looked at Nancy. "I told her she could come along."

"But, she didn't."

"She did not."

"What did you do?"

"I went west, like I said." He looked at her. "I pretty much do what I say I'm going to do."

"Did you tell yourself you were going to get arrested?"

Frank shook his head. "I missed that part."

"What happened when you came west?"

"I worked this and that. Sent my money home. Wrote letters."

"And?"

"I never heard a word from her."

"Why didn't you go back and get her?"

"I - I .." He started to speak but stopped. After a moment he went on, "I've asked myself that a hundred times or more."

For a mile or so, they watched the road in front of them, the wagon's creak and the horses' breathing and clomping the only sounds.

"I came across a pretty good claim in Virginia City. Sent the money back home. Never heard a word from her."

"Perhaps she moved."

Frank shook his head. "No. I think she found someone else and I can't really blame her." His gaze traveled the countryside around them. "I got tired of mining. Sold out. Came over to the Black Hills.

Ended up driving the stage. One night, I was out carousing and come across some friends of mine from Texas."

Something in his manner made her lean forward and pay more attention. "They had brought a herd up from Texas; a herd that several men had contributed to. But, when Joe Collins, the foreman, got paid off, rather than wiring the money back to Texas, he and his men gambled it all away."

Nancy watched his face, noting the sadness as well as the resignation in his face and voice. "What happened, then?"

He nodded, then answered. "They began robbing stagecoaches."

Her eyes scanned his face. "Your friends. Robbed coaches? And you were a driver?"

"They wanted me to tip them off as to when I had a goodly amount of money with me." He shrugged. "But, about then, I had a wreck – horses ran off with me – tipped the coach over – I went flying. Stove me up pretty good."

"Would you have?" Nancy asked. "Would you have tipped them off?"

Frank looked her in the face. "No. Because if they'd been caught, they'd have told on me and I'd have gone to prison, too." He gave a short laugh. "I may have run off from my wife, but I wasn't goin' to help them boys out." Then he added grimly. "But, as they say, Man proposes but God disposes." And he laughed, but did not seem happy.

"What happened, then?"

"Stages weren't payin' much for those boys. At least, the stages they hit. And whatever they got, they spent. It was gone the next day."

Nancy was silent, listening.

"Then, Collins made friends with a man, a conductor for the Union Pacific." His voice rolled on. "He'd been fired from the U.P. and wasn't too happy about it. Collins told him how they could get back at the railroad."

"Rob it," she stated, sitting back on the seat and thinking about his words. "So, what happened?"

"Mr. Collins and company, including one Mr. Sam Bass, robbed the Union Pacific train of sixty thousand dollars in gold coin at Big Springs, Nebraska."

"Where were you?"

"Still in Deadwood. Stove up."

"I've heard of that robbery," she said, slowly.

"You'd have to have been dead or not born yet to not hear of it!"

"Two men were killed, shortly afterward."

"Joel Collins and Bill Heffridge tried to shoot it out with a troop of cavalry," his tone was ironic. "He always said he'd go down shootin'."

Nancy knew he referred to Collins.

"Losin' that money from his friends after sellin' their cattle and knowin' some of them were ruined because of it didn't set well with him."

"So he paid with his life."

Frank slapped Tommy's rump again. Perhaps in the next town, he could get a whip to remind him of his job.

After a bit, he went on. "I went back to Ohio after that." He grimaced a little. "I was still hurtin' and I guess I thought maybe my wife would take me back."

"What happened?" Nancy's brown eyes surveyed his face. "What did she say?"

Frank shook his head. "I went to Springfield. And there she was, at the train station, like she knew I was comin' home. Only, it wasn't me she was greeting. It was a tall man, a minister. I didn't even get off the train."

"But, she was married to you."

He looked at her. "There is divorce," he reminded her. "Even in the Bible."

"I'm sorry," Nancy said after a few moments. "Did you love her very much?"

Frank shook his head. "I've thought about that, too." He looked at her. "Maybe. At first. But, when she let her Mother tell her what to do and expect. And, talk about me. That changed things."

"Yet, you came back for her."

"Well, she was my wife, for what that was worth."

When another mile had rolled beneath the wheels of the wagon, he spoke again. "I got off at the next station, so I could head West. And I heard something that stopped me in my tracks." He flicked the rein at Tommy again. "There was a rumor that I had been one of the Black Hills Bandits."

"The who?"

"The men who robbed the Union Pacific."

"But, you didn't."

He nodded with a grim smile. "That's right. I didn't."

"What did you do?"

"I thought about flattening the face of whoever started the rumor," he confided to her. "But, I was still hurtin' from the wreck, so I went west."

Silence followed his words, broken only by the sounds of travel.

"Where did you go?"

"Texas," was the reply. "I'd heard that my friend, Sam Bass, was lookin' for men to join him."

"But, he was one of the train robbers, wasn't he?"

Frank nodded. "Yep. And he was robbing trains in Texas, too."

"You deliberately wanted to go to the bad?" She asked. "When the accident had kept you from it before?"

His light green eyes slid to hers and he nodded. "I thought my heart was broke. My wife had left me. Married another man. I figured I might as well have the game as the blame." And, his voice was rich with irony at the last.

"So," Nancy filled in. "You robbed trains. And that's why the law wants you."

"No," said Frank. "I did not. The moment I arrived in Denton, Mr. Cobb, my station agent in Deadwood, recognized me and gave me a job."

"Did you see Sam?"

He nodded. "Yes. And he asked if I wanted to join hi gang. They were gonna rob the bank at Round Rock in the next couple of days."

"But, you told him, no."

Frank's lips stretched into a thin smile. "I said, yes."

Nancy looked at him.

"I told him I'd meet him at the camp the next evening and we'd go over the plans. We didn't know, but one of the boys in the gang had turned traitor and was informing the Rangers of the plans. Sam and the boys went to Round Rock to case the joint once more. One of the boys got trigger happy, shot the sheriff and only Sam and Frank Jackson escaped, though Sam was hard hit."

Nancy leaned forward with interest.

"I was out on a stage run. Didn't know all this had gone on. I was driving by a pasture with a big tree in it. Saw a little girl takin' a glass of water to the tree and then run back to the house without it. Then, I saw the blood trail and I stopped the team. Stage was empty, nobody but me. I could be a little late."

She knew he was reliving the moments.

"I come up to Sam, bloody as hell, layin' there, leanin' against the tree. Boy, was he glad to see me. But, he wouldn't let me move him. Said he was done for and didn't want to get me mixed up in it." There was more irony in his voice.

"Mama?" Stella sat up in the back of the wagon. "Are we stoppin' soon?"

Nancy looked about them, suddenly realizing that the afternoon was well advanced. "It's a little early, yet. But, why don't you girls get out and walk a spell?"

The suggestion was put into action and for the next little while, the girls ran and skipped along, picking up rocks and throwing them, then chasing each other about; the wagon rolling beside them. A couple of times, Nancy sat up as if to join them, but each time, she wrapped her arm about her belly and subsided onto her seat.

There seemed no good time to pick up the conversation with Frank, but Nancy drew her own conclusions.

"God," she said.

He threw a sidewise glance at her. "What?"

"God has certainly had a hand in keepin' you from goin' to the bad."

"Well, he's had a damned funny way of going about it. I've just spent the last eight years of my life in prison, for a crime I didn't commit!" With that, he slapped the reins on the rumps of both horses and let them trot right smartly for a bit. It gave the girls a good run to catch up to them.

"Mr. Pascoe, would you mind stopping?" Nancy grimaced and leaned forward.

He immediately stopped the team. "Are you alright?"

"I just want to lay down in the back for a bit."

Immediately he stopped the team, but before he could help her down from the wagon, she had stepped over the back of the seat and into the wagon bed.

"What is it, Mama?" Evie came running up, while Stella, distracted by some low hanging branches, trailed behind.

"I just want to lay down for a bit," her mother smiled at her.

Stella came to stand beside Frank and before she knew what was happening, he tossed her into the wagon beside her mother.

"Hey!" Her eyes flew wide when she landed on the mattress. Then, as quickly, she was back on her feet and said, "Do it again!"

He grinned at her. "Another time." Taking off his jacket, he handed it to Nancy.

There was a question in her eyes, but he motioned that she should use it to as a cover or a pillow. Then, he got back in the wagon and Evie climbed up to sit beside him.

When he rolled up the sleeves of his shirt, it revealed well muscled forearms as well as some long, thin scars along them. She glanced up at Frank who nodded, then took up the reins.

The sound of trotting horses came to them and she looked behind them. "A bunch of men," she reported. "Not soldiers," she said, slowly. They didn't ride anything like her father and his brothers. "Maybe the law," she added. Though raised in the hills, she had seen a few groups of men bent on having justice.

Frank maneuvered the wagon closer to the edge of the road so they could pass.

Instead, they pulled up. Frank glanced up at the riders, five of them, mostly well mounted, but recognized no one.

"Say Mister! You been on the road long?" One of the men in the group spoke up.

Another, apparently the leader on a well bred horse, frowned at him then turned to Frank.

"I'm Jed Rittenour. We're of Mount Joy and we're lookin' for a man, a Jack Davis by name." He was an older man, already sitting his horse as if he was sore from the few miles of riding they'd done.

"We're the Cyrus's!" Evie grinned at him. "We're headed west to start a new life!" She ignored the dubious looks the men gave their wagon.

"We've not seen any Jack Davis." Frank admitted, his manner thoughtful as he stroked his scruffy beard.

"If you do, let the Sheriff know, will you?" Rittenour turned his horse away. "There's a reward for him!"

"Yes sir," was the reply. He figured the man liked hearing 'sir' and it showed that he knew his place; which wasn't on the back of a five hundred dollar horse like Mr. Rittenour.

"Good-bye!" Evie waved at them as they rode passed.

"Good-bye!" From the back of the wagon, Stella chimed in.

When next Frank glanced into the wagon bed behind him, both Stella and her mother were asleep. Beside him, Evie kept up a continual chorus of songs. Dixie seemed to be her favorite.

"They lost, you know," he put in.

She flashed a look at him. "We lost," was her reply, "But that's only what's on the outside. Nobody can take what's on the inside."

"What's on the inside?"

Her fist tapped her chest. "A heart for Dixie."

"What does that mean?"

"It means that no matter what's happening out there," her hand swept in front of her, "I have a home here." She tapped her chest again. "Where I'm free to think what I think and be what I want to be." She leaned towards him. "Which means I ain't gettin' married!"

"Get up, Tommy!" He called to the horse. "Why not?"

"Cause no man is gonna tell me what to do."

"You're gonna tell him what to do?"

Evie shrugged. "All I know is, my Mama is a lot happier with no man around than when Uncle Albert is around. Or the men from church, tellin' her what she has to do. Or that Reverend Deering!"

When she was quiet for a few moments, he asked her, "What if you want children? You have to get married to have children."

"Cousin Garnet didn't. She put the cart before the horse, Mama says. So. When the time comes, I'm gonna put the cart before the horse, too."

There came the sound of another group of horsemen, riding faster than the one before it. Since it was warm, the sides of the wagon were rolled up, making the interior visible from a distance. Just a glance revealed Nancy lying there, her condition unmistakable, with Stella beside her.

The group started to slow, but then their leader signaled to keep going. One man of the group tried to turn and look at them, but the rider beside him blocked his view. He started to draw rein, but the man spoke to him and he spurred on, to follow the rest.

It was clear to both Frank and Evie who the man was.

"Except," Evie said, thoughtfully. "I might marry that Shelby fellow." And she nodded toward the man who was now a quarter of a mile away.

It was all Frank could do to keep a straight face. "Why is that?"

Evie sighed. "Well, for one thing, he saved my life." She looked at him. "You did, too."

"But I don't count."

She shook her head in agreement, then went on. "And for another, when I first saw him in that store at Lester's Landing when he was trailin' you? I felt like I was struck by lightning. My heart stopped and then it started again." Evie looked at him, her hand on his sleeve. "That counts for somethin', don't it?"

Frank nodded somberly. "It does," he said. "It counts for a lot." Though the road was smooth and usually he would have called for a trot, he decided walking was best, to let the riders get well ahead of them.

Since Nancy continued to sleep through the nooning, they didn't stop, but passed biscuits and bacon between them. It wasn't until mid afternoon that she sat up looking more rested. Yet, she continued to sit in the wagon bed, playing with Stella and singing songs.

Near sunset, Frank looked for a good place to make camp. They'd passed by many farms, some in better shape than others, and possibly could have been offered hospitality, but Nancy insisted that they drive on. The two little towns with sidewalks of people who stared as they drove by were equally not deserving of their presence, Evie declared with her nose in the air.

"Sir Walter Scott," Nancy explained her daughter's sudden haughtiness. "Ollie's Grandfather, Colonel Allen, had some of his novels. Read to all the children, boys and girls alike."

"Til I could read them on my own," her daughter said, proudly.

"One of the few who took an interest," Nancy smiled at her.

"He could read and write?"

"His Pap was a Baron over in Ireland," Evie put in. "And His Mam was a Lady."

Nancy nodded. "Yes, he could read. And he tried to teach his sons and daughters the same, but they were too busy carvin' out a livin' on the land."

"The land that he owned." Evie put in.

"Yes," Nancy went on. "Once upon a time, Colonel Allen owned all the land above The Forks. It was give to him for his service in the Revolutionary War."

"But, he sold it." Evie added.

"Farmin' those hills is a hard way to make a livin'. You have to clear the land, plow it, sow it, build a house an' barn," her mother spoke up. "Sometimes you need a little cash money."

"Some of the land he gave to his sons and daughters." Evie scoffed. "Who sold it." It was clear that she didn't hold with the action.

"Evie," her mother reminded her. "We sold our land."

Her daughter fell silent.

"Look!" Stella pointed skyward.

They were on a rise above a wide valley, beyond which, the land stretched, seemingly forever. Above them, the sky had lost its bright blue and had faded to cerulean, with bands of golden clouds horizontal across the horizon and puffs of pink dotted here and there.

Since the wagon was stopped, Nancy and Stella got down from the back, while Evie started to climb down from the front. There was a clunk and a pistol fell to the floorboard.

Frank looked at it, then at her.

"Mama said to keep an eye on you." With that, she picked up the gun and tucked it into the waistband of her skirt. Then she stood, waiting. Frank got down, clipped the weight to Tommy's bit and joined them in the road.

"Look!" Stella pointed. "The sunset! It's so big!"

Nature seemed to be putting on a show, with the sun painting cloud and sky alike with both bold colors and pastel.

"Immense," Evie added. Then, she turned around to see that color tinted the sky behind them as well. "Look! It's behind us as well!"

"Our sunsets are so little!" The little girl exclaimed. She turned in a circle, her eyes never leaving the sky. "Lookit all the colors!"

"Red. Pink. Blue. Orange. Gold!" Evie named them. "And lookit the pink! It's everywhere!"

Nancy looked at Frank. "They've only seen sunrises and sunsets in our little valley. With the hills so close, there's not much sky to be seen there."

He nodded in understanding. "The West is big, girls. Bigger than this. And the sunsets? You've not seen anything like 'em."

Stella looked at him and he knelt, to be on her level. "Then, I wanna go west!"

"That's where we're headed," he reminded her. And when he stood again, she put her hand in his.

Chapter
SIX

THIS NIGHT, THE MOON SAILED A SKY EMPTY OF CLOUDS. It was bright, almost light enough to do work. But, in the camp, Stella was already asleep and Evie's eyelids drooped, though she would occasionally jerk awake. Nancy leaned against a wagon wheel, Stella's head in her lap. Then, she moved away, gently resting her daughter's head on the ground.

"They've adapted well," Frank noted that both girls slept on the ground.

"They're always playin' Indian and makin' camps and sleepin' out." Nancy shifted her position, her hands on either side of her belly. She closed her eyes and breathed out, focusing on the baby inside, then opened them, as if rejoining the camp.

"If you can't have coffee, this isn't bad," Frank took a swallow of tea.

"I take that as a compliment." Nancy smiled, then winced.

"Are you alright, Mama?" As if summoned, her oldest daughter sat up and got to her feet.

Nancy gasped, then moaned, her hands gripping handfuls of grass and tearing it up.

"Baby a' comin'?" Frank asked.

"Yes!" But she shook her head. Sensing Evie's presence, she turned to her. "Baby's a' comin', Evie!"

The girl sank to her knees beside her mother. "Our last bit of Papa?"

Nancy looked away and another moan escaped her lips. Twisting to the ground, she pounded the dirt with her fists. "No, no, no, no!"

"What is it, Mama?" Evie brushed her mother's hair away from her face.

"It's too soon, lovey," the words were a whisper.

"My granny used to say, babies come when they come and they make their own welcome." Frank put in.

"Well," said Nancy. "This one's a' comin'." Another spasm gripped her and she gasped. "Evie's young, yet. No help."

"I can help, Mama!" Her daughter put in.

Her mother shook her head. "No."

Frank started to speak, but she interrupted him. "You been at a birthin'?" Her eyes met his.

"Yes. During the war."

"Soldiers have babies?" Evie asked, frowning.

"Camp followers do," was his reply.

Nancy nodded her head. "You'll have to do."

Later that night, Evie and Stella slept on a blanket, facing one another. The moon was once more playing hide and seek with the clouds. In the wagon, Nancy lay on her back while Frank stood before her, something in his hands.

"Is it . . ?"

Frank looked at her, then at the small form, before bringing it to her.

The baby was small but perfectly formed, like a marble doll, only lacking the spark of life.

"He never stood a chance, did he?" She took the tiny body from him.

"I'm sorry."

Her eyes never left the infant, while she smoothed his skin and made him comfortable in her arms. "I've hated it and loved it. Cursed it and prayed for it."

"Your husband's last child?"

"No," she glanced up at him, then back at the baby. "No. Not Ollie's."

He waited.

"It was at the funeral. His brother Albert. Drunk. Took me." Her words were guttural, said with emotion that was the more intense for its low volume. She lifted her chin, daring him to think the less of her.

Frank jerked, almost taking a step back from the intensity in her eyes and voice. "I'm sorry. I'm damned sorry." His hands flinched as if desiring to do something, anything, to avenge the atrocity. But there was nothing he could do.

She continued to stroke the child, to move its thin hair, fascinated with the impossibly tiny fingers and toes. "I didn't hate him so much as I hated the man who fathered him."

Frank nodded.

"I cursed God for it." Her eyes met his. "But then, I thought, God put him in my body for a reason, and I began to love him." Her voice broke. "Every baby needs love."

"Yes." She seemed to need an answer from him so he spoke the word. His hands made fists and relaxed, made fists and relaxed.

"I guess it wasn't enough." Her voice was tired. "God gives and God takes away."

The LONG WAY HOME

Frank stood before her, not knowing what to do or say, waiting for her.

"Well, that's done," she said softly. "I'm sorry he won't be goin' west with us. Maybe it's just as well that his journey ends here."

He looked up, back the way they had come. "I'll bury him in the road, there."

"In the road?" Nancy frowned, concerned. "Where people will drive over him?"

A tender look was on the man's face as he explained. "It's what you do in the West. The wagon and horse tracks will hide his grave. So the Indians won't dig him up, wonderin' what we buried."

Satisfied with his answer, her eyes went back to the child in her arms. She started to hand the baby to Frank but stopped. "No. Not yet. He has to have a name." Her eyes swept the tiny body, as if getting a clue as to what he wanted to be called.

"Cecil," she decided. "That was Colonel Allen's first name."

"That's a good name."

But still she held onto the baby. "I always give my children Bible names, too." Another few moments passed before she looked up at him. "Joseph. He was taken to a foreign land without his consent. Cecil Joseph Cyrus."

"Can I see him, Mama?" Evie had waked and came to stand beside Frank.

Nancy nodded and the girl crawled into the wagon beside her.

"He's perfect," she touched the cold skin. Like her mother, she lifted each hand and foot, keenly interested in the tiny fingers and toes. "But no spark."

"That's what life is, Evie. Birth and death. And we don't get to choose who lives or dies." Her eyes went to Frank. "For the most part."

"Your Mama is a brave woman. Havin' a baby out here, with no womenfolk to help."

Evie looked up at him. "If Aunt Gert had been here, would he have lived?"

Her mother shook her head. "No, Evie. Mr. Pascoe did fine, just like any midwife would have done. It just wasn't meant for Cecil to live." Tears came to her eyes with the words as she looked at Frank. "Thank you."

This time, she gave the baby to him and leaned back, an arm over her eyes. Evie scooted out of the wagon and looked up at him.

"Could I come with you, Mr. Pascoe? I ain't never had a brother before."

Frank looked at Nancy who nodded. Then, he bent and gave the baby to Evie who certainly knew how to hold one.

"Could you call me Frank?" He asked. "I think maybe I can be allowed some intimacy. We've a long way to go and well, it just seems more friendly."

Nancy looked at her daughter then at Frank. "My mother called my father Mr. Perry as long as she lived. But, I think we can be a little more familiar, Mr. Frank."

"Mr. Frank," Evie grinned up at him.

"Thank you," he gave a slight bow. "Mrs. Cyrus."

And there it was. If they were going to be more familiar with him, then it followed that he should be allowed the same privilege.

"Miss Nancy?" He suggested.

Wearily, she nodded then closed her eyes.

The LONG WAY HOME

Taking the shovel from the side of the wagon, Frank and Evie walked into the darkness beyond the campfire, thankful that the moon had reappeared.

It didn't take long and as they walked back to the wagon, Frank suddenly knelt down, motioning Evie to silence. Men's voices carried to them, along with Nancy's.

"Where's your man? We seen him earlier."

"Cain't you tell I just had a baby? He's gone to the creek to wash him off!" The words were said loud and angry, with enough volume to be heard a good distance.

"Come on, let's not bother her," Shelby's voice came to them. "Sorry, ma'am."

"Where you headed?" Another man spoke up.

In the darkness under the tree, Frank said, "three," as if he was counting them.

"We're headed west to make a new life," she answered. "Same as any on these roads." She paused, then went on. "Where are you headed?"

"We're looking for a dangerous man, a fugitive. Jack Davis, but he goes by Frank Pascoe as well." Shelby told her.

"What's he done," she asked anxiously.

"Well, for one, he's broke jail."

"Don't make him dangerous," was her reply.

"He's wanted for armed robbery."

"Is he armed?"

Shelby hesitated as he made the realization that his next words were possibly true. "By now he probably is."

"And you four men, you come upon a woman that's had life's hardest travail and you accost her and rob her of rest?" Her hands went under the quilt and began rummaging around. "Where's my pistol? I'll show you who's dangerous!"

"Damn, Shelby. Never get a pregnant woman riled!"

In the darkness of the trees, Frank said, "four." He took Evie's hand and began moving forward, to the edge of the line of trees. Three men sat their horses, while Shelby stood before her, reins in hand. Evie looked at Frank, ready for anything he might do or say.

Under the quilt, Nancy found the pistol and raised the barrel to let them know she had it.

"Sorry to have disturbed you, ma'am," Shelby mounted his horse. "Just be on the lookout. Let the sheriff know if you see him."

Around him, the other men turned their horses, anxious to get out of the range of the pistol. All of the men except one. He rode his horse close to Nancy and leaned toward her.

"What husband?" He asked of her. "You've no husband. And you won't have one, neither. None but me."

Nancy's eyes grew wide as she recognized Albert Cyrus. The pistol barrel moved in his direction.

But, his eyes were on her belly and the position of her body. "What did you do? Where's the baby?"

Her lips tightened and she started to bring the pistol to bear. But just then, a spasm rocked her; the afterbirth would not wait.

"Mama?" Stella called from her bed near the fire. When there was no immediate answer, she began to cry. "Mama?"

From the darkness beyond the camp where the other men had disappeared, one of the men called. "Lordy, Cyrus! Now you've stirred up the devil!"

He spun his horse about, ready to leave. "I'll find this Pascoe fellow, get the reward and I'll be back for you."

With both hands, she lifted the pistol in his direction, but before she could fire, he spurred his horse to gallop off, leaving behind his jeering laughter.

Nancy fell back onto the mattress, the pistol clattering on the boards.

"Have you passed the afterbirth, yet?" Frank was there, concern in his tone.

"No," she panted. "I couldn't. Not with all those men there. Staring. Gaping."

Behind them, Evie took Stella back to her bed and sat with her, humming a song to help get her back to sleep.

Frank was concerned for Nancy. "It's got to come out."

"I know, I know." Her head moved side to side. "Evie, Evie! Get Stella and both of you, back to bed."

"Yes, Mama," Evie's voice seemed little and thin in the late night air. She gripped Stella's hand the tighter and with her eyes squeezed shut and lips moving, prayed for her mother.

Nancy moved about the wagon, restless, as if trying to find something to hold onto. Her hand found an object in her movement and picked it up. It was the pistol. She looked at it, then at Frank. He held out his hand and she gave it to him, which he put in his waistband. Then, he reached for her hand again, but she grabbed the side of the wagon. Then, her eyes closed as she began to push once more.

The next morning found them on the road again, Stella sitting beside Frank, alternately asking him questions and singing to him. In the back of the wagon, Nancy lay on the mattress, her face flushed and feverish. Beside her, Evie sat dabbing a cloth on her forehead every little bit and murmuring softly.

Once, when the wagon jarred on a bump, Frank could hear her more plainly and realized she was reciting from Psalm 23. "Yea though I walk through the valley of the shadow of Death, I will fear no evil: for thou art with me, thy rod and thy staff they comfort me."

He shot a quick glance at Stella, but she was focused on making her corncob doll dance in the air.

Above them, the sky had clouded over, an unremitting ceiling of gray. A raindrop hit his sleeve, then another and another. As a matter of course, he pulled the wagon off the road and rolled down the canvas curtains. Glancing inside, he could see that Nancy was fretting, her head moving side to side. Evie looked up at him, but did not speak. That the girl was worried did not need to be said.

"Stella," he called to the little girl on the wagon seat. "Do you want to ride inside? Out of the rain?" He added the last because it was starting to rain harder.

With a grin of assent, she walked to the edge and he picked her up, depositing her under the canvas. In another moment, she had crawled up to her mother and lay down at her side. Evie gave him a look of gratitude and once again dabbed the cloth on her mother's face and lips.

Frank looked around them, trying to make out landmarks but it was hard in the rain. Picking up the reins, he gave both horses a resounding slap with them.

"Where are we going?" Evie asked, alarmed at the quick pace.

"I know of a place," he assured her.

Behind him, the girls settled in beside their mother, both cushioning her and lending warmth from their bodies.

Rain roared on the metal roof of the corn crib. Thankfully, it had enough of an overhang that it did not come inside. Between each board was a small opening, but it kept most of the rain out. The hard packed dirt floor didn't raise much dust except in the corners where corncobs were littered.

"Like it couldn't come down fast enough," Evie noted. She sat beside her mother, gently spreading drops of broth on her lips. It was dab, let her lick her lips and dab again. Though Frank had offered to help, she kept the spoon and bowl to herself.

It was slow going and in between dabs, she looked around.

"She's happy," Evie pointed the spoon at Stella, who was making families of leftover corn cobs, even to great uncles and great aunts.

A coffee mug in his hand, Frank walked around, looking out of the building, first one side then the other. All that could be seen was rain that had dropped a gray curtain all around them.

"Nothing beats a good cup of coffee," he said.

"It was good of Mr. and Mrs. Gardner to allow us to stay here."

Frank nodded.

"And give us food."

"Very nice," he agreed.

Though the Gardners had offered Frank and the girls the hay loft, there wasn't much room, since the first cutting of hay was already stacked there. As they had driven into the farmyard, Evie had noticed the corncrib which had more room, since the corn had not yet been harvested. They had a smokehouse, too, but no one thought it tenable. So, at her suggestion they moved into the corncrib just as the heavens let loose.

Turning, Frank looked at her, realizing she had a reason for her words.

"How did you know where they lived?"

He squatted down and watched as she wiped her mother's face with the towel, then offer her another dab of broth. "I've known Red Gardner these many years. We served together." And he did not refer to which side he had served on.

"Mama's pretty sick."

"Yes, she is."

"I wish we were home. Aunt Gert would know what to do."

Stella looked at her. "Aunt Gert is scary!" She pointed to her nose. "She has a big wart, right here!"

When no one replied, she went back to her corncob dolls. "And this one," she picked it up and shook it, "is not Aunt Gert!"

"You helped with the birthin'," Evie went on. "Are you a doctor?"

"I helped out some. During the war." It seemed like every time he tried to get away from that time which showed the difference between them, it seemed that it wouldn't be avoided.

"I heard you talkin' to Mrs. Gardner," the girl's eyes met his. "Sayin' that if anythin' happens to Mama, who would take us in?"

Stella looked up from her play. "I don't wanna go to an orf'nage. I wanna go home to the Forks." Tears began to well up in her eyes.

"Now girls," Frank held up a hand. "Nothing is gonna happen to your Mama."

"Why did you ask her, then," Evie looked at him accusingly.

"I'm thinkin' that little pitchers have big ears, is what I'm thinking."

Stella stomped her foot. "Grown-ups is always sayin' that. What does it mean?"

"It means we hear what we ain't supposed to," was her sister's reply.

They were quiet for a few moments, then Evie asked, "Where are we?"

"I'd say we're close to Texas," was his reply.

"I hope she makes it to Texas," the girl said, simply, brushing her mother's hair from her face. "So we can say she made it 'west'."

Frank looked over at the wan face, stood up then knelt again, close to Nancy. He put a hand to her forehead. "She'll make it," he told her.

"Do you know that for a fact?"

Frank looked around them. "Isn't it about your bedtime?"

"It's just dark because of the storm." When he did not reply, she added, "It will make trackin' a lot harder."

"Don't you have something you could be doin'?"

Seeing that her mother slept, Evie got up and went to the carpetbag. She drew out a deck of pasteboard cards. "None of our grandmothers would let us play. But, Mama does."

"Surprise, surprise." Frank glanced at Nancy. Was she resting better or was it only his hope for her?

The sound of the cards being shuffled drew his attention and he sat down a little ways apart, near the open door, for the better light. Stella came to sit on one side of him, Evie the other.

"What do you play?"

"Poker."

"Better and better," Frank rubbed his hands together, then cut the cards when they were offered to him.

Evie began dealing, but there was still something missing.

"Bring some of those pebbles over here," he told Stella. "And ante up."

The next morning, Frank got up and looked out the corncrib door. Fog hung thick around them and the air was so moist, it seemed that he breathed water. Behind him, Stella lay beside her mother, while a little further away, Evie was curled around a mound of pebbles.

As he looked out the door, he noticed the team in the small field next to the barn. They were on good grass and making the most of it. His fingers tapped the handle of the pistol at this belt. Then, he took a deep breath and let it out, as if he'd decided something.

He started to step outside, then stopped. Turning about, he walked between Nancy and Evie and knelt down beside the woman. A clamp of his hand on her forehead confirmed what he'd learned the night before. She was resting easy, the fever gone. It was likely she'd be weak for a few days, but she was strong and would come out of it.

Standing up, he walked quietly to the door.

"Before you go, you might want to check the loads in that pistol."

Frank halted, his hands sort of up. From the sound of her voice, he expected a pistol in her hand when he turned. But, both of her hands were still under the quilt. "What?" His smile was uneasy. "Why?"

"Check 'em." She motioned and only then did he realize she held a pistol under the quilt.

He was careful about drawing the gun from his waistband, keeping the muzzle pointed down. When he opened the gate and spun the cylinder, it was clear to see it was empty.

Nancy brought her pistol out from under the quilt. "This one is the twin to that one. Ollie got 'em during the war off some officer. Probably ill gotten gains, but come in handy, now and again."

Frank started to put the pistol on the ground, but she waved him off.

"Carry it." Her pistol wavered and her eyes closed, but just for a moment. "Evie!"

The girl got up immediately, which let him know she'd been awake the whole time.

"Give him a bullet."

Evie went to the carpetbag and pulled out a pouch clearly full of cartridges. She handed one to him.

"You might need it." Nancy sank back on the mattress from the wagon and closed her eyes.

Frank looked at Evie, who looked back at him, a certain hardness around her eyes and mouth. "I was just goin' to see about breakfast," he told her.

But, from the look on her face, she didn't believe him.

Frank slid the bullet into the chamber, then put the gun in his waistband. Whistling, he left the corncrib.

A short while later, Evie heard voices and came to the door, her Mama's pistol in her hand. Frank came walking up, Mrs. Gardner beside him. He waved at her and grinned, raising both hands, showing a basket in one and a pitcher in the other. "Breakfast is served!"

Chapter
SEVEN

From the back of the wagon came the cheerful voices of the girls as they played together; the Gardners had been very charitable with their corncobs which made for some happy children. Stella was especially pleased and promptly named all of them. It was up to Evie to make up the stories of their lives and what was to happen next.

Frank glanced over at Nancy. She was feeling better, yet gripped the wagon seat any time the road got rough, which it had been a lot lately.

A bump bounced them almost together, but the next moment, he had scooted back to his place on the seat.

Nancy sniffed and moved away from him.

A glance her way showed that her eyes were on the road, her knuckles white from gripping the wagon seat. It seemed she was determined not to bump into him again.

There came a buzzing sound and a large deer fly zipped by him on its way to one of the horses before him, no doubt. Quickly he took off his jacket, then used it to swat the fly as it landed on the spine of Tony.

Rather than startling at the action, the horse seemed grateful to leave the deer fly in the dust behind them.

"Well done," Nancy commented.

He grinned at her and swung his jacket around to slide his arms back through, but halted. Suddenly the reason for her aversion came to him. "I stink."

"You shoulda stood in the rain last night," Evie sang out over the sound of the wagon on a suddenly rocky road.

"I didn't even think of it," he said. "Had other things on my mind," his eyes slid to Nancy beside him. Then, he stroked his whiskers. "You got a razor in that Pandora's box?" He glanced over his shoulder at the carpetbag.

"No. Papa didn't shave." Evie replied. "But, he did bathe. We all bathed, every Saturday night."

"Guess it'll have to wait," Frank slapped a rein on Tommy's rump. That horse was going to have a rude awakening one of these times, he told himself.

"It's been Saturday a couple of times since we've been on the road," Evie's clear voice came from the back. "And there's one comin' up in two days."

Frank nodded. "Good to know." But, he told himself, he was going to bathe one way or the other beforehand.

The afternoon was hot and lazy; the horses were only walking, seemingly half-asleep. Frank clucked to them and they responded with a faster gait. He kept his jacket off and rolled up the sleeves of his shirt, it was that hot.

Beside him, Nancy looked around them, noticing the landscape and the various animals, though most had sought shade by now.

A lone horseman came riding up and passed them, his horse gaiting so that he scarce moved in the saddle.

"I used to have a horse like that," she murmured, watching them move down the road. "Belle. Best horse. I rode her to church, sidesaddle, but without the saddle." She smiled with the memory. "The boys would ask to escort me home, but none had a horse to keep up with her when she hit her stride." Her mind went back to the time Albert, frustrated that his horse couldn't keep up, began beating Belle with his whip as they raced alongside. One of his blows had hit her when she had tried to protect her horse. It cut through the cloth of her sleeve and bloodied her arm. He never noticed.

"Then, Ollie went to Memphis and brought back a fancy horse. Cost him almost a year's wages and his share of the timber. Black Diamond, the horse's name was. Almost as pretty as Belle." She smiled a little. "He caught up to us and that's when I said he could come courtin'." Her fingers smoothed her dress. "That's the horse he left to go fightin' on. Lost him right off to an officer. Seein' how things was, he thought Diamond would have a better time of it with the officer." She shook her head. "Officer and horse died in the first battle. That's about when they made a sharpshooter out of him and he was glad."

"What happened to your horse. Belle?"

"Yanks," was the short reply.

There it was again; a reminder of their differences.

She held a hand over her eyes to shield them and looked around. The horseman was no longer in sight, but a group of three riders were coming toward them. She looked for a long time before she sat back in her seat. "Three riders. Probably headed to town with their wares," for there were three packhorses along with the riders.

They were silent until the men passed, tipping their hats to Nancy, and nodding to Frank.

Once they were out of earshot, she spoke. "This Shelby Sinclair wants you almighty bad."

"Seems so," was his reply.

"Are you sure it's just for the train robbery?"

"Maybe it's pride. Maybe nobody ever slipped his jail before."

"Pride means a good deal to a young man."

"Any man," Frank put in.

"Any man," she repeated in agreement.

The afternoon seemed to stretch as long as the vista before them. For as far as they can see, there are no hills or mountains, just land.

"Mama?" Evie's head appeared between them as she knelt on the wagon bed.

"Yes?"

"They's a horse followin' us."

Nancy turned to look and when Frank had a chance, he glanced back as well.

Indeed, there was a horse following them. It meandered along the roadside, grabbing mouthfuls of grass here and there, but in the main, it was keeping up with them.

"Do you see that often?" She asked him because in the hills, every animal had an owner and everyone knew who it was.

"Nope," he said and wondered if he was becoming as laconic as the Cyrus's.

"I think he's hurt," Evie frowned.

Nancy looked again. Every little bit, the horse would limp or take a funny step.

"Whoa," Frank pulled the team to a stop and waited.

As they watched, the horse came up to the wagon, seemingly interested in the girls who sat at the back. Evie held out a bit of a biscuit. "It's Stella's from this morning."

The horse seemed familiar with the treat and took it gently from her fingers.

"I wanna horsie!" Stella clapped her hands together.

At the sudden noise and movement, the horse shied away. But, when Evie held out her hand again, the horse came forward.

Frank eased out of the wagon and approached the horse. "He's not hurt. Just a loose shoe."

"She," Nancy corrected from the wagon seat.

"Can you get it off?" Her daughter stroked the nose of the horse, allowing Frank to walk around it.

He did not attempt to touch the horse, just looked it over. "Got some pliers?"

Evie shook her head.

"Well, it might come off on its own, if he, if she keeps travelin' with us." He got back up in the wagon seat.

"Wonder who she belongs to?" Nancy was turned, watching the horse as the wagon began to move.

Frank shrugged. "No brands anywhere."

"Come on, girl!" Evie called to the mare, offering the last piece of the biscuit. When the horse followed, she bounced up and down a little with excitement. The horse hesitated at her action, so she settled for smiling instead.

That evening's camp was much different than the night before. Nancy, though weak and leaving a good bit of the chores to Evie and Frank, sat upright against the wagon wheel, Stella snuggled close by her side. All of them were glad to have her back in the land of the living, as Evie said.

There was another reason for the girl's ebullient spirit. The horse.

"We're out of corn," Frank showed them the empty bag . "Your horse likes corn, too," he motioned to Evie. "Keeps tryin' to get his share."

"She's still out there?" The girl's smile seemed wider than her face.

"Yep. And if that shoe doesn't come off," he deliberately emphasized the next word, "She's gonna tear a bunch of hoof off with it."

"An' we've nuthin' to get it off with!" Evie was as crushed as she had been happy before. She well knew that a horse with a torn foot was of no use to anyone for a while, and might possibly need doctoring in the meantime.

"There's a little town, not too far from here," Frank looked at Nancy. "Probably have a blacksmith."

She nodded. "We could use some flour, soda and salt."

"And coffee."

A slight smile came across her tired face. "And some honey or some kind of sweetenin'."

"And a peppermint stick?" Stella roused from her half-asleep state.

"We might be able to find one," her mother assured her, then looked at Evie. Her oldest daughter was on the cusp between child and young woman. Too soon, in her opinion, but life was what it was. "Or two."

Evie smiled in relief, happy that she wasn't too old for the treat.

"So, it's agreed. We go to town?" Frank asked again. Though, like the rest, he wanted, no, needed to go to town, there were certain dangers there. For one thing, there was Shelby. The kid seemed bound and determined to take him to jail. For another, this was Texas and at any time, he could meet some of the old crowd, which might make it uncomfortable for him. And of course, there was his old nemesis, whisky. After his one binge in Mount Joy, he'd held off indulging. But now, too much had happened and he felt it was owed him.

"What if she won't follow us to town?" Evie spoke up with sudden worry.

Nancy held up a rope braided from cloth torn from her petticoat. "I think she will."

The town of Red Top wasn't much compared to bigger cities. But, for this part of Texas, it was pretty much expected. A few of the buildings were built of brick or stone, but the rest were wooden. Strips of wooden sidewalk lined most of the buildings which were built on either side of a wide street. Perhaps the only change from other towns of its size was the fact that a church was one of the first buildings built there. Since it occupied one end of the street, the two saloons were at the other end, one facing the other.

On a corner halfway down Main Street where the Austin road bisected it, was the blacksmith shop. It was a gathering place for men when it was too early for the St. Regis Saloon, just a few doors down, to open. As Frank pulled up in front of the blacksmith shop, several men abruptly left, headed for the saloon. He watched them go and licked his lips when they disappeared inside.

"We'll get some shopping done," Nancy got down from the wagon.

He wondered if she'd noticed his lapse in attention and lack of manners. His gaze went back to the saloon, then across the street when he heard a door slap shut. A group of men had come out of an office; it looked to be a sheriff's office.

Frank came around to the back of the wagon as Evie helped Stella down.

"You'll need some . ." Nancy put her hand in her reticule.

He waved her off as he reached for Evie's horse's lead and a stray thought wondered where the purse had come from, probably the carpetbag. Reaching down, he tousled Stella's hair and tugged on one of Evie's braids, and they grinned back at him. All of this kept his head down and back turned while the group of men came slowly up the boardwalk.

The blacksmith shop was cool and dark, but he didn't walk all the way in. Not until he knew what was happening behind him as well as before him.

"What can I help you with?" A blonde man, not tall but broad, smiled at him. "I'm Billy Hartford, the blacksmith."

Frank hesitated, wondering what his response should be. "Cyrus," he said. "Good to meet you, sir." He glanced over his shoulder. The group of men were still making their way toward the blacksmith shop. "Could you take a look at this horse?"

"I sure will!" Hartford walked outside and then around the mare. "That's one fine horse!"

"She needs that shoe reset."

"Well, I've got a few ahead of you," he looked at the horses in the two stalls nearby.

Frank frowned a little. "My family and I want to get back on the road as soon as possible." Though he didn't know the reason for the group of men, where they were heading or if they had anything to do with him, somehow, he had the feeling they did.

Hartford sighed, his hands on his hips. "My helper is home nursing a broken leg, damn mule. If you know how to use the tools, help yourself."

Another glance down the street revealed the group of men getting closer.

"Why thank you, sir. Much obliged," Frank led the mare into the shop. Under his breath, he cursed the fact that Shelby wouldn't give up the trail while he blessed him for the fact that he wore a new white hat. It made him stand out in a crowd and he was grateful.

Thus, when Shelby Sinclair and three other men walked by the blacksmith shop, all they would have seen in the dimness were two men, their backs to the street, shoeing horses. Of the men, only Shelby glanced inside. The others walked past unseeing, their attention on the St. Regis Saloon.

In the Red Top Mercantile, Nancy moved among the counters shopping for various items, Evie her shadow. In an open space near the front, Stella and another little girl about her age played with a toy tea set. They sat down at a child sized table and poured invisible tea for one another.

The counter full of bolts of cloth ran along a window facing the street, so that one could tell their true colors. Nancy looked at this one and that, feeling their softness or thickness.

"I like this one, don't you?" She asked Evie as she held up a bolt with a red background.

"I like this one," Evie's hands trailed over a blue and yellow plaid on a field of white.

"That's fancy," Nancy looked at her daughter. Yes, she was growing up. It was a pattern she wouldn't have picked a year ago.

A form blocked the light from the window and Nancy looked up to see Albert leering at her through the glass. Surprised, she took a step back. He laughed at her response, a jarring sound, even through the glass. Then, he turned to walk down the street, laughing as he went.

"I don't like Uncle Albert," Evie confided. "He drowned two of Betty's puppies for no good reason."

"For meanness," Stella put in from her nearby table.

"Let's keep shopping," Nancy turned Evie away from the window.

"What else did you find?"

Evie led her to the knife case and pointed. "If I had the cash money, I'd buy one of those."

"What would you want with a knife?" Nancy asked in a low voice, surprised at her daughter's fierceness.

"To keep you safe."

"I am safe," Nancy smiled at her.

"Not when Uncle Albert is around."

She looked at her daughter, her brown eyes searching Evie's blue ones, so like her father's. What did she know? Then, she patted the girl's shoulder, trying to lighten her mood. "I've raised a bloodthirsty child."

"Or," Evie went on, "I'd give it to Mr. Frank. So he could keep you safe."

Nancy looked at her daughter again. It seemed that children could know more than they were telling as well as adults.

"Look, Evie!" Stella pointed at a basket of kittens in the corner. Immediately, both girls were sitting beside it and playing with the black and yellow balls of fur. Even the Mama cat came in for some petting.

Nancy went back to her shopping, carefully considering what was needed and what she could afford. It wouldn't do to spend all of her money on supplies. They would need money where they were going, and she had no idea what land in Texas would cost.

Then, she realized what she had just thought. Texas. Was Texas home? Standing at the window, she glanced up at the cloudless blue sky above and asked again. Was Texas home?

A movement outside caught her eye and she saw Frank and a young woman walk out of the back of the saloon across the side street. The woman swung her hips and laughed, while Frank nodded and smiled, a whisky bottle in his hand. As Nancy watched, he opened the door to one of the little cabins that lined the back of the lot and followed her inside.

"How can I help you, ma'am?" One of the clerks broke in to her thoughts.

"Yes," Nancy turned to him. "Here's my list," which she handed to him.

After walking about the store a bit, making sure there was nothing more she needed, Nancy went back to where her daughters sat on the floor, playing with the kittens. It was hard to resist their entreaties to take one with them. But, Nancy was adamant. There was no place for them on the road, and what would they eat?

"Biscuits!" Stella put in and they all laughed.

A shadow passed in front of the window and she looked up to see Frank walk by, headed for the main street. Though all she could see was his hat, she recognized it. Then, she turned her attention back to her daughters and their play.

The clerk came by to say that her purchases were ready and she stood up to follow him to the counter. From what she'd seen of Frank with the whisky bottle, she would have to arrange to have them taken to the wagon.

Their purchases made, Nancy led the girls from the Mercantile. She held Stella's hand, but Evie walked a little behind, looking at the buildings all around them.

Beyond the little town, the prairie stretched, seemingly nothing else in sight, except the shrub lined creek. All through the town, men walked here and there, bent on some business or another. A thought occurred to her and she turned all the way around, but no, there were no women or girls in sight. As Evie finished her turn, she nearly ran into a man walking along the sidewalk.

Dodging her, he still had time to tip his hat to her, and she held her head a little higher. But, something made her look back at him, just in time to notice that he slowed his step, his eyes on a rider coming up the street.

Since the sun was in the horseman's eyes, he probably didn't notice the man move into the shadow of an overhang. Evie watched him, then the rider as he passed.

She didn't think she'd ever seen a getup like his, with silver buttons down the sides of his pants and long roweled silver spurs on shiny black boots. His hat brim was larger than most and around it were more silver buttons.

His horse was one to take anyone's eye, a blood bay high stepper with silver adorning the saddle, breastplate and bridle. His head bobbed with every step, the long black mane and forelock, bouncing and waving. The horse's long, thick tail was like black smoke floating behind him.

When the rider turned to look her way, she noted his thick black moustache, much like the man who had nearly run into her. But this man, somehow, gave her pause.

"Evie!" Her mother beckoned to her from the other side of Austin Road. Quickly, she caught up to her, but still she watched the man on the fine black horse ride down the street. Just before she followed her mother into the blacksmith shop, she noticed that the first man stepped from the shadows and continued to watch the rider as well.

"There's our wagon," Nancy pointed out. "The horses must be in the livery stable."

"Eatin'." Stella put in.

It was dark inside and took a moment for their eyes to adjust to the gloom. Looking about, it seemed that only the blacksmith was there, but he turned and grinned at their approach.

"Excuse me, sir. Do you know where my man is?" She thought this was a safe way to refer to Frank, since he could be a worker or a husband, God forbid. "He brought a horse to be shod." Then she added, "One foot," since most everyone brought horses needing to be shod.

"Yes, ma'am. He's down by the creek bank." And, he pointed to an area beyond the saloons.

"What's he doin' down there?" Evie asked, as puzzled as her mother.

"He's racin' that blood horse you got."

"What?"

"Your horse, the one with the shoe half off. Some men come through here, said they had a horse that ain't never been beat. Your man took your horse down to the bottoms to race it."

Nancy looked in the direction he pointed, but saw nothing but open range. Apparently the racing grounds were behind the buildings opposite. As she looked, a group of men came out of the St. Regis Saloon. They were arguing, some pointing toward the bottom land and others up the street.

Suddenly, she recognized both Albert and Shelby, though why they should be together, she did not know. Drawing Evie and Stella to her, she stepped further into the darkness of the blacksmith shop. "Do you know how long it might be?"

"Depends on how likkered up they wanna get."

Nancy looked again in the direction of the creek bottom.

"What are we gonna do now, Mama?" Evie asked.

The clump of boots on the boardwalk drew her attention to the men walking toward them. One of the men was Albert who peered intently into every store front. The other was Shelby Sinclair who kept his gaze on their wagon.

"Looks like we'll have to wait," she moved further into the dimness of the shop.

"My wife and I live the next house over. You could set yourself down and rest a bit. You and your girls," the blacksmith offered. "She'd admire to have another woman to talk to."

"Well, hello!" Shelby Sinclair stood at the front of the shop and he swept off his hat when he saw them. "We meet again!"

"Under considerably better circumstances," Nancy's tone was cool.

The young man colored visibly. "Yes, ma'am. Considerably better."

"You've come far afield, Mr. Sinclair," she noted.

"I go wherever the trail leads," he smiled at Evie who stood beside her mother, her eyes big.

"I wish you wouldn't chase Mr. Frank," she said.

"Why?" His attitude was that of humoring a child.

"Because he saved my mother's life."

"Well, I guess there's some good and bad in all of us," Shelby glanced around the blacksmith shop.

"Amen," Nancy said, wryly.

The young man's face flushed again.

"And, and . ." Evie looked down, suddenly shy.

"Yes?"

Before she could reply, Albert Cyrus pushed past Sinclair. "Hello, sister-in-law!" It was clear he'd been drinking and Evie's face wrinkled up, while Stella sought shelter behind her mother.

"If you'll pardon me, gentlemen," Nancy smiled at Shelby. "We have an appointment." Taking Stella's hand, she started to turn, but Albert blocked her path.

"Where you goin'?" He leered at her. "Don't you wish there was still that Biblical thing where a widow has to marry her husband's brother?"

"Come girls," Nancy took a hand of each daughter in hers. "It was nice to see you again, Mr. Sinclair."

Before she took two steps, Albert reached out and took hold of her arm.

Shelby grabbed his other arm. "Now see her, Cyrus. We don't accost women like that!"

Albert pulled out of his grasp and started forward again, but Evie whirled on him, her knife at the ready. "Stay away from my mother!"

For a moment, there was silence in the blacksmith shop, broken only by the sound of a shotgun being cocked.

"Your friend is right," the blacksmith spoke up. "We don't treat women that way." Though he held the gun with the barrels pointed upward, it would only take an instant to bring it to bear.

"Aw, I was only foolin'," Albert laughed. "Good day to you, Miz Nancy," he doffed his hat. Then, he shot a look at Shelby. "And don't touch me like that again!" Slapping his hat to his head, he stomped out of the building.

"Your friend is a little touchy," Hartford spoke up.

"He's not my friend," the young man told him. "He joined our group for the company."

"You might want to unjoin him. Out here, we don't manhandle women. Nor make unsavory remarks."

The LONG WAY HOME

"I'll keep that in mind." He tipped his hat to Nancy, then to Evie. "You certainly have a protector in your little girl."

Evie's chin came up. "I'm not a little girl anymore. I'm just shy of marryin' age. And, I can shoot as well as any boy at the Forks!"

Barely concealing his amusement, Shelby said, "I'll keep that in mind." He turned to follow Albert out of the building.

"Come, girls," Nancy motioned to her daughters. "And put that knife away, Evie. I didn't buy it for you to wave around five minutes later!"

She slipped it into the sheath that was mostly concealed by the folds of her skirt. Though her mother held out her hand, Evie looked at it for a moment, then ignored it. "I'm gonna marry Mr. Sinclair, Mama. Just as soon as I'm of marryin' age."

Noting her determination, Nancy's amusement faded. "I wouldn't be surprised, Evie. You take after your Pa that way. Settin' your mind to somethin' and not lettin' go."

"No, Mama," Evie put her fist to her heart. "I feel it here."

Chapter EIGHT

Though Mrs. Hartford and her husband offered to house Nancy and the girls for the night, she declined.

"We'd like to get an early start in the morning," Nancy told them with a smile, "And would not want to disturb you."

Mrs. Hartford protested that it would be no trouble at all, yet Nancy was adamant.

Stella pouted, because her new found friend was the Hartford's daughter, but she was pacified with the promise of another peppermint stick.

The wagon was loaded with their purchases, then Nancy took the reins and they once more headed west. On their way out of town, Evie sat beside her mother, eagle-eyed, looking for Shelby. But, he was nowhere to be seen.

She did see the man in the black hat and big black moustache coming out of the sheriff's office. Again he tipped his hat to her as they passed and she sat up a little straighter.

Once beyond the buildings, they could see the crowd of men along the creek bottom and from the dust, it seemed that horses were racing. But, their view was blocked by the backs of the men and Nancy seemed satisfied to let them be, urging the team to a trot as they left the town.

Since they'd gotten a late start on the road, they weren't far out of town when they stopped to camp. Evie helped her mother unharness the horses and then picket them on a patch of grass.

"Always stop where your animals have good feed," Nancy told her daughter. She had halted for a moment, her hand on the wagon for support, the other on her abdomen.

"Yes, ma'am." Evie replied. "Are you alright, Mama?"

Nancy nodded. "Still weak."

"I can get dinner."

Her mother smiled. "Yes. Please do that."

It wouldn't be hard since they still had the stew that Mrs. Hartford had sent along. Evie took pride in the fact that she'd been making biscuits for the last two years, so that wouldn't be difficult, either.

After dinner, they sang some songs, but mostly, Nancy listened to her daughters sing. At bedtime, she braided their hair then let Evie braid hers.

"You have lovely hair, Mama."

"That's what your father always said."

"I'd like to have hair like yours someday."

Nancy looked at her daughter's blonde strands. "You'll have prettier hair than me some day." Picking up her braid, she looked at the dark hair. "Mine isn't truly brown or truly black."

Evie suddenly leaned forward and enveloped her in a hug. "It's the most beautiful hair in the world, Mama."

Tears started to Nancy's eyes as she patted the hands clasped around her. "And, I've got the most beautiful girls in the world." Her other hand stroked Stella's hair, for the little girl had almost thrown herself into her mother's arms.

For a long moment, they remained embraced, then Nancy tapped Evie's hands and Stella's bent head. "Time for bed, girls. And let's not forget to thank God for getting us this far."

"Yes, ma'am," came the chorus back to her.

The fire was a mound of embers when a step crunched nearby. Through protests, Nancy had insisted that the girls sleep in the wagon that night. She, however, lay under it and at the sound turned to face the intruder, pistol in hand.

Frank stepped forward, a smile on his face. He kicked at the fire, rousing it to flame. "Hello the camp!" From his laughter, she knew he was drunk. "We've made some money this day!" Pulling out a flask, he took a swig.

"We could have been down the road another twenty miles or so," she reminded him, her voice even. She noted the fact that he was shaved and wore new clothes.

Frank shook his head. "We made money, I tell you! And we wouldn't have if we'd been on the road!" From another pocket he pulled out a sheaf of bills. As he rifled it, he laughed again, exultantly.

"You're drunk."

"I am," he nodded, unabashed. After eight years, it was owed him. "That mare we found is a racer! And she out raced everythin' they could find to put against her!"

"Where is she now?" She moved to where the pistol was pointed in his direction, but he was oblivious.

"Sold her." He rifled the bills again. "Three hundred dollars! Do you believe that?"

"You sold my daughter's horse?"

He looked at her blankly. "Your daughter's?"

"Didn't she find the horse? Get it to come to her? Brush it? Untangle its tail?"

"It would still be limpin' if not for me!" He was indignant.

"Thank you for savin' my life, Mr. Pascoe, but this is where we part ways." Her voice was dead quiet.

Frank stared at her. "What for?" Though drunk, he was rapidly sobering. "I thought we had a deal. Travel together til Denton."

"We don't need you anymore, Mr. Pascoe. Especially a man who would benefit from the loss of my daughter's horse."

"You want me to go? I'll go!" He started to turn but stopped.

"Good night, Mr. Pascoe."

But, he stood as if rooted to the spot. "You're gonna need protection."

"I've got protection," she motioned with the pistol. "Besides, I've a notion to ask Mr. Sinclair to join us. We seem to be going in the same direction."

Frank brought his lapel to his nose and sniffed. "I smell good."

"Good night, Mr. Pascoe. I wish you safe travels and Godspeed."

"Sure would be a sight easier to get to Denton together."

"You'd best be headin' down the pike." She cocked the pistol.

"Damn it, woman! You know there's a posse after me! At this point, they'd probably string me up as soon as take me to jail!"

"I do know it," Nancy said, calmly. "I just wondered if you remembered it."

Frank looked around, still angry and drunk. "Alright." He took a deep breath. "Alright. What does it take? What do I have to do?" He shuddered, as if repulsed by the thought of bargaining with her.

There was a sound and Evie's face appeared over the side of the wagon. "Mr. Frank!" She called to him excitedly, then looked around. "Where's my horse?"

"Shush, Evie," her mother said, quietly, "Go back to sleep." Then, to Frank, she added, "I think you know the answer to that."

"That's three hundred dollars! We could take the stage! Get to Denton a heap sooner! Stay in hotels instead of sleeping on the ground!"

"Knowing a little about horse racing, myself, Mr. Pascoe, I wouldn't be surprised if you bet on the horse yourself."

Frank looked caught.

"And, if so, then you have more than three hundred dollars."

"I may have spent a little bit," his hand smoothed the new vest and the watch fob that dangled across it.

"But, you've more." When he didn't respond, she went on. "I'm not asking for any of the money you won off my daughter's horse, just for the horse."

"Damn, you drive a hard bargain." He thumped one fist into the other palm in frustration.

"How old are you, Mr. Pascoe? Too old to remember how it feels to be ten years old? To lose your Papa and then your home? To give your heart to a lost horse and have it follow you around like a dog?" Her tone was flat when she added, "Do you want to tell her that you sold it? That it's never coming back?"

Frank sighed and looked up at the stars. After a few moments consideration, he said, "If I'm not back by the time you start out, I'll catch up."

The LONG WAY HOME

"We're headed out early. If you don't catch up by noon, I'll know you're not comin'." The words were said evenly, matter of factly.

For answer, he turned on his heel and strode into the darkness. "Women! Girls! Horses!" Though he was not shouting, the words were clearly heard. Then, he hit something in the dark and groaned. He kicked it, then groaned again. "God!"

"You think we'll see him again, Mama?" Evie's face appeared over the side of the wagon.

"We'll see him when we see him, I reckon." Nancy got out from under the wagon and scraped the scattered the coals together. It wouldn't do to start a prairie fire.

When she was satisfied with the fire, she crawled back to her bed. "God knows, Evie. God knows."

"Thanks for thinkin' of me, Mama," Evie said from above, in the wagon bed.

Nancy smiled, realizing once more how mature her daughter was becoming. "Did I ever tell you about my gaited horse, Belle?"

The next day dawned with no clouds. Around them, the land seemed flat, but was cut up by draws. The horses walked the descent but trotted up the incline. On a whim, Nancy let Evie handle the reins of the team.

"You're doing well," she told her.

"I didn't know the reins would be so heavy!"

"You'll get used to it."

"Where are we going, Mama?" Stella asked. "Austin? San Tone?" She was repeating the names she'd heard back in Red Top.

"Home," Nancy replied. "We're goin' home."

"Well, where is home?" Stella frowned as she looked into the distance.

"Home will be where we decide to make it."

"Where will we make it? Here? There?" With her hand, the little girl swept a long arc, ending at a lone tree standing in the distance. "Can we go say hello to that tree, Mama? It looks lonely."

"Head for that tree, Evie," Came the calm direction.

Evie moved the reins over and the horses obeyed in a smooth motion, as if leaving the road to travel the country was their usual routine.

"As for home, we'll know it when we see it," assured her mother.

"What about Mr. Frank? Will he be home, too?"

"I think that Mr. Frank's idea of home is different from ours."

Stella stared at her. "Different?" She bounced her corncob doll in the air before her. "No! I like Mr. Frank. He plays tea party with me and Dolly."

On the other side of her, Evie spoke up, "Well, wherever home is, Mama, please don't make it up some holler. Mr. Sinclair has to find it."

They pulled up next to the lone cedar and got down out of the wagon. Stella walked up to the tree and hugged the area she could reach.

"I like trees, Mama," she confided. "They make me happy."

"Yes," replied her mother. "They make me happy, too. I like to touch them and say thank you."

"Thank you?" Evie asked.

"Thank you for the shade you provide, for the wood in winter and the fruit from your limbs."

Stella looked at the lone tree. "Trees are my friends and you always say hello to your friends."

Beside her, Evie looked at the tree, then at her mother. "Is that an Indian thing, Mama? Thanking trees?"

"Indians give thanks," was the reply.

"Like Christians."

"Like a lot of people." Nancy helped Stella back into the wagon. "Being grateful makes you feel good."

Stella leaned forward, hugging her. "I like that, Mama. I like saying thanks to trees."

"Me, too," Evie spoke up.

"Saying thanks any time is a good thing," Nancy settled in beside her. "Now, let's find the road again."

It wasn't long after that, Stella's little voice came from the back of the wagon. "I'm hungry!"

Nancy smiled a little, then glanced down at the horses' shadows. They were trotting on them, so it was noon. "Alright, Stella. We'll stop and eat some of the biscuits saved from this morning."

Looking about, there seemed to be a likely place for stopping, near another lone tree. "Take us over there, Evie." She glanced at her. "You have to be careful. Sometimes, wagons turn over when they leave the road. Angle it a little."

Evie's face was tight and her lips pursed together.

"Do you think you can do it?"

"Yes, ma'am," was the reply. And, true to her word, she turned the wagon at an angle and let one wheel at a time leave the road. It was a little bumpy, and the horses almost came to a stop once or twice, but she did it. She continued driving over to the tree her mother had singled out.

"Very good!" Her mother smiled at her. "You did it! And, you did it very well."

"Thank you, Mama!" Evie grinned.

"Yahoo! Evie's a driver now!" Her little sister crowed.

The sound of a trotting horse had them all turning around. It was Frank, riding up on Evie's horse.

The girl called whoa to the team and tossed the reins to her mother; out of the wagon almost before it stopped rolling. "Gypsy!" In another moment, she had her arms wrapped around the horse's neck, for the mare had lowered her head to her. Though Evie buried her face in the horse's mane, she pulled away for a moment. "Thank you, Mr. Frank! Thank you!"

He handed her the reins, then stepped away. It was obvious the connection the girl had with her horse, how could he have missed it? Though he dreaded looking at Nancy, when he glanced up, he was greeted with a pleased smile.

But, he wasn't ready to give up his temper just yet. "You sure started early! That was a good fifteen miles of riding! Bareback!"

"Stella woke up early. We decided to get on the road before it got too hot."

As if prompted, Stella leaned out the back of the wagon. "Hello, Mr. Frank! Want to play tea party?"

"Not now," Nancy told her. "He's probably wantin' a meal."

"I am at that," he was pleased that food was in the offing. Though the mare had smooth gaits, trotting that distance with a pounding head had not put him in a good mood. Not that he'd been in one anyway when Mr. Dickerson, the man he'd sold the mare to, insisted on making a hundred dollar profit selling her back to him.

"I'll get the biscuits!" Stella disappeared back into the wagon to dig out the leftover food from breakfast.

Evie was petting her horse and murmuring to her, so that left Frank standing before Nancy with some degree of privacy.

He tilted his head, a grin on his face. "Surprised to see me?"

"I admit that I am," she said, frankly.

"Glad to see me?" He walked in front of her and waved his hands so that his cologne would waft towards her.

"What's that you're wearin'?" She wrinkled her nose in distaste. "Eau de cathouse?"

He bent his head to take a sniff of his vest. "First, I smell. And then . ."

"You stink!" Stella leaned out of the wagon to give him his biscuit and bacon and laughed at her own comment.

"Girls!" Frank took the food from her. "Women!" He didn't look at Nancy. "There's no pleasing them!"

Nancy looked at him but said nothing. Instead, she passed out biscuits and ladled out a serving of beans from the Dutch oven. He took a seat by the wagon, using the wheel as his backrest and enjoyed his meal. At the finish, he took out a flask from his pocket and tilted it on his lips. Then, he wiped his mouth with the back of his hand. "Nothing finer than Tennessee corn," he grinned.

Nancy motioned to her oldest daughter. "Come with me."

The girl followed her mother as she walked away from the wagon. Every little bit, Nancy would pick up a rock or point out one that Evie should get. After a few moments of watching, Frank realized that she was setting up targets.

He smiled at the sight and got to his feet, pulling his holster into position. It and the pistol in it were some of the things he had acquired with his winnings. But, when Nancy came back, she walked by him and went to the wagon. Unwrapping a bundle, she pulled out one of the Winchester rifles and handed it to Evie. She took the other one for herself.

While he watched, Nancy had Evie lie down on the ground and fire the rifle. Each target that her mother pointed out, the girl hit.

"Nice shooting." He commented and his praise was genuine.

Then, she had Stella take Evie's place. This time, she put a rock under the barrel so that the little girl did not have to lift it.

Though she did not hit her targets square on like her sister, she was close enough to do some damage.

Still ignoring Frank, Nancy stepped forward and turned her left shoulder to the targets. Then, she snapped the rifle to her right shoulder and fired as rapidly as she could work the lever, a steady roll of sound. Bits of stone flew as bullets hit rock and then ricocheted away. Of the rocks that withstood their bullet, there were white scars, dead center.

Frank looked at her, amazed at her skill. Mountain women were a different quantity, to be sure. He started to speak, but the look on her face stilled the words.

Satisfied with her work, Nancy turned and looked at her daughters. "Let's clean up."

Evie left her rifle by the wagon wheel and with Stella, picked up the plates and put them in the little wash bucket. They'd come across enough water that they'd used it to wash with instead of sand.

With the girls busy with their chore, Nancy stepped forward, the rifle still in her hands but held low across her body. Frank looked at it, then at her.

"What's goin' on?" He asked, his voice slurring a little. That little bit of whisky added to what he'd imbibed the day before had an effect.

"This is the end of the road," she told him.

"What do you mean?" He raised his hands a little. Was she going to shoot him? If only he could take the string off the hammer of his pistol.

"I mean, we part ways."

"I thought we had a deal."

Nancy's gaze was hard. "Maybe we did. But, I'm breaking it off."

"You need me," he said. "You won't get far. A lone woman with two little girls."

A slight smile tilted her lips. "I think we just showed you that we can."

"What about the horses? The wagon?"

"This is as far as you go, Mr. Pascoe," she informed him. "That boy, Shelby, is just down the road a ways. Passed us this morning. I'll pass word to him where you are."

Frank looked around, then at her. "I don't get it. What's goin' on? What changed your mind?"

"You did, Mr. Pascoe." Nancy told him. "You reminded me that I can't trust men."

"What are you talking about?"

"My mind was almost made up last night. When you come back without Evie's horse." She admitted. "But, it was decided today. With that." And, she nodded toward the flask he'd left lying by the wagon wheel.

"What do you mean?"

"Whisky," was the short, flat reply. "Gets men to doin' what they might not ordinarily do."

Frank looked at her and started to speak, but stopped.

"He saved our lives, Mama," said Evie, quietly.

"I'm savin' more than that right now." With the muzzle of her rifle, she motioned that he should step aside. "I won't tie you up. And I won't take your pistol. You might have need of it before that boy gets here."

Slowly her words were cutting through the haze in his mind. "I understand what you're saying. But, I'm not your brother-in-law. What's his name?"

"Albert," Evie put in.

"I don't do the things he did."

Nancy never took her eyes off of him, but called to her daughter. "Get packed up, Evie."

Quickly the girls got all the dishes put away and the Dutch oven stowed. The older girl helped get Stella into the back of the wagon, then climbed onto the seat.

"Take the reins, Evie."

The girl did as she was told.

Nancy put a hand in her pocket and took out a gold coin. "This should make us even," she told him. "Pay for your services." There was irony in her voice.

"You need me," he told her.

She looked him up and down. "You're a man," she said contemptuously. "And I don't need any men."

With that, she backed away to the wagon, put a foot up on the step and climbed aboard. Frank watched the wagon roll away from him and kicked the dirt in disgust. Then, drawing his pistol, he whirled and fired at one of the targets. Chips of rock flew up and he almost fired again. But then, he thought his bullets might be put to better use and holstered the weapon.

Looking about him at the vast undulating land, he considered what he should do. From his vest pocket, he drew out the gold coin.

"Heads, west. Tails, east." Tossing the coin into the air, he caught it and placed it on the back of his wrist. He glanced at it then straightening his shoulders, he turned his steps to the West. Even if young Sinclair found him, at least he was going to be as far west as he could make it.

"Why did we leave Mr. Frank back there?" Stella asked her mother. "He's gonna be mighty lonely."

Nancy surveyed the landscape and noted that they seemed to be the only living creatures. "He did some bad things."

"What kind of bad things?"

"You know I don't hold with drinkin'."

"Aunt Gert did it."

"That's one of the reasons I don't like it."

"And Uncle Albert drank," Evie put in from the front of the wagon.

"Let's find something else to talk about," their mother suggested.

After some moments of silence, Evie asked, "Mama, what about forgivin'?"

"What about it?"

"When people do somethin' bad, ain't we supposed to forgive 'em?"

"Yes."

"Well, could we forgive Mr. Frank?"

Nancy sighed. "What is it with you girls and Mr. Frank? Can't you see he's . . ."

"He's what?"

She could feel the wagon slow because Evie's attention was on the inside and not the outside.

"He's not a nice man."

"He plays with me and Dolly," Stella spoke up.

"He brought Gypsy back to me," reminded Evie.

"Let's keep goin', Evie, or we're never gonna get where we're goin'." Nancy told her.

The girl spoke to the team and they again began to pull with a will.

"Don't we need him, Mama? To keep goin' west?" Evie asked after a few minutes of silence.

"I need him," Stella informed them. "No one else swings me up in the air like he does."

"I wish he were here," came Evie's voice. "These reins are heavy and my arms are tired."

"Pull over," her mother told her. "I'll drive."

Thus it was that Nancy was driving when the road sloped down a grade and into a shallow creek. Shallow as it was, the crossing seemed it should be straightforward, but at the last moment, Tommy shied into Tony, forcing him to the side. The wagon followed and was suddenly in deep water. When Nancy urged the horses forward, she found one of the wheels was stuck fast between two rocks.

"How did that happen?" Giving the reins to Evie, she waded to the hole. "Turn them to the left."

The team moved to the left, then as told, to the right. But, the wheel was stuck.

Nancy tucked her skirt into her belt, to give her legs more freedom, then bent to try to lift one of the stones that held the wheel. Neither one would budge. .

The LONG WAY HOME

"Now what, Mama?" Evie asked.

"Back them up."

The girl tugged on the reins and the horses backed, but still the wagon did not move.

Nancy looked around for a limb or a branch that she could wedge the wheel with. But, all about was water and smooth stones.

The wind picked up and she looked skyward. Tall clouds had been looming and building all afternoon. Now it seemed, they threatened rain.

Bowing her head, she asked for God's help. Should they abandon the wagon? Should they unharness the horses and ride into the nearest town? Was the closest town before them or behind them? Was there a nearby ranch where they could get help?

"Mr. Frank would know what to do," Stella put in.

"Yeah. He drove a stage," Evie added.

Nancy sighed. It seemed that no one was happy with her choice of breaking with Frank. With a girl on each side of her, she walked to the top of the grade and looked around. There was nothing as far as the eye could see. Where were Shelby and his posse? Surely they were somewhere about.

"Storm comin'," Evie pointed out a dark gray cloud that reached from ground to sky. "Headed our way."

"Let's go," Nancy walked back down the grade, the girls following. She looked at the wagon, seeming so forlorn in the creek bed. Should she unload it and leave it? Yet, with the coming weather, she thought perhaps they could get some shelter from it.

When the storm hit, lightning flashed and thunder shook the ground. Rain lashed the canvas and sprayed in between the curtains. Nancy and her girls huddled in the middle of the wagon, while the team did their best to turn their tails to it. With the first clap of thunder, Gypsy pulled loose but was nearby.

"Mama?" Evie's voice came through the tumult of the storm.

"Yes, Evie?"

"Crick's comin' up."

Nancy looked through the canvas curtain to see that her daughter was right. "Not again," she sighed. Were they going to be forced from this refuge, just as they had been their home?

"Lord, what should I do?" She asked. The water was still low enough that they could still get to shore. Should they abandon their craft?

Suddenly through with waiting for answers, she went into action. First, she carried Stella to the shore. Then, she handed the carpetbag, cooking utensils, what food she could carry and of course, the rifles to Evie who put them on higher ground. Even as she worked, she could see the creek rising.

Then, she went to the horses and began unhitching them from the wagon. The leather was wet and hard to pull apart from its wraps. Tommy began to toss his head and thrash about, though Tony was quiet, waiting.

She had the thought that she should go to the shore and get Evie's knife but a sudden surge of water knocked her off her feet. Thankfully, her grip on the harness was good enough that she wasn't swept away.

When she regained her feet, she could tell that the water had risen. Though her skirt was swept up and the hem tucked in her waistband, it was like a sail that the stream used to try to force her downstream.

She shook the water from her face and looked toward the creek bank. The rain was almost a solid curtain and she could vaguely see her daughters. They were wet and bedraggled, anxious looks on their faces..

"Mama!" Evie called, motioning with her hand. "Come to us!"

Her heart clenched because she knew she couldn't let go of Tony's harness else she would be swept away. "And then, my girls will watch their mother drown," she told God. "Is that what you want?"

Yet, she had to do something. She raised her face to the sky, the driving rain forcing her to close her eyes. "God!" She called out. "Help me, please!"

Beside her, Tony flipped up his head and Nancy turned to see what caused it. A dark figure held onto the horse's bridle as he made his way around to her side.

"What the hell are you doing here?"

It was Frank. Relief flooded through her even while the current grew stronger.

"The wagon's stuck!"

"Where?"

She held onto the harness and then the wagon, to work her way to the wheel. Quickly, he bent over, even to ducking into the water, to feel about the wheel.

Then, coming to the surface, he put his hands under the bed and pushed up. "Not anymore!"

As she stared, the wagon rolled forward a little. The vehicle was buoyant enough that the water, along with his upward shove had freed it. "Thank you! Thank you!" She cried.

"Let's go!" Quickly, he clambered up to the wagon seat, while she followed him. He turned and would have helped her, but she was already up. Taking the reins, he slapped them on the backs of the horses and they plunged out of the flood, snorting and shaking their heads.

On the bank, the girls jumped up and down when they saw them drive out of the water.

"Mr. Frank! Mr. Frank!" Stella called to him, happy even through the driving rain.

"Thank you, Mr. Frank!" The older girl's voice was deep with emotion.

"Yes," said Nancy, as the wagon came to a stop alongside their belongings. "Thank you."

Under the protection of the trees, the rain wasn't quite so heavy. Frank looked at her, then slid his hand into his jacket and came out holding the flask. "Got somewhere to stow this, Miz Cyrus?" He asked.

She looked at it, as if leery of touching it.

"Medicinal purposes only."

Her eyes met his as she took it from him. "Yes, Mr. Frank. For medicinal purposes only."

Though Nancy would rather not have admitted, there was a certain comfort in having Frank with them. She didn't think it was just because he was a man.

"He's like a rock, Mama," Evie had told her as they put their belongings back in the wagon.

And, she had to agree with her. There was something about his quiet confidence. Yet, she wondered, could she truly depend on him, like one could a rock. Her eyes slid over to him. He hadn't been too dependable when racing Gypsy, then selling her.

And, of course, there was the fact that he had served time in prison. Of course he said that he was innocent, but that was pretty much what they all said, wasn't it? She also had to admit that guilty or not, he had served his time. Yet, he had broken out of jail. That was against the law and there was no getting around it.

There was also a posse after him; a mark in the negative column. Perhaps having lived through the war had given her a different outlook on that particular situation. She tended to weigh a person's heart and how they treated others against whether one was right or wrong. Too many people had been killed or sent to prison for being on the 'wrong' side and many others had been taken advantage of by those on the 'right' side. And, in the country around the Forks, the 'right' side changed to the 'wrong' side more times than she cared to think about.

Frank called to the horses and drove them up the creek bank while Nancy continued to weigh him in her mind. He was a good driver, a good man with the horses, and he treated her and the girls with respect. Evie liked to regale him with stories she made up and listen to his which probably weren't. Of course, Stella adored the man because he would swing her up high, which she did not remember her father doing, and he would play tea party with her and the corncob dolls.

Of all the songs they sang, there were a few songs he knew the words to and would join in with them. He would bow his head when they prayed, whether he believed in the words or not.

Most telling, from her point of view, was that he was always ready to help with the camp chores, even after the horses were unharnessed and picketed. He would start the fire, bring water from a creek and then clean whatever animal had ventured into rifle range. The animal might be one she shot or Evie or even by Frank, since one of the Winchesters was always within reach on the wagon's floorboard.

Everyone did their part, of course, but it was nice to not hear complaining about duties. Not only that, other than a few references, she noted that he did not talk of the war and would occasionally join in singing Dixie.

All in all, he seemed like a good man and it was possible that being sent to prison was truly a case of mistaken identity.

Nancy glanced sideways at him. But, she was still on her guard. She was a woman alone in a vast land with very few people about. And, she'd learned there were men that couldn't be trusted, even of her own family. Her main concern was to keep herself and her daughters safe, even while following a most harebrained scheme.

Patting the pistol in her waistband, she believed she would be able to protect her family, even if Frank proved untrue.

After the cloudburst, the sky had given way to sunshine and warmth, for which all were grateful. If only she could take down her braid and let her hair dry in the soft breeze. But, she knew, that would never do. No matter how much of a rock Frank was.

Behind her in the wagon, Stella was quiet, only occasionally having her dolls quarrel at one another. Evie sat on the tailgate, legs dangling, singing to herself as she watched Gypsy walk or trot behind them.

Alerted by her horse, Evie called out, "Mama!" And she pointed at the road in front of them.

A column of cavalry was trotting their way, and beside the lieutenant, the white hat and white faced horse of Shelby Sinclair was unmistakable.

"Is them Yanks?" Stella peered through the curtains at the front.

"Yes, child. Them's Yanks." From the angle they were approaching, it was unlikely they would have seen anything but the wagon and team. Nancy motioned for Frank to get in the back of the wagon. Stella was thrilled with this development and sat down beside him.

Because of the lay of the land continually undulating, the wagon and team disappeared into a draw and when they rose out of it, they met the Army column. The lieutenant held up his hand to halt his men, then rode up to the wagon.

Nancy held the reins while Stella stuck her head through the curtains, eyes wide. At the back of the wagon, Evie sat holding the reins of her horse. Because of the heat, the other curtains of the wagon were rolled up revealing Frank laying there a quilt over him and one arm over his face to keep out the sun.

"Good afternoon! I'm Lieutenant Rogers," the officer tugged at his hat brim.

"I'm Mrs. Ollie Cyrus, Lieutenant Rogers," Nancy told him. "This is Stella and Evie's in the back. My man is in the bed. He took bad sick this mornin'."

Lieutenant Rogers urged his horse forward and looked at Frank who laid there, his shirt off and sweating. "We've an infirmary at the fort."

"Well sir, I give him an emetic already. Should be workin' pretty quick now."

Rogers backed his horse away. "Yes. Well. I think I can smell it already."

"Yes, sir!" Nancy said proudly. Then she looked at Shelby. "Good afternoon, Mr. Sinclair."

Shelby tipped his hat to her but did not speak. This was the Army's situation, not his.

"You know this man?" The lieutenant asked with some surprise.

"Yes, sir. He pulled my eldest out of a river in high flood. She might have drowned otherwise."

Evie turned to look at her mother, eyes wide, as if this is news to her.

"He says he is looking for a fugitive."

"I'm sorry to hear that." Nancy did sound sorrowful.

"Why is that?" The lieutenant looked from her to Shelby.

"My daughter has set her cap for Mr. Sinclair," she said, simply. "And I don't want her marryin' no man-hunter."

"Well, yes, I see." Rogers looked away from Shelby. "Not a reputable profession."

Beside him, Shelby visibly lost some pride.

The officer stood in his stirrups and looked around. It was time to get back to his duty. "Well, Mrs. Cyrus, you're going to have to come with me."

"Why is that, Cap'n?" She didn't think there was any harm in promoting him.

And it seemed the lieutenant did not see reason to correct her. "We're collecting everyone along the road and taking them back to the fort. The Indians are causing trouble and only large groups are allowed to travel."

Nancy nodded. "Do we have to be inside the fort, Cap'n? Could we be a campin' outside? I'm not sure you want my man in close quarters."

He glanced at the wagon bed, his nose wrinkling. "We'll see what we can work out."

Perhaps it was an answer to Evie's prayer or perhaps the lieutenant had a wry sense of humor, but Shelby was asked to escort the wagon to the fort, trailing along behind the column. At first, they trotted a good bit, but as the number of wagons and lone horsemen grew, they only trotted every little bit.

Rather than stay up beside the team, more often than not, Shelby's horse would fall back to walk beside Gypsy, giving Evie a chance to talk to the young man.

"What happened to yore posse?" She looked at him, then her horse. It was hard to know which to look at, her horse or her intended.

He was only being polite, he told himself. "We decided to part company."

"They didn't hold with man-huntin'?"

"I'm not a bounty hunter," he informed her. "I'm a deputy, duly sworn in by Sheriff Wynn Tucker of Clark County. I'm just doing my duty."

"What else is yore duty?"

"I help collect taxes." Though he was only recently sworn in, he knew it would be one of his duties once he got back to Ohio.

"My great, great grandfather didn't hold with taxation. That's why he fought the redcoats."

There wasn't much to say about that. Shelby looked at the country all around them. "I arrest drunks." This was something else he hadn't done, yet. But, he knew it was part of the job.

"People say that my great Uncle Oscar is a better man drunk than sober." Evie thought for a moment. "But, my Uncle Albert is a terror when he's drunk."

"And, Aunt Jess, too." Stella had crawled into the wagon bed and made her way to the back, careful not to disturb Frank.

"Aunt Jess likes her likker, that's certain," Evie said, thoughtfully. "She makes a good bit of it, too."

Frank coughed and from the wagon seat, Nancy called to them. "Girls! Can you think of something else to talk about?"

"How old are you?" Stella asked him.

"I'm twenty years old," and he seemed proud of it, too.

"Are you married?" Her eyes were big and wide.

He was caught off guard by the question. "No. I'm not married."

"You sweet on somebody?"

"Girls!" Their mother called from the front of the wagon. "Can't you leave the poor man alone?" She turned a little so that she could see him. "I apologize for their forwardness, but they've heard it often enough at the Forks. Discussin' a man's prospects."

"You don't have to apologize, Mrs. Cyrus. I've heard my sisters talk." He tipped his hat to them. "I think I'll go find out how much further it is to the fort."

As he rode away, Evie whispered to her horse, "I'm glad he's not married, because I'm gonna marry him."

Stella looked around them with the land stretching to infinity and the only living beings in sight those on the road. "But, who am I gonna marry?"

Frank yawned, relieved to be able to breathe freely. With young Shelby away, he thought he could stop hiding.

"How old are you, Mr. Frank?" Evie asked, musingly. She watched as a horseman came riding up, apparently in a hurry to get to the front of the line. Suddenly, she recognized the rider as the man with the big black moustache and black hat. He tipped his hat to her and started to ride by, but he hesitated, reining in his horse a bit when he heard Frank's reply.

"Too old for you to marry."

At the sound of his voice, the passing rider glanced in the wagon and Evie wondered what would happen next. Frank laid there, no weapon in sight and she wondered how she could get one to him. Yet, in the next moment, the man rode on, not even stopping to talk to Shelby a little further down the road. It was a puzzle to her, but she did not speak.

"What about me?" Stella moved up beside Frank. "Could you marry me?"

"Much too old!" And with that, Frank gratefully put his other arm over his face.

At the fort, the parade ground was filled with wagons of various sorts and sizes, as well as campfires burning. With the various lamps lit here and there, it almost seemed to be a little city.

In the bright moonlight, clouds could be seen piling up to the north and west. From the way the wind gusted, they would be headed southward soon.

Men walked here and there and soldiers tramped their duty on the catwalk along the walls. Once or twice, one could hear the soft voice of a woman calling to her children or for her husband to take care.

All in all, the evening had a wild, expectant aspect to it.

Just outside the open gates of the fort, the spring wagon sat with its own little fire and lamps. On the seat, Evie sat, a pistol in her lap ready to hand, though concealed from passers-by. Walking about the fire and putting away sand washed plates and utensils Nancy moved, with Stella as her shadow.

"Good evening, ladies!" Shelby walked up to the camp, removing his hat with a flourish. There was an air of excitement about him, explained by his next statement. "Lieutenant Rogers says you need to come in, now. He wants to close the gates."

If their lack of response disappointed him, he didn't let it show. "He thinks we'll see action by morning!"

Nancy glanced worriedly at the wagon. "I'm not sure that's a good idea. My man is pretty sick."

"Your man?" Shelby stepped forward as if to peer in the wagon. "Where did you get him?"

"I was told I shouldn't head west without one," Nancy told him. "And this man said he wanted to get to Texas pretty quick, so I hired him."

Interested, Shelby stepped closer but Nancy put herself between him and the wagon. "I'd hate for anyone else to get it."

Nothing could diminish Shelby's enthusiasm and he gave a little bow. "I am merely the messenger, since the lieutenant is busy getting his men ready for the attack."

"Well, we don't want to be caught out with the Indians," Nancy put the pans in the wagon bed. "We'll get moving." She glanced at him, "Thanks for comin' to tell us."

"What can I help you with?" He looked around, still grinning with anticipation of the coming battle.

"Would you mind putting this in the wagon?" She handed him the Dutch oven. "Careful. It's still pretty warm."

Shelby swung it onto the tailgate of the wagon then started to turn to see what was next. Instead of seeing the camp, he saw stars as Frank's fist hit his jaw. Before he could react, there were a couple of loops of rope around his arms, a cloth stuffed into his mouth and he was dumped unceremoniously into the back of the wagon.

Evie quickly brought the harnessed team out of the shadow of the fort walls which Frank hitched to the wagon. Nancy stepped up and took the reins, while Frank and Stella got in the back. In another moment, they were wheeling away from the fort with no one the wiser. At least, no one called for them to halt.

The morning dawned bright and hot, too hot for jackets. In his shirtsleeves, Frank drove the team, alternating between walking and trotting them.

"Do you think there's Indians, Mr. Frank?" Evie rode her horse beside the wagon. Though her mother told her that young ladies rode aside, she rode astride, like a boy. Nancy was willing to allow it, due to the conditions of the road and the length of their journey.

"Likely." He continually scanned the land around them.

Behind them, Shelby moaned. The cloth that had been in his mouth now bound his hands and a rope was around his feet. Nancy sat beside him, while Stella rested against her, half-asleep.

"Good morning, Mr. Sinclair," Nancy greeted him.

Shelby moaned again, then opened his eyes, squeezed them shut, then opened them again.

"Good morning, Mr. Sinclair," Evie said sweetly, having reined her horse back to look in on him.

But, he ignored her. "Is that you, Pascoe?"

"It is."

Shelby looked at Nancy. "What have you done, woman?" He struggled to sit upright, but lay back down with a moan. "Where are we?"

"Somewhere in the middle of Texas," was Frank's laconic reply.

"Indians?"

"We've seen smoke, but no fire."

"I'm glad you're not hurt too bad," Evie smiled at Shelby.

"What do you call 'too bad'?" He frowned at her.

"Mr. Frank has a flask," Nancy put in. "If you're in need of a pain killer."

"I-I don't need anything." Shelby tried to sit up again, but a jolt of the wagon made him flinch.

"Isn't that right, Mr. Frank?" Nancy asked of him.

For answer, Frank let the silver flask drop into the wagon bed.

"There's no shame a' takin' it as medicinal," she took the stopper out. "It's all in the intention." She offered it to him. "Medicinal."

Reluctantly, Shelby downed a couple of swallows, grimacing between each one.

"Mr. Frank hit you, it's true, but I believe the real damage was when you hit your head on the Dutch oven as you fell."

He took another swallow.

"If you'll lie back, I can put this on your head." She held a wet cloth in her hand.

"Where are you taking me?" He muttered then gave a grateful sigh. The cool cloth felt good.

"We were right sorry to do this to you, Mr. Sinclair," Nancy assured him. "But we had to leave the fort and this seemed like the only way to do it."

"Take me along?"

"We knew the Cap'n would send someone to tell us to come into the fort," she informed him.

"We thought it might be you, but didn't know for sure," Evie reined her horse back to walk beside the wagon. "You seemed deadset on meetin' up with Indians and Mr. Frank said you'd probably get your wish if we took you with us."

Shelby shuddered, "Thanks for thinking of me." He rose up to look at Frank's back. "So, you've added kidnapping to your list of crimes."

"I'm as much a prisoner as you are," Frank neglected to add that his pistol and holster were in the carpetbag, close to hand. He nodded to Evie, who held a pistol across her lap

She smiled and nodded at the young man.

"Why Mr. Sinclair," Nancy exclaimed. "Kidnapping is a serious charge! Haven't you been followin' us right along? Why, we're jus' makin' it easier for you to keep up."

Shelby looked at Evie, who grinned and lifted the pistol, then at Nancy who nodded and smiled at him. He followed her gaze to the rifle that was within her arm's reach. Then, he lay back and closed his eyes.

After nooning, they switched places in the wagon and Nancy sat beside Frank on the wagon seat, a rifle across her lap. The canvas curtains were lowered, making it hot and stifling inside. Evie sat on one side and peered out, a rifle in her hands, the tip of it parting them so that she could see between them. On the other side of the wagon, Stella was supposed to be doing the same, but the warmth of the space, along with the motion of the wagon put her to sleep. The derringer she was holding slipped out of her grasp and onto the floor of the wagon.

Between them, Shelby laid, his hands and ankles bound. Since it was warm, the quilt was piled up beside him and he put his hands under it, trying to work loose from his bonds. The wagon hit a bump and the derringer slid a little toward him. He stared at it, as if it willing it to come closer. A moment later, there was another bump and his wish was granted. He turned onto his side, as if sleeping. After a little bit, he managed to flip the edge of the quilt over the little gun.

As if alerted to his movement, Evie turned her gaze from the road and looked at his back. "I think he's gonna make a fine husband," she said with a smile.

It was late afternoon when they stopped again. Frank drove the team down a slope and into a swale. A small stream with shrubs lining its banks coursed at the bottom of one of the draws. From the amount of water and wood for a fire scattered about, it looked to be a good place to camp for the night.

Frank unhitched the team and Evie took her horse for a drink at the creek.

"Get down and walk around some," Nancy untied Shelby's legs.

"I appreciate it," he told her as he stretched.

Fresh from her nap, Stella ran along the stream and sometimes in it, making the water splash high on her dress. "Mama, come look!" She tugged on her mother's dress.

Nancy nodded that she heard, then spoke to Shelby. "Do you know how to drive a team?"

"I know how to drive a single horse. A team on this road?" Other than the up and down of the terrain, the road was fairly straight. "Couldn't be that different."

With Stella pulling on her hand, Nancy followed where her daughter led.

Behind her, Shelby went to the back of the wagon and his bound hands rapidly searched for the hidden derringer. When he touched it, he smiled.

It was a bucolic scene, with the light of late afternoon creating a golden haze in the little hollow. Frank watered the team, while Evie sat her horse and let her eat and drink at will.

Shelby walked from behind the wagon, the derringer in his right hand, but concealed by his left hand resting on the other. "Any way I could get loose for a bit?"

Frank glanced up at him. "Sure. As soon as the horses have got their fill."

Further up the creek and just out of sight of the camp, Nancy splashed water on her face.

"Look, Mama!" Stella climbed the slanted wall of the wash where some yellow flowers bobbed in the slight breeze. It was the work of a moment to grab a handful of stems and pull. They came loose, but much more quickly than Stella had anticipated. Losing her balance, she turned and ran, almost falling, back down to the creek and into the water. On the other side were some rocks lining the creek and she stepped up on one.

There was a warning rattle and an immediate scream from the little girl. "Mama!"

Nancy was there, pulling her child to the side, then picking up a rock, throwing it at the retreating snake, which coiled again, ready to strike. "No! No! No!" She threw rock after rock until the snake was a bloody mass. Then, she turned and pulled off Stella's boot.

Two holes pierced the pale skin of her little foot. Nancy bent her head and tried to suck the poison out, but there was little liquid when she spat. Quickly she gathered Stella into her arms and began running back to the wagon.

Evie was still on her horse, lying on her back face to the sky, while Gypsy grazed along the creek bank relishing the green grass when something made her sit up. She looked around, rifle at the ready, to see her mother running with Stella in her arms. Quickly, she slipped off her horse and ran beside her. "What happened?"

"Snake!"

Spinning on her heel, Evie ran ahead of her mother to the camp, coming around the corner just as Frank looked up from starting to loosen Shelby's hands. "Mr. Frank! Mr. Frank!"

Shelby was loose when Frank stepped away, his face full of concern for the girl.

"Snake!" Evie told him.

She turned just as her mother came running up, Stella in her arms.

Frank took the girl from Nancy and carried her to the back of the wagon.

Quickly, Shelby slipped the derringer into his pocket. "What can I do?"

"Evie!" Nancy gasped. "Get the sweetinin'!" Then she looked at Shelby. "I need a fire."

Langdon Pierce

Frank looked up just before he put Stella on the mattress. "Put it under the tree there. Hide the smoke." Then he rolled up the canvas curtains. "Damn hot in here," he muttered.

It didn't take long to get the fire going for the wood scattered about was very dry.

"No one's been along here in a while," Frank commented.

"Indians," said Evie, and he nodded in agreement.

In the wagon, Nancy sat holding her daughter's head and encouraging her to drink from the flask. When she thought she had enough, she put a rag in her mouth. Stella tried spitting it out and squirming from her grasp, but her mother soothed and reassured her. Then, she took her wrists in her hands.

At the tailgate, Shelby stood holding both of the little girl's ankles in his grip. Beside him, Evie stood poised, ready to do whatever was asked of her.

Frank walked up to the wagon, Evie's fire cleansed knife in his hand. "Ready?" He looked at Nancy.

"She smells like a drunken sailor." It was her attempt at levity in the dire situation. "But, we're ready."

Stella jumped when the knife cut her skin, but Shelby and Nancy held firm. She tried to cry out, but the cloth wouldn't let her. When the blood came, Frank bent his head to it, sucking it up and spitting it out. Stella tried to struggle.

"We need a Dutch oven," Shelby referred to what had knocked him out the night before.

"Ready?" Frank looked at both of his helpers. At their nod, he held out his hand to Evie.

She handed him the hot knife and he touched it to Stella's skin.

The little girl stiffened, her body arcing with the pain, then slumped limp to the bed.

"Thank you," Nancy's eyes met Frank's. Then she looked at her oldest daughter. "Evie?"

Evie handed her the jar of honey.

With deft hands, she smeared the golden liquid on the wound, then bound it with a cloth.

"I'll make her a crutch," there was a catch in Frank's voice. It was too bad that something like that had to happen to the young girl. "I doubt she'll be walking on it for a while."

Nancy put a hand on his arm. "First, we pray."

Evie crawled into the wagon beside her little sister. "Yes, let's pray."

"Yes, let's." Shelby's tone was sarcastic.

Nancy looked at him standing behind Frank who had his hands up.

"You're my prisoner, Frank Pascoe!" The young man was exultant. He looked at Nancy. "He's my prisoner!"

"Are we your prisoners, too?" Nancy asked quietly.

Shelby hesitated.

In a voice equally quiet as her mother's, Evie said, "Indians."

Chapter
NINE

A LL EYES FOLLOWED HERS to watch six Indians ride up to the camp. Quickly, Evie untied the canvas curtains, letting them drop closed.

Exasperated, Shelby let the derringer slip back into his pocket while Frank glanced at the rifle that leaned against the wagon wheel. It was too risky to try to get to it, so he stayed put.

"They're hungry," was Nancy's observation. She went to the wagon and took the frying pan and cornmeal that miraculously appeared from between the curtains.

"I hope so," said Frank, under his breath.

The Indians drew rein in front of the wagon, noticing both what Nancy was doing and where the rifle was.

One of the Indians, apparently the leader, held up a hand in greeting. Frank held up his hand as well and they held a short conversation, split between verbal and sign language.

"Would you bring me the side meat, Shelby?" Nancy asked, pointing toward the wagon.

"Yes, ma'am," the words seemed to stick in a throat suddenly dry.

Evie pushed the burlap sack with the side meat in it toward him, the movement revealing the pistol lying in her lap. As he took it, he noted that the other rifle lay between her and the side of the wagon.

"I'll be back for that," Shelby said in a low voice, his dropped gaze indicating the rifle.

Evie shot him an angry stare just before the curtains closed, but he had already turned and didn't notice.

"Get down and eat," Frank motioned to the fire.

The skillet warming over the fire held the scent of meals past and the area already smelled good. Needing no further invitation, the Indians slipped from their horses and gathered around the fire.

It wasn't long before the sidemeat was ready and shortly after that, hoe cakes began appearing on the plate near the fire. The Indians took them from the plate the moment any were put on it. Not only that, the leader tried to take one out of the pan, only to find that it was too hot to handle and it fell into the fire.

The Indians sat cross legged near the fire and ate voraciously, continually pushing empty plates toward Nancy. She said little and kept cooking even as their food supplies dwindled. Frank sat beside the leader, while behind them Shelby tried to unobtrusively get to the rifle leaning on the wagon wheel.

Nancy turned away from the fire when it leapt up from spilled grease. As she did so, the butt of the pistol in her waistband could be seen. One of the Indians noted it and pointed, saying something in his language. The other Indians laughed, while Frank looked up at Nancy, understanding what they said.

"They're calling you the Queen Bee,:" he told her. "We are the workers," he indicated himself and Shelby. "You're the only one with a stinger."

Nancy looked at the Indian and nodded, acknowledging his comment. Then, she turned back to frying side meat and making hoe cakes.

As he turned back to face the fire, Frank saw the wagon curtains move and the barely visible muzzle of the rifle. Knowing that Evie was behind it and would be looking, he rubbed his nose as he shook his head and it disappeared.

When the side meat was gone, Nancy held up the frying pan to show that it was empty. Then, she picked up the Dutch oven and tilted it so that the Indians could see nothing in it as well.

They spoke and nodded, but continued to sit. When she waved her hands and her apron, shooing them away, they laughed indolently and stood up. Frank walked the leader to his horse then stepped back as he leapt astride. Moments later, the Indians trotted away from the camp and into the shadows of the creek as they followed the stream.

Frank turned back to the camp, noting the muzzle of the rifle in the wagon. "Thanks, Evie. You can put it away now." He walked over to the fire and began kicking dirt on it.

Shelby had picked up the other rifle and kept it in his hands as he watched the Indian ponies climb out of the wash and disappear over the horizon.

"You've got grit, Mrs. Cyrus," Frank told her. "You certainly have grit."

It was as if his words released whatever had been keeping her upright and going for the last hour, for she stopped to look up, then wobbled. But when he stepped forward to assist her, she held up a hand and shook her head. Then, slowly, she made her way to the wagon and got in it.

"What's wrong?" Evie asked, worriedly. "What's wrong with Mama?"

"She had a miscarriage a couple of days ago and she's at the end of her tether. That's all. Can you make her comfortable in there?"

"Yes, sir," Evie replied.

Inside the wagon, Nancy lay back on the mattress. Evie followed her in with a damp towel to dab on her forehead.

"What a lot of fuss," Nancy tried to sit up, but almost immediately fell back.

"We'll break camp, get a few more miles down the road," Frank told them, then turned to look at Shelby who still held the rifle. "That is, if it's alright with you."

The young man watched as Frank put away the utensils, made sure the fire was out, then brought in the team who had been grazing along the creek. Since Stella's accident with the snake had happened before Frank had a chance to unharness them, it was the work of moments to hook them to the wagon.

Evie tied Gypsy to the tailgate of the wagon so that she could stay near her mother and sister. Concern crossed Frank's face when he unwrapped Stella's foot. It had swollen to twice its size. He felt of the little girl's forehead and his lips thinned. "It's up to God, now," he told Evie.

The girl grabbed his hand, her eyes meeting his. "Let's pray, Mr. Frank, for we surely need the help."

Slowly, he nodded and bowed his head, letting the girl speak the words.

"Heavenly Father, You know our troubles. Would You pass Your healin' hand over my mother and sister? And, Pap, if you got any say up there, now is the time to speak up. Amen."

When he opened his eyes, he noted her fierce, determined look. "Amen."

Shelby sat in the wagon seat and watched Frank step up. When he took up the reins and called to the team, the young man stuck the rifle barrel in the older man's ribs. "Wrong way. Turn around."

"Can't you converse like every other human being?" Frank asked, leaning forward, as if to help the team climb out of the draw.

"Turn around. You're my prisoner."

"And you're a parrot who only speaks three words," Frank said, irritably. "At this point, Denton is closer than any town back there," his head indicated behind them.

"The fort. We'll go to the fort."

Frank looked at him. "Who is gonna get you your reward? The Army?" He asked, derisively. "Or the Texas Rangers?" Lifting his hands, he indicated the direction they were going. "There's Rangers in Denton."

"You're offering to drive to Denton, where you'll be handed over to the Rangers?" Shelby was suspicious.

"There's a doctor there. I'm thinking of Stella."

"And, Mrs. Cyrus?"

"And, Mrs. Cyrus," Frank repeated.

Shelby sat back which he took as assent. With a cluck to Tony and a rein slap on Tommy's rump, he turned to the road toward Denton, headed west.

They were only able to continue on for a few hours before darkness stopped them. A fire was built, but that was all they had to eat except for tea. Evie kept their mugs full, but it wasn't food.

On a nearby stone, Frank sat mending harness. Whenever the going was easy, Tommy had a habit of reaching over and gnawing on Tony's bridle. Shaking a rein at him or turning his head to the side only worked for a little while. Then, he would go back to annoying his partner.

Frank's stomach growled and he frowned at it, as if that would help.

"Sure wish those Indians hadn't eaten so much."

"She shouldn't have cooked everything we had!"

The older man looked at him calmly. "If she hadn't, it's likely we wouldn't be having this conversation."

"We could have taken them, "Shelby scoffed. "The rifle beside the wagon was only two steps away."

"You ever tried to outrun a thrown knife?" Frank looked down at his work. "Besides, the Chief's rifle was pointed in that direction."

Shelby abruptly stopped pacing, clearly surprised at this revelation. "Mrs. Cyrus had a pistol."

"For herself."

Whether it was because of his nonchalant attitude or the words he spoke, Shelby stared at him.

"Well, Evie had a pistol as well."

"If you think a ten year old girl could aim and fire that pistol to any effect . . ." Frank shook his head. "That was for Stella. And herself, if she had time."

Shelby stared at him. "You – you had that planned?"

"We've had it planned for some time," Frank went on. "This isn't the East, Mr. Sinclair, with towns and sheriffs around every corner. This is the West. It's a great place. Lots of room. Freedom to do what you want. But, it comes with a price. Everything comes with a price."

The young man latched onto one word, "Price! That's right! And the price you're paying for your past is the one on your head!"

Frank shook his head. "You've got me puzzled. How come you to be in the law game?"

Somehow, the question nettled Shelby. "I – I had my reasons."

"Why'd you come after me? That poster, that reward. That's pretty old."

For a long moment, Shelby stared at him, debating how much to say. "I came after you for the money."

"So, you are a bounty hunter."

"No!" Shelby flared up. He paced back and forth in front of the fire. "I'm a duly sworn officer!"

"That works in the East," was Frank's mild reply. "This is Texas."

"I told you, I had my reasons!"

"Any of those reasons involve Wynn Tucker?"

The young man whirled to face him. "How did you know?"

"I know Wynn," was the calm statement. "I know he'd go to about any lengths to get me." He shook his head. "He send you after me?"

"No," he burst out, then he dropped his head. "Yes. Sort of. He showed me the wanted poster."

"For Jack Davis?"

"Yes." Shelby shot a look at him. "Jack Davis is you."

Frank laughed. "Wynn." He shook his head, "Can never let bygones be bygones."

Before him, Shelby frowned, not understanding.

"I don't care about any of that. You broke the law. I'm taking you in."

The older man slanted a glance at him. "That's your plan?"

"That's my plan."

Frank looked around the camp then patted his vest pocket. "I'd smoke," he said, "if the Indians hadn't taken all the damn tobacco."

While they were talking, clouds had overtaken the sinking sun. Lightning streaked through the sky, followed seconds later by a crash of thunder. One of the horses called out in fright. Frank looked up and sniffed the air. "If we get rain, it will be a soaker. I'm going to stand with the horses." He hesitated, as if to say more, then turned his steps away.

There was nothing else to say or do, so Shelby watched him disappear into the darkness where the horses were picketed.

It didn't take long for the storm to pass, mostly full of wind and fury and very little rain. Frank made sure the horses would stay tied, then came back to the camp. Under the wagon, Shelby lay, using his jacket for a pillow. Peering into the wagon, he could see Evie lying on one side of Stella and Nancy on the other. He felt of both Nancy's and Stella's foreheads and noted that they were hot.

"Are they gonna be alright?" Evie whispered, her eyes gleaming in the darkness.

Frank looked at her and wondered what he should say. This was the West, after all, and dreams of new lives and renewed hope came at a cost. "We'll know in the mornin'."

"I'd like to pray again, Mr. Frank."

He nodded, then bowed his head.

Evie got up and crawled to where he stood. Rising to her knees, she put her hands together and made sure that Frank did, too. "God," she said, "Please have mercy on us. Heal my Mama. And heal my baby sister." She hesitated, then said, "They're all I got left in the world. Thank You." Then she added, "Thy will be done."

"Amen." The word sounded final in Frank's deep voice. Then, Evie chimed in. "Amen."

Due to the continued thunder of the night before no one slept well and the next morning, Frank and Shelby moved about the camp, stumbling and bleary eyed.

An overcast sky filled with gray clouds shielded the sun, though heat made it through.

Regardless of his lack of sleep, Frank went to the creek and made his ablutions. He smoothed his hand over his face, satisfied with the result of shaving with no mirror. As he made his way back to the wagon, Shelby passed him carrying a bucket. The young man ignored his greeting and kept walking.

At the wagon, he pushed aside the curtain and peered inside. Nancy opened her eyes and looked at him, then at Stella who lay in the crook of her arm.

Flipping back the quilt, he looked at Stella's foot. It was swollen, as if it would burst the bandage.

Nancy's eyes met his, an anxious look in them.

Frank shrugged. "She's in God's hands."

Something about his tone made her look at him a little harder. "You don't believe in God."

"He's done me no favors," was the admission. Then, he turned to greet Evie who rode Gypsy up beside him.

"I just doctored it," she interrupted their conversation. "With the sweetenin'." Her eyes were worried.

"Good girl." Frank nodded, then looked at her. "Gonna ride the race horse today?" He walked over to the campfire and the girl and her horse followed.

The girl glanced at the team that stood in their harness at the front of the wagon. "I don't think they're in the best shape, Mr. Frank." She leaned forward to pet Gypsy. "All the travelin' we been doin' and the poor grass near the trail. I thought I'd save 'em a little weight."

"And, it's a little weight," Shelby walked into camp, the water bucket full. He kicked a rock out of his way. "You're no bigger than a minute."

"I'm big enough!" Somehow his words had struck her as being negative.

Frank took the bucket and emptied it on the embers of the campfire. "That's good thinkin', Evie," he smiled up at her, continuing their conversation. "If you take care of your horse, you horse will take care of you."

Shelby kicked another stone, larger than the first. But, it didn't move as easily, so he stubbed his toe and cursed quietly.

"There's a man who could stand some coffee," Frank observed.

"And food," muttered the young man.

"Now that's something we don't mention in polite company, is it, Evie?"

She grinned at him. "Not where I come from!"

Frank looked at the fire once more and kicked more dirt onto it. Then, he walked to the wagon, got in and picked up the reins.

"Wait for me!" Shelby seemed surprised that they might leave without him.

As he clambered in, Evie rode up beside the wagon.

Frank called to the team and they put their weight into their harnesses. Once out of the hollow, the road west stretched long before them. As was his habit, he walked the horses a bit, trotted them a mile or so then walked them.

"How's your mother this morning?" He glanced at Evie who rode beside the wagon. Partly it was to make conversation, but he wanted to know what the girl thought as well.

"Better. But she's a' worryin'," was the reply. "Stella's really feverin'. Foot's swoll up big, too." A sigh escaped her lips. "I done the best I knew how."

Frank's glanced at her and nodded. "You'll do, Miss Evie. You'll do."

She looked at him with surprise and gratitude in her eyes. It was the first time he'd called her Miss, acknowledging her maturity. Then, she looked at Shelby who had his eyes on the road ignoring everyone, and she gave a little smirk. He might not think she was yet a young woman, but Mr. Frank had just acknowledged her as such.

It was well into the afternoon and it was hot. He pulled the team down to a walk. They'd been trotting at a good clip and were sweating with lather on their chests and between their quarters. Frank and Shelby sat on the wagon seat, jackets off, sleeves pushed up.

"You're pushing the horses pretty hard," Shelby commented.

"Aye. There's need of it."

The young man glanced behind them. The canvas curtains were rolled up and Nancy crooned a song to Stella. Every little bit she would grow silent, though her lips moved. Following the wagon on Gypsy, Evie knew that then she was praying.

"You think she'll make it?" Shelby asked and it was hard to tell if he cared or was being polite.

"God knows," was the tight lipped reply.

Before them, the road stretched long, continually appearing and disappearing as it breasted the rises then fell into the hollows.

"Are you my father?"

The question was abrupt, bringing Frank's attention back from where it had wandered under the hot sun.

"I don't know. She never told me." He looked at Shelby.

"I'm twenty years old. You've been gone twenty years."

Frank nodded. "I'm telling you. If she was pregnant, she never told me." He flicked a rein needlessly on Tony's rump. "And she could have."

"Do you think I am your son?"

The older man turned and looked at him. "You resemble my father, I'll say that. As for anything else, she gave you my middle name. Tarrant."

"So. You're my father." Shelby's tone grew deeper and contemptuous. "A train robber."

Frank looked at the young man, then back at the road. "Any man can be a father. As my grandmother would say, 'men are careless of their seed.' But, as to truly being a father, providing, protecting. No. I am not your father. I'd say that Reverend Sinclair has done a better job of it."

"I'll say!" The words were forceful.

They drove on for a mile or more before Frank spoke up. "And no. I am not a train robber."

"Wynn Tucker says you are."

Frank looked at him. "So, it was Wynn."

The young man looked down, chagrined that he had given it away.

"I'd like to get something clear. Son." His voice was deep and brooked no interference. "I am not going to defend my actions. I went west to start a new life. I asked your mother to go with me. She refused. Perhaps because she was pregnant with you. I don't know. As I said before, she never told me."

Frank noticed that Tommy seemed to be listening, too, and had forgotten he was supposed to be pulling the wagon. He snapped the rein on the horse's rump. "I did a lot of things, worked a lot of jobs, had a mine at one point and a ranch, too. Any time I had money, I sent it back to your mother. She says she never got it, nor my letters."

A herd of antelope in the distance attracted Shelby's attention.

"She's right," he said, finally. "One time, I was looking for a necklace for Grandma. You know, Mother's mother. She sent me upstairs to get it, since her rheumatism had flared up. I went to her jewelry chest like she told me, but couldn't find it. So, I opened up the top drawer of her chiffonier. In the back of it was a bunch of letters bundled up. Addressed to Mother. With postmarks from all over the West."

Frank glanced at him, feeling relieved. The young man had given him the answer to why Cecilia had not replied to his letters.

"When I asked her about them, she swore me to secrecy and said, they were nothing but trouble."

Shelby looked down at the horses, then at the older man. "I'd forgotten about that, til now."

Frank was silent, going back in his mind and wondering if anything would be different if the woman had not interfered.

"I guess she didn't like you," was Shelby's conclusion.

"I guess not."

Silence dropped between them until finally, the younger man said, "Do you hate her for it?"

Frank looked at him, then back at the road. "No. What's done is done."

"That's pretty big of you," Shelby went on. "I think I'd be pretty mad."

"What good would it do you?"

The young man shrugged. "Nothing, I reckon. But, I'd still be mad."

A slight smile crossed Frank's lips, then he called to the horses, urging them to a faster gait. The road had leveled out and they could make good time.

The next time the team walked, Evie rode up beside the wagon. "I don't believe you're a train robber."

Frank shot a glance at her. "I appreciate that. Too bad the jury did not share your opinion."

"He's a train robber alright," Shelby assured her. Though he might give the man the benefit of the doubt on being his father, he had hard proof of the robbery. "I've got the wanted poster."

The older man shook his head. "You're some persistent with that belief."

Evie glared at Shelby. "He's not a robber."

"How do you know?"

Taken aback, the girl was at a loss for words. Then, she put a hand on her heart and replied, "I know it here."

Shelby shook his head. "Girls."

"Have you heard of women's intuition, by chance?" There was a light note in Frank's voice. But, in the next moment, he called to the horses once more. "Come on, Tommy! Tony! We're burning daylight!"

Evie followed the wagon on her horse, walking when the team walked and trotting when they trotted. Watching Frank drive, she noted how he found the smooth parts of the road and avoided potholes and ruts. At the same time, he kept an eye on the country around them, making comments about it. She marveled at his ability to do both so easily.

All around them, the prairie stretched endlessly, an ocean of green grass rising up and down like waves below a cloudless blue sky. She knew that her heart would have sung at the sight, except for concern for her mother and sister.

"How much farther, Mr. Frank?" Evie called to him.

He glanced behind him at Stella and his lips tightened. A lift of the reins sent the team once more into a trot. "Too far."

It was night when they came into the little town. The first house on the right had a picket fence around it and on a whim, Frank pulled up. He sent Evie to read the sign that hung from the post.

"Is this Denton?" Nancy asked from the back.

"No," Frank replied. "Bastian. If we have any luck, they have a doctor here. Years back, they did. Don't know about now."

From the sign post, Evie sounded out the name, "Doctor Robert Cutright."

"Looks like we're in luck." Shelby slipped out of the wagon and went to knock on the front door.

Meanwhile, Frank went around to the back of the wagon and was handed Stella. Then, Nancy got down out of the wagon and followed him to the house.

Doctor Cutright was immediately concerned for Stella's well being. After she was put on the examining table, the doctor's wife, Mabel, shooed all but Nancy into the parlor.

"The Doctor will take good care of her," she assured the others. "Are you too tuckered to eat?"

Grateful eyes swung her way and she went to the kitchen, Evie following her to help.

Thus it was that they had a late dinner provided by the doctor and his wife. Evie struggled to stay awake long enough to eat and moments after finishing was asleep sitting upright in a parlor chair.

Frank had not seen to the horses before his meal as was his normal wont. Rather than confess to being loathe to leaving Nancy and her children, he gave himself the excuse that he'd needed sustenance to take care of them. Now refreshed, he went to unharness them and make sure they were well fed.

Nancy came into the dining room and picked at the food she was offered. At Mrs. Cutright's insistence, she drank coffee and had a piece of dried apple pie. She offered to help clean up the dishes, but the woman insisted that she sit down and rest.

Shelby came into the parlor from his visit to the privy and looked around to see Evie curled in a chair and Nancy leaning back in another, both with their eyes closed. "Where's Frank?"

There was a curt note in his voice and Nancy roused up. "What?" She looked around and blinked. "Stella?" Her eyes went to the door to the examining room.

Feeling bad that he'd caused her more worry, Shelby sat down, feeling hollow, though he'd just eaten quite a bit.

There came the stomp of boots on the porch and when the front door opened, along with the thin night air along came a skinny, scruffy man wearing a peaked hat with a hole in the crown and tall boots with his pants tucked in the tops. Shelby looked at him and felt himself a stranger in a strange land. It seemed that anything could happen at any time.

"Where's the doc?" The creature cried out, his voice a screech.

Shelby noted that he had no teeth, at least none that were visible.

"Jessup's gone an' fell down the steers agin!" He announced to the room. "We need the doc!"

Mrs. Cutright came into the room and soothed the man. "Now, Link, settle down and tell me what's happened."

"It's Jessup." The man pulled off his hat at her entrance, revealing tufts of long white hair around a bald pate. "He's done fell down the steers agin!"

The woman nodded. "The doc has an emergency right now," she told him. "But, I'll let him know."

Link continued to stand in the middle of the parlor, his hands skimming the brim of his hat as it went round and round. "What's a feller to do, Mrs. Doc?" He looked worriedly about. "You know. Until doc can come."

"You go and sit by Jessup," she told him. "He'll be right there in a little bit."

Mollified, Link put his hat back on his head, then left the room, his spurs clinking softly before being drowned out by the clump of his boots on the boardwalk.

He hadn't been gone long before Mrs. Cutright came back into the parlor. "Mrs. Cyrus?"

When Nancy didn't respond, she put a hand on the woman's shoulder and shook it a little.

"Mrs. Cyrus?"

Nancy stood up in reaction, though it was plain to see that she wasn't clearly awake. "How is she?" Her eyes focused on the woman. "How is my baby?"

"The Doctor wants to see you." Mrs. Cutright led the way to the hall.

Though Nancy followed, her legs seemed to be asleep and she walked woodenly. The woman opened a door and motioned her in.

"How is she, Doctor?" Nancy looked at her daughter in the bed and was by her side in two long strides.

"She's got a fever, as you know." Doctor Cutright might have been in his fifties, for his hair was graying. Though not tall, he was broad and as hill people would have said; well fed. His eyes noted her movement, smoothing Stella's hair away from her face. "Where are you from?"

"The Forks," was Nancy's immediate response. Then, she added, "Tennessee," because most flatlanders did not know of The Forks.

"I thought as much," Cutright nodded. "Your remedy of the honey poultice was just the thing. We'll know more in the morning, but it might have saved her foot, as well as her life."

Nancy flashed a smile of relief at him. "That would be good news, Doctor Cutright."

"Yes," he agreed. "You need to get some sleep," he told her. "I'll see you in the morning." Looking at her, he wondered if he should order it, rather than suggest it.

"Would you mind if I saw her a little bit, right now?" Nancy's eyes and tone had a pleading note.

Far be it for him to separate mother and child at this stage, he thought. "Yes," he replied. "Yes, of course."

When Frank walked in the front door, both Shelby and Evie looked up at him in unison; like a pair, he thought. "Where's Mrs. Cyrus?" His tone may have been a little sharp, but he was tired. "Is the child alright?"

"She's in the back, sayin' good night to Stella."

"Seems like the honey poultice may have done the trick. Saved the child's life." Shelby put in.

"And her foot," added Evie.

"That remains to be seen," Shelby added.

"Well, I've made camp a little ways out of town. Bought some grain from the livery stable and the horses are sure making it disappear." He smiled at Evie, so that she knew which horse was eating the most.

When Evie woke the next morning, it was to the sound of a town coming to life. At first, she was unsure of where she was, but the beams that crossed above her reminded her: the room under the eaves at Doc Cutright's house.

Her mother had stayed downstairs with Stella, but she had assured Evie that if anything happened, she would let her know.

Though she knew she should be up and doing, the girl reveled in the clean sheets on the thick straw mattress. This was livin', she told herself.

Voices wafted up to her as well as the sound of a merchant sweeping the walk outside his shop. A team walked by, a wagon creaking behind them.

"Grease," she spoke aloud. The wheels needed grease. She'd helped grease their wagon's wheels often enough; she should know. Swinging her legs over the side of the bed, she went to the little window and looked out.

As her ears had told her; there was the man sweeping the walk in front of his shop, the team with the creaking wagon, as well as two men standing in front of the freight office arguing about something.

Just down the street, the door to the café opened and a man, vaguely familiar, stepped onto the boardwalk. When he put on his hat, she laughed to herself. It was the man with the thick black moustache. She hadn't recognized him without his hat.

It was the work of a moment to slip on her blouse and skirt. Her boots she carried in her hand as she went down the narrow staircase. An enticing smell came from the kitchen and her stomach growled.

"Good morning!" Mrs. Cutright smiled at her.

"Good mornin', ma'am," Evie replied. On the table were four plates and she wondered at their number, since their party was five and their hosts made seven. An uneasy feeling rolled through her body and she glanced in the direction of the examining room.

"Your mother's eaten already. And Stella." The older woman assured her. "She's such a pretty little girl."

Evie agreed with her. Little sisters didn't come much prettier or more angelic. It was the angelic part that worried her. Was she wanted in Heaven so soon?

"Said she loved my pancakes," it was obvious the woman took pride in her cooking.

As Pa would say, if a person took pride in their work, it was gonna be well done.

"Mr. Pascoe has been in, checking on your mother and sister." Mrs. Cutright seemed to blush. "He's – he's an unsettlin' kind of man." After this admission, she stared at Evie, as if she'd said too much.

"I speck so," was the nonchalant reply.

While Evie was eating the pancakes, which were pretty good but no match for her mother's hotcakes, Nancy walked into the dining room. Mrs. Cutright had gone to see whoever had jangled the bell at the door of the doctor's office.

"Mornin'," mother and daughter greeted one another. Nancy sat down at the table across from her.

Before Evie could ask, she went on, "Stella's awake. Much better. Doctor Cutwright says she should stay off of the foot. Probably should stay here for a couple of days."

"Here?" Evie asked, pointing at her plate with her fork.

Nancy shook her head. "We can't stay here at the Doc's, it would put them out too much. Frank says he's made camp a little out of town, where we won't be a bother to no one."

Something in Evie's chest fell a little and she looked down at her plate. Nancy noticed her crestfallen look.

"We've some shoppin' to do. We'll come to town, too."

Evie brightened. Though she liked traveling, it was tedious and at the same time, hard work to stay on the alert, looking for Indians or Yankee soldiers or whoever. The town was a welcome change.

Mid-morning, Frank came by to get them. He rode Gypsy with the plan being to borrow the Doctor's buggy, at his insistence, to drive Nancy and Stella back to camp. Evie, of course, would ride her horse. Shelby, he told them, was in town, doing he knew not what. And, it seemed, he didn't care.

Evie wondered that he wasn't afraid Shelby would get the law of the town to come arrest him. But, if he wasn't worried, she wasn't going to be concerned.

Before heading to camp, there was shopping to do. Stella was napping, which all agreed was a good thing. So, Nancy and Evie went to the Bastian Mercantile while Frank went to the feed store.

Though she liked being in the store, Evie wasn't as interested in shopping this time, since it was mostly foodstuffs that were wanted. Wandering to the front window, she heard young voices laughing and calling. She went outside on the porch and watched while several young boys, two at a time, raced down the street, a stick in their hand and keeping a hoop going.

She realized it was a relay, with three boys in one line, two in another. They were racing to the water trough in front of the blacksmith shop and back. Without even thinking, she went down the steps and got in the shorter line.

At first, the boys didn't notice her, but when they did, they stopped.

"Can I play?" Evie asked with a grin.

There was some hesitation between the boys.

"It will make the teams even," she suggested.

From their attitudes, it was clear they didn't think she could do it.

"It will make the teams even," one of the boys spoke up. His hair was almost white, a towhead, and his eyes as blue as any bluebonnet that graced the Texas plain. "She can be on my team."

"Are you sure, Freddie?" The other boy on his team asked, slowly. He was taller and a year or so older.

"Yes, Stan," was the firm reply.

Reluctantly, the boys lined up again, with Evie the last one in the line.

Freddie raced against Little Bill, down to the trough and back, the easy winner. As he handed off the stick and hoop to Stan, the older boy bobbled the transfer and started off late. His opponent was Big Bill, who wasn't big at all, just bigger than Little Bill.

By the time Stan got back to the line, he wasn't that far behind. Yet again, his hands fumbled in trying to hand the stick to Evie. But, once the stick was in her hand and the hoop was going, she gathered her skirt and ran.

It was tricky, though, because she couldn't go faster than the hoop. If it hit a bump or a hollow in the road, it would try to take off in a new direction. The key was to keep it going fast, which helped keep it on a straight path.

At the turnaround, the boys circled, keeping the hoop going, but Evie stopped the hoop for the brief moment that it took to run around it then head back up the street. In this way, she saved time and distance and quickly outdistanced Neil, her opponent.

Grinning and seeing that victory was in her grasp, she looked up to see stricken looks on the boys faces. In that moment, she faltered and the hoop wobbled. But then, she noticed Frank standing in front of the feed store, watching. In that moment, she gave another effort and brought the hoop home, her team the winner by inches.

Freddie smiled and congratulated her, elbowing Stan to do the same. When she glanced around, she could see that the other boys were glum, until Freddie chided them about it.

"That was a good idea about running around the hoop," Neil admitted, smiling.

Beside her, Freddie agreed. "We should have thought of that sooner."

Finally, all of the boys were smiling and agreeable, which made Evie feel better. Remembering their errand, she looked up at the Mercantile to see her mother standing at the window. She wondered how much she'd seen.

"I have to go," Evie told the boys, but Freddie said they were all going fishing and asked if she wanted to come along.

Nancy had come out of the store by then and she nodded her permission.

While fishing with the boys, Evie learned several things. One, that the town had no girls their age; for one reason or the other. Either the expected child was a boy or if a girl, died young. Mostly the townspeople seemed to have boys.

"My mother says it's the water," Neil informed her.

And Evie marveled that water could have an influence on whether a boy or girl was born. Perhaps if her family had come to Texas sooner, they'd have had a boy. That lived, she added to herself.

She also found out that the townspeople had been ordered to leave and go to the fort. In this way, the Army would have a smaller area to protect until the Indian menace had been dealt with.

"When are you leavin'?"

"Tomorrow or the day after," Freddie replied. "Pa wants to get as much harvested as he can before we go."

"How come you run so fast," Stan asked. He glanced at the two fish that lay beside Evie and threw down his fishing pole.

"That's how we get around at The Forks."

"What's The Forks?"

"It's where Em'ly and Holdy meets the Wolf."

"Are those rivers?"

"Cricks. Creeks." She told them. "And, below The Forks is good bottom land. Above the Forks is mostly hills. We build our houses and farm on the side of the hills. Or in the little bits of flat land beside the creeks."

The boys listened intently.

"And you run the hills?" Freddie asked.

"Yep."

"Even grown men?"

"Oncet yore married, womenfolk don't run 'em no more. They have husbands to drive 'em here or there. Or, you ride the work mule."

"But everyone else runs?"

Before she could answer, she heard her name called.

"Hello Evie!"

She looked up to see Frank standing on the creek bank downstream from them. "Hello!" She stood up and grinned only then aware that the boys had made a circle around her as they listened to her talk.

"Think it's time to go?" He asked.

She smiled and stood up. "Thank you for a lovely time," she'd read the line in a book somewhere.

The boys stood up, suddenly diffident; whether it was Frank's presence or the fact that they'd spent time with the opposite gender.

"Good-bye!" Evie picked up her stick with the fish on it, trying not to notice that the other boys only had one fish, if they had any at all.

It didn't take long to catch up to Frank and as she walked beside him, she gave a skip every now and then. He stopped briefly to pick up a stick with six fish on it.

"You were here?" She asked. "All this time?"

He glanced around them. "Bastian may be a town, but it's Indian country," he reminded her.

They had dinner that night at the Cutwright home at Mabel's insistence. Nancy allowed Stella to sit on her lap, though that didn't last long. The little girl ate a few bites and was back to sleep. Frank took her to the bedroom at the back of the house, Nancy following.

When they returned, it was to find that Shelby had joined them.

"Well," he told Evie. "You're the talk of the town."

Doctor Cutwright looked up. "What do you mean, young man?"

"A young girl, hiking up her skirts and racing boys!"

Nancy came into the room and sat down at the table. "She's ten."

Shelby had his mouth full of food and couldn't reply.

Evie looked from one to the other of them, unsure of what was going on.

"Had you ever played with a hoop and stick before?" Frank followed Nancy out of the hall and into the dining room.

Evie shook her head.

"So. You not only beat them at their own game, you'd never played it before?" He asked, thoughtfully.

"She barely won," Shelby put in.

Frank looked at Evie. "You turned the corner at the trough differently than the boys."

"Yes, sir."

"I heard about that. You come up with that idea yourself?" Doctor Cutwright asked, gently.

"Yes, sir." Evie looked at him. "The boys said they were gonna use it, too. It would save time and distance."

The doctor nodded, a smile beginning on his lips. "An innovator. That's good."

"Just seemed logical to me," was her reply.

But, Shelby wasn't through. "And then, she went fishing with them!"

"They're ten years old." Nancy reminded him.

"One of them is twelve!"

Evie frowned. "What's wrong with fishin'?" She asked. "It sure made a good meal!"

He looked down at his plate, suddenly realizing what dinner had been.

"It's – it's going around with boys," he replied.

"There's no girls in this town." She looked at her mother. "Neil's mother says it is the water."

Nancy made no reply, but continued to eat her meal.

"Alone!" Shelby stated.

Evie looked at Frank. "He was just downstream of us. Is that alone?"

Shelby looked at the man who looked back at him, an eyebrow raised. "Well, it's still all over town."

"They'd best be worrying about getting their things together to leave," Mabel Cutwright put in. She looked at Evie with worry in her eyes, but the young girl's gaze seemed to have nothing to hide.

When dinner was over, Nancy volunteered Evie and herself to wash dishes. Mrs. Cutwright protested briefly but let them, which satisfied everyone that the right thing was being done.

As Nancy placed the dishes in the hot water, she spoke to her daughter. "You were about to win that race by a good bit, weren't you?"

"Yes, ma'am." There was something in her mother's voice that made her concerned.

"Why did you falter?" She asked. "Because of the boys? What they might think of you?"

"Yes, ma'am," Evie said then sighed.

"Don't," her mother told her. The water fresh from the tea kettle on the stove was hot and she rested her hands on the rim of the dishpan.

"What?"

"Don't falter. Run as hard as you can. Don't give up because of a boy."

"Yes, ma'am." This was different from what she thought her mother might say.

"The right boy will find a way to win or win your heart."

In the doorway came, "Amen," as Frank walked in with a load of dishes in his hands.

Chapter
TEN

THE NEXT DAY it seemed that there were more wagons and teams in the street than there were people. Their own wagon stood outside Doctor Cutwright's office where Frank had gone inside to get Stella.

Evie sat on the wagon seat, her attention on the boys that crowded around. They wanted to know why her family was headed west and not east, like the rest of the town. Freddie said he would miss her and wanted to know where he could write to her. She told him she didn't know and thought no one else in her party knew either.

Though she'd enjoyed the camaraderie of the day before, she was anxious to get on the road. Her gaze went from the doctor's door to the Mercantile where her mother had gone for some last minute items. This attitude of cool nonchalance was new to the boys and drew them like flies to honey.

As she sat there, her attention was drawn to a crowd of men standing outside the Mercantile. When her mother came out, she was greeted by a line of men who one by one, took off their hat and asked her a question. At first taken aback, she then allowed it to continue. Not that she would give them the reply they sought, but to honor their request.

Frank walked out of the doctor's office, and with Mrs. Cutwright's suggestions, made Stella comfortable in the back of the wagon. When he went to the front of the wagon, his attention was drawn to the crowd outside the mercantile as well. His hand with the reins dropped, as he thought to go to Nancy. Then, when one of the men dropped to one knee and looked up in supplication, he realized what was going on.

When he was refused, kindly, with a smile, another man stepped up and presented her with a paper. Even that was not enough to get her approval.

"Do you know what is happening?" Frank asked Evie, his voice brittle.

"They're proposing," was her reply.

He seemed not to hear her. "Half of Texas is lined up asking your mother to marry them."

"Yes sir," she was nonchalant. Men were always asking to marry her mother, even when her father was still alive, but had as everyone knew, no hope of recovering. So far, Nancy had turned all of them down.

Something in Frank's voice made her turn and look at him. His eyes, usually a light blue or green, were silver and glinting. She looked from him to her mother, but it was beyond her understanding.

"Ready." Shelby rode up on a white horse that gleamed in the sunlight. He informed them that he had bought the horse from the liveryman who said it needed a certain type of rider and wasn't good for the general public.

"I think he wanted to get rid of a horse that stuck out like a sore thumb, like a spotlight to Indians," was Frank's observation. The horse was such a bright white, it really stood out.

Finally, the last man made his pitch to Nancy, getting the same response as all of the others. He did, however, help carry her basket to the wagon. As they approached, Frank got out of the wagon to help her into the back, where she sat down beside Stella. Evie crawled over the seat into the back as well to sit beside where her sister lay. Then, she raised the curtains to let in some air.

It took some time to situate Stella on the mattress. When Nancy sat down beside her, she pillowed her daughter's head on her lap.

Glancing behind Shelby at the street, Evie noticed two men come out of the feed store. One bumped into the other and pointed at their wagon. Her blood stilled for she was sure she read, 'Frank' on his lips.

She noted that the first man wore black clothing, a short jacket over a white shirt and pants with silver buttons up the sides. He was the same man who had ridden the prancing bay horse down the street in Red Top, and she wondered at the coincidence.

Then, as if she would never see that man without seeing the man with the thick, black moustache, there he was, standing in the shadows of a nearby alley.

Following the pointing man's hand, he noted the driver and then, his eyes slid to Evie and he tipped his hat to her.

"Are you ready?" Frank asked Nancy, his voice seeming lower than usual.

"Yes. Thank you."

He walked around to the front of the wagon and got in. It was likely his back was turned to the street when another group of wagons rolled by with several riders as escort. One of the riders looked twice at their wagon before being blocked from view.

Evie's heart stilled. She knew the rider; it was Uncle Albert. Then their wagon jerked and started rolling and she was glad.

Yet, it seemed that they weren't ready to leave Bastian because Shelby rode close to Frank and when he pulled his hand out of his pocket, it held the derringer.

"You're my prisoner," he told Frank. With a jerk of his head, he indicated the direction the other wagons were taking. "Let's go."

"Right now? You'd take me in right now?" Frank was incredulous.

"There's a sheriff's office right there," the young man motioned down the street.

"What about them?" A jerk of his head indicated those riding in the back.

"They can find another driver if they need one," he motioned with the derringer. "Let's go."

From the back of the wagon came the sound of a pistol being cocked. "I like the driver we have," Nancy spoke up.

"I'm the law," reminded Shelby.

"That's true," Nancy agreed. "Would you mind taking us to the Sheriff's office, Mr. Frank?"

Everyone was silent as the wagon pulled up in front of the building. It seemed vacant, as if it hadn't been used in a long time.

"Looks empty," was Nancy's observation. "Doctor Cutwright said that the sheriff was killed by Indians a couple of months ago. The town hasn't elected a new one because they don't know if they'll be here from one day to the next. Due to the Indians."

Shelby sighed and put the derringer back in his pocket.

"Looks like you'll have to wait til Denton to arrest him."

"Why do you have to keep movin' west, anyway?" Shelby asked, crossly. "Why not go back to the safety of the fort? The East?"

Nancy smoothed Stella's head that lay in her lap. "Because if it's like it was when my great-grandpap came over the mountains, the Indians won't be here long. The white men will keep coming with their families, with their sense of right and wrong and ownership. And, like them, maybe I can find a piece of land worth fightin' for and makin' somethin' of for my children."

"I think you just heard manifest destiny," Frank tapped the reins on the rumps of the horses. "Spoken by a woman."

Yet, Shelby wasn't ready to give up. "Why are you heading west? To escape the law?"

Frank shrugged. "Maybe to make my fortune as well."

"As old as you are?" He scoffed. "What fortune?"

"Why are you headin' west, Mr. Sinclair?" Evie had been leaning against her mother, but now straightened. Her voice was more firm than anyone had ever heard it.

"To take him to justice."

The wagon had turned and Shelby followed it back through the town to follow the road west. With the turn, Evie was aware that her heart seemed to hum as if her soul was well pleased.

"That's all?" She asked. "You're not makin' a home out here?"

"Why would I?" Shelby frowned. "What's here, anyway? Nothing! A hardscrabble people barely making a living!" He looked at her. "It's too dry. Too brown. Too . . ."

"Big? Too big?"

Shelby looked around them at the enormous bowl of sky above and the endless prairie that held little of civilization. "Maybe." He was angry enough that truth came from his lips.

Getting to her knees, Evie gripped the side of the wagon and declared, "Well, I tell you now, Shelby Sinclair, in front of God and everyone, I'm unsettin' my cap for you!" With that, she walked to the back of the wagon, whistled Gypsy to come up close and slid onto her back. Then, she rode away to scout the trail ahead.

"What is she talking about?" Shelby asked, astounded at the turn of events. "What is she? Ten? Eleven?"

"Sometimes it happens early," Frank's tone was mild, hiding his amusement. "Girl picks out a man."

"What is she talking about, setting her cap for me? She's ten!" The young man was incredulous. He would have spurred his horse and galloped ahead, but Evie was there. "When the time comes, I'm doing my own picking out!" Since he couldn't go forward, he pulled back on the reins, to fall in behind the wagon.

Nancy smiled to herself. "That arrow went home."

The sun was almost directly overhead when Frank turned from the road and drove down the lone swale in the area.

"What are you doing?" Shelby had not lost his anger in the hot, dusty morning ride.

"They need rest," he indicated the team. "She needs rest," and everyone knew he meant Stella. "I know of a place. Nice little spring. Some shade."

Since she rode ahead, Evie found it first. Gypsy quickly slaked her thirst while the girl dropped to the ground and splashed water on her face.

Trees shaded the spring that bubbled into a small pond, then trickled into a stream as it left. Around it, the ground was soft, cut up by the hooves and feet of many animals who came to drink.

"It's a little bit of heaven!" Evie cried out.

"I've always thought so," was Frank's reply as he put Stella on the ground and let her lean against a tree trunk.

"I would think that this," Shelby motioned toward the glare of heat that shimmered in the distance, "would be your preference." His tone was sullen.

Evie led her horse to a spot of grass, hobbled her, then took off the bridle. As she passed him, she tossed, "You're mean," over her shoulder.

"We are all hot and tired," Nancy accepted the bucket of water that Frank offered her. Soaking a cloth in it, she then used it to dab on Stella's face and neck. "I'm sure some shade and fresh water will revive us all."

"Let's use buckets to water the horses first," Frank suggested. "When we get ready to leave, we can let them have their fill."

"So they don't muddy the water," Evie caught on.

"Right you are," Frank smiled at her.

Matching action to words, the horses were watered, then staked out. The water barrel on the wagon was filled as well.

When the horses were watered, Frank motioned to Shelby. "Bring your horse over here." He stood on the bank where the mud was deep.

"Why?"

Frank motioned and the young man did as he was told. Scooping up handfuls of mud, the older man began smearing it on the horse's neck.

"What are you doing?" Shelby pulled the animal away.

"If you're not smart enough to figure it out, then you need to take a different trail." Frank was hot, tired and at the end of his patience with him.

"He's changing the color of your horse," Nancy's quiet tone was calming. "So that he doesn't stand out so much."

Out of patience, Frank flung the mud from his hands and stalked away so that Shelby was left to do the chore himself. However, Evie felt some sympathy for him and helped on the places she could reach. Of course, much of the mud would dry and flake off, but the dirt would remain.

After his horse was picketed again, Shelby began picking up scattered limbs. "Are you wanting a fire?"

Nancy shook her head. "Thank you for the thought, Mr. Sinclair. But, Mrs. Cutwright has supplied us with enough food to last til evening."

With nothing to do, Shelby flung himself down, his attitude one of irritation.

"Lookit, Mama!" Leaning on the crutch Frank had made, Stella pointed into the pond. A school of minnows flitted this way and that.

Nancy stood beside her daughter. On a whim, she picked up her skirt and waded into it. "Why, it's not just a puddle!" She said in amazement. "It's deep enough for a -." She looked at Frank.

"A bath. That's what I was thinking, too." He glanced around. "Mr. Sinclair and I will take a little walk up the draw and you ladies can bathe."

Evie sniffed as she walked past Shelby. "What about you-all?"

"We'll be next." Then, he quickly added, "While you go pick daisies or something."

"That will take some time," Nancy said, slowly.

"Are we resting?" Evie asked.

"Isn't that what Sundays are for?"

Nancy stared at Frank, then smiled. "You're right. It is Sunday. What with everything else goin' on," she looked at Stella then back at him, "I'd clean forgot." She looked at the wagon. "I've a Bible in the wagon, yonder."

"And it's heavy, too!" Stella added.

"What is this?" Shelby asked irritably. "A Sunday-go-to meeting

The LONG WAY HOME

place?"

Frank looked at him. "This is a new country and church is where you find it." Then he added, "Some people set store by religion."

"Thank you for thinking of us," A soft smile was on Nancy's face and her voice was full of emotion.

Hearing it, Evie wondered if she would cry.

"Your consideration was unexpected, but is very appreciated."

This time, the girl's eyes opened wide. It was rare her mother spoke thusly, like you would read in a book. Almost as if she was in one of Sir Walter Scott's novels.

Frank nodded, then walked up the creek, Shelby following.

Yet, Evie had a question. "But, the stores were open, Mama. On Sunday."

"There are exceptions to everything, Evie. Those people were leaving town and the business owners wanted to sell as much as they could, because they can't take it with them."

The girl nodded. "I guess God knows."

Nancy smiled. "God knows."

It was nearing dusk when their ablutions were done. Everyone was cleaner and as a result, felt a lift of spirit. Though wearing the same clothes, care was taken to make them less dusty, and in the case of the men, their shirts were washed then dried in the sun.

As the last rays of daylight merged to shadow in the little hollow, they stood in a circle, both Frank and Shelby with bared heads.

"Give us this day, our daily bread. And forgive us our trespasses as we forgive them that trespass against us." Nancy intoned the words.

Shelby made a noise of disbelief and Evie glared at him.

"And lead us not into temptation, but deliver us from evil," Nancy went on.

There was silence and everyone looked at Shelby, whether expecting another outburst or thinking that he was the evil spoken of, he did not know.

"For thine is the kingdom," Evie's clear voice took over.

"The power, and the glory," Nancy joined her daughter.

"Forever and ever," Frank's voice blended in.

"Amen," the word was said by all except Shelby who picked up his hat and left the camp.

"G'bye, Mr. Sinclair," Stella said, simply.

"He's not leaving," Evie looked at Frank. "Is he?"

Frank shrugged.

"Why don't we sing?" Nancy suggested.

And so, when shadows overtook the wash, they were held at bay by a small campfire around which the weary travelers sat, singing hymns until their repertoire was depleted and then various songs until it was full dark. Sitting on the plain above them, Shelby looked up at the stars, felt the heat rise from the land and watched as a myriad of lights filled the sky from horizon to horizon.

Chapter
ELEVEN

Though Evie tried to save her horse any undue exertion, it was hard when Gypsy wanted to run. So, she let her run for a bit. It was hard to pull her back and then insist on walking until the wagon caught up. When it was close, she let the mare run again.

Behind her, the wagon swayed and squeaked, the lone vestige of civilization in all that great expanse of land. Frank drove, with Shelby sitting beside him, neither saying much.

Evie wondered at Shelby's anger and frustration that continued unabated. She looked about. How could anyone be angry on such a wonderful morning as this? Above, the sky was a cloudless blue, the tall grasses bowed with the breeze, birds called and swooped and a wonderful future called!

Shelby was a hard person to understand. When she'd asked him if he was going to name his horse, he muttered something unintelligible and walked away. So, she took it upon herself to name him, "Angel," for his former whiteness. Stella wanted to call him Snow, but as far as Evie knew, he did not call his horse either name.

In the back of the wagon, Nancy sat with Stella beside her. She'd been telling her a story, but upon looking down, realized that the girl was asleep. "How much further, Mr. Frank?"

"Horseback, you could make it by evening. We'll be there tomorrow."

"Thank you," Nancy settled back.

"It's a town with a sheriff," Shelby spoke up.

"That it is," was Frank's mild reply.

"What then?" The young man asked. "Am I still your prisoner?"

Frank looked at him. "My prisoner? You've never been my prisoner."

"Their prisoner, then!"

The older man continued driving.

"What do you call this?" Shelby held up his hands to reveal nothing in them. Nor was the derringer in his jacket pocket.

Frank nodded at the rifle lying in the floor of the wagon. "That rifle's been within easy reach. If we need it, use it."

"It wasn't there yesterday," was the sullen reply.

"It was."

Shelby looked away, clearly not believing him.

"That's the thing with being angry. You can be so focused on staying that way; you miss what is right in front of you."

Evie turned her horse and came cantering up to the wagon. From the look on her face, she had something to say, so Frank pulled the team to a stop.

"They's a wagon a comin'." She pointed in the direction she had come.

Frank looked down the road and Shelby picked up the rifle from the floorboard.

Yet, the wagon coming in their direction did not seem a threat. A young man, probably only a little older than Shelby was driving, with a young woman sitting beside him, a small child in her arms.

"I'm Grayson Ferris and this is my wife," the driver introduced himself. Though young, he seemed to have a defeated attitude about him, his shoulders bent forward.

"This is the Cyrus wagon," Frank replied. "This is Shelby, our helper."

"You'll need all the help you can get in this country," Grayson replied, his wife nodding in agreement.

"Where you headed?"

"To the fort. Everyone is supposed to go to the fort."

"What about Denton? There's a fort near there, isn't there?"

"Well, truth to tell, if the Indians burn us out, we're headed back east, to her folks." Grayson went on. "This is a hard country, sir. A hard country."

"You'd ought to turn around and go with us. Seein' as you have your wife and those young-uns." Mrs. Ferris spoke up. Since their wagon had come abreast of them, she could see Nancy in the back of the wagon. Evie rode her horse to one side, trying to quiet Gypsy who still wanted to run.

"What do you say, Mrs. Cyrus?" Frank asked over his shoulder.

"We've a schedule to keep and people to meet," was her answer. "I guess we're headin' on."

"There's plenty of Indian sign," Grayson cautioned them. "The Harpers got burned out."

"Thank you for your concern," Frank gathered up the reins.

"Well, God bless you and good luck to you then," was his salutation when he saw that they were continuing on.

The baby in Mrs. Ferris' arms began crying. She bounced it, trying to quiet it, but the crying got louder.

"If it was up to her, we'd keep goin' clear to Pittsburgh!" Grayson picked up the reins and slapped them on the backs of his team. "Git up!"

"Good luck to you!" Frank called out as the wagons parted.

Behind him, Nancy watched the other wagon rolling eastward and put a hand over her heart. "May God have mercy on us all." She wondered if she had made the right decision, but in truth, it was the only decision to be made. Behind them was nothing, while before them was the promise of a future, if only the Indians would leave them alone.

By mid-morning, it was hot. Evie and Nancy traded places, with the girl in the back of the wagon napping with her sister and her mother astride Gypsy. Nancy had debated which way to ride the horse, aside or astride. But, since there was no saddle, she decided that astride might be safer, even if less decorous or in good taste.

Frank had to admit that the woman could ride and spent a few moments admiring her on Gypsy as Nancy found a lone log to jump.

Beside him, Shelby grumbled. "Mother would have a fit if she saw that."

"Takes some skill to jump a horse bareback," Frank replied.

"She's riding astride. Like a man," complained the young man.

"That's the way Indians ride."

"She's not an Indian."

"Isn't she?"

Shelby looked again at the woman with the high cheekbones, sleek dark hair and dusky skin. "Not a plains Indian."

"No," Frank agreed.

"And, her children are blonde haired and blue eyed."

Frank was silent, his attention on something further up the road.

"Aren't you afraid to get to Denton?" Shelby asked. "You're going to be arrested. Again."

"You've been barking up the wrong tree for some time," Frank informed him.

"What do you mean?"

"I'm not Jack Davis. Never have been. Never will be."

"That's your face on the wanted poster."

"A resemblance, that's true." Frank noticed that Nancy had seen the smoke as well. "You're not the first one to think it."

"So? How do I know you're not Jack Davis?"

Frank looked at him. "I knew Jack Davis. Met him a time or two in Deadwood. If you saw us side by side, you'd not think we looked much alike."

"You knew Jack Davis?" Shelby was dumbfounded. "What about the picture?"

"I don't know who put that on the poster. I wish I did. He cost me eight years of my life."

"What do you mean?"

Frank looked at him. "I went to prison for Jack Davis. And for a crime I did not commit."

"I don't believe you."

"The jury didn't either."

"Then, you're Jack Davis."

"I'm telling you, I'm not." Frank stopped the wagon and stood up, his attention on the smoke off to the side of the road.

Nancy rode up beside them.

"Can you prove you're not Jack Davis?" The young man asked.

"I guess not," said Frank. "And the man who could is dead," he said, slowly. "But, I can prove I'm Frank Pascoe." His tone was sharp for once more he was running out of patience with Shelby.

"How?"

"Ask your mother."

Immediately, Shelby was angry. "Leave my mother out of this!"

"You wanted proof," Frank guided the team off the road and stopped them.

Shelby held a rifle across his lap. Whether it was by accident or on purpose, the rifle was pointed at Frank.

"Let's not be hasty." He gently pushed the barrel aside then motioned for Nancy to ride up beside the wagon. When she did, he stepped to the side so that she could dismount into the wagon. Handing her the reins, he got on the horse and rode to where the column of smoke rose from the prairie.

Nancy drove the wagon, following him. Soon they could see that the smoke rose from the remains of a cabin, barn and haystack. The corrals, for the most part, had not burned. As she pulled into the farmyard, Frank was coming out of the smoldering cabin.

"No one home," he informed them.

"Thank God," Nancy responded. Seeing the farm in ruins brought forward the realization of the danger that lay about.

"Now do you wish you'd turned back?" Shelby asked.

Frank glanced at him. "Let's keep a good lookout." He tied Gypsy to the back of the wagon.

Meanwhile, Shelby saddled Angel and rode ahead, a rifle across his saddle.

"You ride him hard," Nancy nodded toward the young man.

"He's pretty stuck on putting me in jail."

"He thinks he has good reason." When Frank was quiet, she went on. "Does he?"

Frank spat to the side, though he didn't know where the spittle came from. It was pretty hot and dry. "Was there a wanted poster with my face on it? Yes. But, I've served my time." He shot a look at her. "Like I told him, it was for a crime I did not commit."

"You let him arrest you."

"I was drunk. The first time in eight years." He grimaced. "Drinking always gets me in trouble." He slid a glance her way, but his tone was light. "I don't know why I keep it up."

"You were drunk in Lester's Landing?" She thought back to when the girls had met him and what he had done for them; rescuing them from would-be kidnappers.

"Yep." He glanced at her. "I'd been drinking just about all day, waiting for my turn to cross the river. I went to the Mercantile to get some tobacco, saw what was happening with your girls and got to feel some flesh hit my fist. Felt good." He grinned. "To celebrate, I drank some more."

"Did you know Shelby was there?" She remembered Evie telling of the lightning between them.

"I didn't know he was there at the Landing. I'd already met up with him at a town upriver, where he tried to arrest me. But, I thought I'd given him the slip." His lips tightened in a mirthless grin. "That's what liquor can do for you. Make you careless."

"So, Shelby arrested you." She said slowly. "And then, you were drunk when you pulled me out of the river?"

"No," he shook his head. "By then, I was pretty sober. I'd had to wade out to get on the boat. That water was cold!"

"Why didn't you tell him, then, that you'd already done your time?"

"I tried. He wouldn't listen." Frank heard a sound and turned around to see Evie looking at him, her eyes wide. Beside her, Stella was stirring. There may have been a time he wouldn't have told his story with little ones around. Now, however, not knowing how their trip would turn out, he figured it wouldn't hurt. Honesty was supposed to be the best policy, anyway.

"Which is when I broke jail."

"Why?" Nancy said, slowly. "Why did you break jail? Why didn't you tell the authorities? Someone higher up than the sheriff?"

"Well, it seems that Sheriff Bellville Tucker was the cousin or some relative of the sheriff of Clark County, Ohio, Mr. Wynn Tucker. After the first telegram to Springfield, he was in no hurry to let me go."

Nancy nodded. "Still, things would have been sorted out eventually. And, you wouldn't be a fugitive."

Frank looked at her and smiled. "Mrs. Cyrus, Miss Nancy," he used the name they had agreed upon. "I begin to think you care."

Behind them, Evie held her breath and Stella squeezed her hand. They both looked from one to the other.

Nancy thought for a moment. "I try to care for every one of God's creatures."

"Now, I'm a creature?"

A smile crossed her face. "A creation. As we are all God's creation." Her eyes met his glance. "I did want to apologize to you, Mr. Frank. Mr. Pascoe."

"I like Frank, better."

"I've used you for my own ends, namely to make our way westward." She looked around them at a seemingly empty land. "But, it may get you killed."

"Miss Nancy," he replied, "until you and your girls came along, I was well on my way to drinking myself to Hell. I don't see much difference between liquor and Indians, since the result is the same."

"Well," said Nancy, "Since you see it that way, I'm glad we were able to spare your life for at least a little longer." A slight smile crossed her lips.

Evie sat back, as puzzled as ever as to what was going on between the two, if anything. For the most part, they could have been neighbors, nodding in passing. But now, her mother mentioned that their trip held danger unspoken of before. She and Stella exchanged looks. They would just have to wait and see. Meanwhile, Evie promised herself to keep an even closer look on the land around them.

As much as he could, Frank kept out of the road, since their passing raised dust. Instead, he drove along the side of it or even several feet away from it. All around, as far as they could see, the land seemed to continue on forever, with a trackless sky above them.

"It's like we're the only ones in the world," Evie spoke the thought aloud.

"Don't let that fool you," Frank said. "This is a deceivin' land. Could be a band of Indians over yonder rise or up the next wash and you wouldn't know it."

Evie noticed that her mother sat up a little taller. Even Shelby, who rode off to the side, seemed to be more alert.

That night, moonlight spilled over the land, making silver the grass all around them. Above, a flood of stars shimmered and sparkled, leaving little room for darkness.

"I don't know if I'll get to sleep," Evie remarked. "The sky is so bright!"

"Sleep under the wagon with your sister," was Frank's suggestion.

Before them, the fire had dwindled to nothing and their dinner plates were stacked to one side, already cleaned by the sand they'd used to scrub them.

"I wish we could sing," Stella whispered in the quiet. "And, I wish there were some hello trees."

"There are trees in Denton," Frank assured her.

"I will say hello to them," she smiled.

"Any coffee left?"

"I think so," Nancy sat close to the fire, mending Stella's blouse.

Sitting close to where the dishes were stacked, the little girl handed him a cup.

Rather than switch hands, Frank reached for the coffeepot with his left hand. "Ow!" He cried out, almost dropping the coffee pot into the fire.

Immediately, Nancy was on her feet, Evie behind her.

"Are you alright, Mr. Frank?" The older girl asked.

"I'm fine. Just had my mind on other things," he admitted.

"Here's the cloth!" Nancy held a folded cloth and offered it to him.

Grimacing, he took it, wrapped it around the coffee pot handle and was able to pour himself a cup of coffee.

When he put the coffee pot back on the rock it had rested on in the fire ring, Nancy walked up to him and asked, "May I see it?"

Frank held out his left hand to her.

The LONG WAY HOME

"It's already raisin' a blister," was her comment. "I've got some salve for it." She glanced at Evie who at once went to the wagon and dug it out of the carpetbag.

"And a bandage, Evie," Nancy called to her.

The girl had been about to jump down out of the wagon, but turned and went back to the carpetbag. Then, she appeared again, salve in one hand, a roll of bandages in the other, and jumped down out of the vehicle.

Nancy held out her hand for Frank's and when he gave it to her, there was a sudden snap.

They looked at one another in surprise.

"Must be the storm that's coming," he said.

"Yes," was her reply. "It must be."

Evie looked at the sky from horizon to horizon. "What storm?"

No one answered her as her mother tended to the injury. When the hand was bound up, Nancy went back to her sewing and Frank walked over to check on the horses.

He was only gone for a few minutes, then sat down nearby to enjoy his cooled coffee.

A coyote called and Evie leaned forward, a pistol in her lap.

Was it an Indian or a coyote, was the question in everyone's mind.

"Are we close to Denton? Shelby spoke up, irritably. He had tried hard not to speak to Frank at all.

"Close enough. Maybe noon tomorrow."

"Would Indians come that close to town?"

Frank gave a little smile. "They've driven folks out of San Antonio before. That close enough for you?"

The young man leaned back against the wagon wheel, a rifle across his lap.

Evie looked around, noticing that all of them were armed. Frank sat next to a rifle that leaned against a wagon wheel. Shelby had the other rifle as he sat with his back against the back wagon wheel. As her mother moved about, cleaning up after the meal, the butt of the pistol in her waistband could be seen. Looking down, Evie looked at the pistol in her lap, then her gaze went to Stella. She was lying down under the wagon, the derringer beside her.

Anyone trying to surprise them might get a surprise themselves!

As the fire died down, she saw Shelby walk a little away from the camp and sit down. He had the first watch and Frank would relieve him in a few hours. It was something they'd done since leaving the fort.

Her mother sat down near the fire, using its light to sew a patch on Evie's skirt. The girl had torn a hole in it when climbing some rocks that day at nooning. Frank came up to the fire and poured a cup of coffee.

"Well, Miss Nancy," he said. "You've heard some of my story. What is yours?"

She looked up at him, her eyes searching his face.

"Why are you headed West? Running from something?" There was humor in his question.

Nancy continued to look at him, as if gauging him. "Alright. I'll tell you. I'm a girl of the hills," she said. "But I always wanted to see what was beyond them. Livin' in the hills and hollers was enough while Ollie was alive. But, once he died, I had no peace there."

Her hands dropped to her lap and she looked out at the darkness beyond the camp. "It felt like there was somethin' I was supposed to remember. And, I didn't know what it was until I stood on the bank of Lester's Landing and saw all those people, headed west. And, I knew

I wanted to be among them."

Her eyes sought his for understanding. "I know there's people who would say what I did wasn't right. That I was riskin' the lives of my children as well as my own. There's plenty that would say I was a loose woman, strikin' out on my own that way." She gave a shrug of her shoulders. "It doesn't matter."

"What about Albert? Did he have anything to do with your decision?"

Her gaze went back to the darkness. "He might have." Yet, she shook her head. "No. I think it was just me. Ollie and I talked about goin' west more than once." She smiled ruefully. "About ever' time he had a reverse. Like when he was sold land that didn't belong to the seller. Or when he bought a mule that wouldn't ride or drive."

Frank was surprised to hear this bit of news. "How did that happen?"

"He was drunk," was the simple reply. "And, he liked the color of the mule. Red, with a yaller mane and tail. It was pretty."

"What happened to it?"

Nancy smiled a little. "I taught it to ride and drive afore he sold it."

"How did you do that?"

"Biscuits," she smiled. "He loved biscuits."

Frank looked at her. "You loved him. Ollie."

"I did," she admitted. "I was happy with him. Even with everything." Picking up the mended skirt, she looked it over. "But, you know. I never grieved his passing."

Her eyes met his. "After all the prayin' and bargainin' with God, when he passed, it was just time. He was ready to go and I had to let him." Her eyes glistened in the firelight. "I missed him. I missed him somethin' fierce. But, I didn't grieve him." She looked at him. "Maybe that was wrong. But, I had two children to raise, a farm to look after and . ." Her arm crossed protectively over her belly.

Silence fell between them while before them, the fire popped and glowed red with dying coals.

"Now, you're headed West."

"I am." Nancy looked up at him. "What about you? Happy to be headed West?"

"I am," he replied.

"You said you'd been West already. How came you to be West in the first place?"

They had been talking, with Nancy sitting on a rock near the fire and him standing. "Do you mind if I sit?"

Nancy spread her hand beside her, offering him a bit of ground.

He took advantage of it, and Evie noticed, sat perhaps a little closer than he should have.

Unlike you, I did not love my wife."

"What?" Nancy frowned. "That cain't be true."

"It's the only answer I can come up with as to the reason I went west." Frank stared straight ahead into the night. "We started out alright. As you say, we had some reverses. I had a few jobs, lookin' for one that felt right, that I could stick to."

"Sometimes it takes a few," she agreed.

"I worked for her father in the Mercantile until he died. And then, I worked for her stepfather as well." Frank shook his head. "He wasn't much of a businessman. Ran the Mercantile into the ground, but Marge, Mrs. Mansback, resurrected it." A small smile passed over his lips. "After she got rid of him."

"What? Got rid of him? How?"

The LONG WAY HOME

"He died. Drank too much. Walked home from the saloon and got run over by a wagon."

"So," Nancy leaned forward, to change her posture. "Mrs. Mansback took over the Mercantile."

"And did well with it." Frank admitted then glanced at Nancy. "She did so well, she didn't need me." He thought for a moment. "Came to feel like I wasn't much needed at all. By anyone."

He looked around the camp. "I even tried farming." He sighed then shook his head. "The land was worn out. I was worn out."

"So, you went west."

"To make my fortune."

"Why didn't you take your wife with you?"

Frank's lips stretched, but it was no smile. "She wouldn't go. Didn't want to leave the comfort of Springfield." His gaze went to Shelby. "If she was pregnant, she didn't tell me."

"But, she promised to cleave to you, didn't she?"

"She did," he admitted. "But, I promised to cleave to her as well."

Nancy leaned forward, frowning. "So, you went West."

"I did." He grimaced. "I had to. It was like Springfield was too small for me, like I couldn't breathe with all the closeness of the buildings and the people."

"Had you been west before?"

Frank glanced sidewise at her. "Yes, during the War. I was in Vicksburg and then, went on to Texas."

"And you liked Texas."

"A lot of what I saw was like the East. Green. Rolling hills. Farms everywhere."

She frowned at him. "What did you like about it, then?"

"Being free. Feeling free. There were farms, but it was still so new. Not a lot of rules and restrictions. Not only that, the further west I went, the flatter it got and the more open it seemed."

"What did you do?" She asked. "What did you work at?"

"Whatever I could. Made some friends. Went up to Alder Gulch with them and tried my luck. Found a little gold, did well. Bought myself a house and some land. Planned on going back to Springfield and bringing Cecilia back out."

"What happened?"

"She never answered my letters. House burned. I moved on." He shrugged.

"What then?"

"I worked on the railroad for a while. Hunted buffalo for them."

Nancy turned a little to look into his eyes. "I've heard of that. Herds of buffalo as far as the eye could see."

"And with it, the smell of blood and death." His voice held a bitter note. "Reminded me of Shiloh. I quit it."

Nancy nodded.

"I laid track for a while."

"What was that like?"

Frank smiled a little. "It was backbreaking work but I was good at it and I gloried in it. And then at night, I would drink and gamble." He glanced at her. "I liked that, too. But, there was something else. An excitement. The glory of achievement. We were putting down rails, civilization, in an untamed land. We were uniting a country, when just a few years before, we were fighting a divided country."

He went on, "There were Irishmen, Chinamen, Russians, any country you could name, men, as well as ex-slaves. Men were fleeing debt and prison and families. It was a stew of men working together in a magnificent achievement."

Slowly, he nodded his head. "That's what I remember, now. The feeling of being united in a purpose."

"Did you work til the joining of the railroads?"

He glanced at her. "No. I had moved on by then."

"Where did you go?"

"I went to the Sandwich Islands on a ship."

"As a sailor?"

He smiled. "I was pretty dang good at that, too. Had a good captain, good crew. But, when we got back to San Francisco, I was ready to do something else."

"What did you do?"

His gaze roved the camp and when Evie thought he was looking her way, she quickly shut her eyes. "I joined up with a traveling show of marksmen, about the same time Bill Cody started his show, The Scouts of the Prairie."

"You've certainly lived a life!" Nancy looked at him, marveling at his adventures.

"I was the pistol expert, Josh Pedego was the rifle marksman and Luke Stewart was the knife thrower."

"And you traveled with this show?"

"Yep. Mostly in the East. They would pay to see anything that seemed to be of the West."

"Are you?"

"What?"

"An expert with a pistol?"

Frank smiled a little. "I was at the time." He looked at her. "Besides, anyone can be an expert when there's no one shooting back at you."

"In the War, there were men shooting back at you."

"That's true. But, in target shooting, there's none of that."

She nodded then waited to see if he would say more.

"When the Black Hills gold rush started, we broke up and headed west. We figured there were easier ways to make money," he gave an ironic laugh.

"What does that mean?" Her eyes narrowed as she looked under the wagon. Evie had risen up on her elbows to listen more intently, but sank back to her blanket.

"It means I'm not cut out to be a miner," his smile broadened. "I went to driving stages, freight wagons, anything to make money." He glanced at her.

Her attention was on him.

"Which is where I met up with Sam Bass."

"How?"

"He robbed my stage. One of his men fired a pistol, sent some wood off the stage into my arm. When I ran into him in a saloon, he bought me a drink as an apology."

Nancy noted that he rubbed the upper part of his right arm, as if it still hurt.

"When Sam found out I didn't have a job because I was laid up with that splinter, he offered a spot in his gang to me."

"So, you did know Sam Bass."

"Yep, I sure did. And, that fact has caused me a heap of joy and despair."

"Joy?" Nancy was puzzled.

"Sure. Sam was a fine fellow and he laughed at my jokes."

"Despair?" Her voice softened.

"Someone put my face with a name that wasn't mine on a wanted poster." He looked at Nancy. "As a member of Sam's gang."

"But, you didn't join the gang. You were hurt from a wreck. Or were you?"

"I was." He admitted. "Just when I was beginning to think I could make more money and be appreciated a little more in Sam's gang, my horses spooked and bolted, ran for half a mile and turned it over. I went flyin'."

"So, you couldn't take part in the robbery," she said, slowly.

"Just my luck," was his reply.

"No," said Nancy. "It was God. He kept you from robbing the train."

"I still went to prison for it."

She looked at him, as if suddenly aware of his nearness, then stood up. "God has His ways. We don't often know the reason for things at the time."

Frank got to his feet as well.

"You went to prison for something you didn't do," she said, slowly. "Were you angry?"

"Hell yes," was sudden, harsh reply. Then, he spoke more softly. "Yes, I was."

Under the wagon, Evie compared his answer to what he'd told Shelby earlier.

"For the first year, I probably spent more time in The Hole than I did in a cell. Then, one day, I was out in the yard. I looked up at the mountains just beyond the prison. And, I saw how aloof they were, just being there. Aloof and beautiful. They didn't care if it was snowing or if it was Spring or Fall. And, they didn't care if I was angry or not." He looked at her. "I don't know if that makes sense, but I stopped being angry. I decided it wasn't getting me anywhere besides more time in The Hole." A soft smile was on his lips. "I knew that I wanted to be outside, looking at those mountains, any time I could. And, that's what I did."

"You were looking at God," Nancy told him.

"I thought it was mountains."

"God's creation. He made you look up. Appreciate the beauty in your life."

Frank shrugged. "At any rate, from then on, I tried not to be angry – at anything." His eyes went to where the horses were picketed. "Even a young man who insists he needs to arrest me."

Nancy nodded. "I know you have suffered hardship," she said. "But, I'm glad you didn't rob the train."

With that, she made her way to the wagon and lay down under it beside Stella. On the other side of her sister, Evie turned on her back and looked out at the stars.

They got on the road early the next morning. Whether it was the excitement of coming to town or the almost incessant cry of coyotes, everyone woke before dawn and they were on the road shortly afterward.

Shelby took a turn at driving, his rifle on the floorboard while Frank sat beside him, a rifle across his knees. Behind them, Nancy sat with Stella, telling her stories and listening to her telling stories of her own.

Turning Gypsy toward the wagon Evie came trotting up. "I seen some riders," she looked at Frank.

From the back, Nancy said, "Saw some riders."

"Where?" Frank looked around.

"They're ahead of us."

"Coming this way?"

Evie shook her head. "Nope. Goin' the same way we are."

"White men?"

"They had hats on. Dark horses."

"How many?"

"Six."

"We must be close to Denton," his tone was light. "Might see some more before we get there." He smiled at her. "That's fine work; a good lookout."

Evie brightened. "Thank you, Mr. Frank!" She put heels to Gypsy to go back to her scouting position.

Shelby watched her ride away. "She hasn't said a word to me since the other day. Never knew a little girl could keep a grudge like that." He looked at Frank. "I guess it starts young."

"It starts when anyone feels wronged," he said, mildly. "Regardless of age."

"Sounds like you're referring to me. But, you don't know me."

Frank looked at him. "Maybe I was referring to myself."

Chapter
TWELVE

Perhaps it was the excitement of knowing they would be in Denton that day that hastened them on their way that morning. It was just as well, for once the sun was up, the day grew rapidly warmer.

Nancy was glad to have had enough supplies to prepare a good breakfast, so good that even Shelby commented that it was one of the best he'd eaten.

Even so, Evie noticed that it seemed her mother wasn't happy with Frank, for she kept her eyes down as she handed him a plate and was in a hurry to get away from him.

Yet, all that was dispelled when they were on the road, for Nancy sat beside Frank who drove the wagon. Evie rode Gypsy to one side of the wagon, while Shelby ranged far ahead on his mud splattered horse.

In the back of the wagon, Stella was playing with her corncob doll and singing Dixie.

Sometimes, Evie would join in. After a few times through, she glanced at her mother who looked off into the distance and she wondered why she didn't say something. Stella had a tendency to stay on one song until everyone was tired of it.

"Nice singing," Frank spoke up. "Could we have another song?"

Stella poked her head between him and Nancy. "Don't you like that song?"

"That is a good enough song," was the reply. "But, I thought maybe we should have a different one for the next ten miles."

Nancy looked at him, smiling a little. "She doesn't have to sing anything, if you'd rather."

But, he shook his head. "She's a good little singer. I thought it might be nice to have another."

Stella grinned up at him. "I know a good ten mile song," she said, then disappeared into the back of the wagon.

"In Scarlet Town, where I was born," Came the little voice as she started on Barbry Allen.

Evie rode up close to the wagon and joined in, "There was a fair maid dwellin', and every youth cried well a way, for her name was Barbry Allen."

This song seemed to suit Frank for he nodded his head in time to it. As she rode along, Evie could smell the dry earth and feel the coolness of the morning breeze. Trees were becoming more frequent and it seemed that each of their leaves glistened. All in all, it was a golden morning.

Evie sang a little louder, her voice blending with the others, "They buried William in the old churchyard, and Barbry there a nigh him. And out of his grave grew a red, red rose and out of hers, a briar."

"They grew and grew in the old churchyard til they could grow no higher."

Nancy and her girls looked around because Frank had joined in.

"And there they twined in a true love's knot, the rose around the briar."

They finished in soulful unison.

"I didn't know you knew that song," Stella informed him.

Frank grinned. "Well, if I didn't know it before, I know it now." He put a finger in his ear and rubbed it, as if it hurt from the repetition. "You sure do like that song."

"It's so sad," Stella spoke up. "Sometimes I cry."

"Found out she loved him a little too late, don't you think?" Frank raised an eyebrow.

"She was mean," Evie added. "Makin' fun of him, when he loved her so." Then she lifted her voice and sang, "Mother O Mother, come make my bed. Come make it long and narrow. Sweet William died for me today, I'll die for him tomorrow. That's my favorite part."

Frank nodded, her mother's eyes met hers with a smile and Stella settled into the back of the wagon, her eyelids growing heavy. Almost out of sight rode Shelby on his white horse, the only things moving on a wide open plain. Evie gave Gypsy a little more rein and let her trot forward. Perhaps she would see if Shelby would care if she rode beside him.

Just as Frank had predicted, it was noon when they rolled down the main street of Denton, Texas. As they had approached the town, he could see that not much had changed since he'd been there last. The land still rolled, trees filled the little creek valleys and habitations were few and far between.

There were plenty of buildings, many more than Bastian. But, the town seemed just as vacant, due to the lack of people and traffic.

Evie noted there were hardly any women there, at least not in view. As they drove down the street, a man came out of a doorway and stood watching them pass, his thumbs hooked in his gun belt. She recognized the man with the thick, black moustache. As usual, he tipped his hat to her. Somehow his gesture made her feel conspicuous riding her horse astride. She swiveled one leg around to ride aside, like a proper young lady.

While she was getting her skirt situated, she looked up in time to see two men walk out of Gibbs' Saloon. Upon seeing the wagon, they stopped and stared at it. Behind them, the man with the silver conchos on his pants came out of the saloon and ducked his head to listen to what they had to say.

"Mama," Evie called out. "I think I just saw Uncle Albert."

Nancy was riding in the back of the wagon with Stella, somewhat concealed by the half rolled up canvas curtains, her field of vision obstructed. "Where?"

Evie tilted her head toward the saloon, but there was too much shadow and distance to make him out.

Whether it was to frighten Frank or for some other reason, Shelby rode his horse to the Sheriff's office and dismounted. Evie watched him go to the door and try to enter it, but it seemed to be locked. She knew a certain gladness because of it. Yet, the young man was undeterred and headed for the nearest saloon. They would know where the sheriff was.

As Frank turned the team toward the livery stable, Evie was surprised to see that the man with the thick black moustache stood at the corner. He sure had hurried to get there, she thought. It was funny how he kept turning up wherever they were.

Turning her head to the front, she saw Frank give a nod and she wondered if he knew him. When she glanced at the back of the wagon, she knew her mother had seen it, too.

"Whoa!" Frank pulled the horses to a stop.

The livery stable owner, Wash Peters, limped out of the barn. "What can I help you with?"

Frank grinned, "Glad to see you haven't gone to the fort. They could stand a good bit of corn."

"Not runnin' til I know what I'm runnin' from," was Peters' reply.

"My horse, too," Evie slid off Gypsy.

The livery owner smiled. "I'll see that they get it."

"Where do you want the wagon?"

"My boy and I will handle it," Peters indicated a slight boy of about twelve.

He took the reins from Evie and grinned at her, but she didn't seem to notice.

"How long will you be stayin'?"

Frank had walked around to the back of the wagon and glanced up at Nancy. "It's up to her." He held out his hand, as if to help her down.

"Probably just the night, Mr. Peters," she gave Frank the carpetbag.

He handed it back to her. The look on his face made her look the way they had come.

Three men had just turned the corner and something about them took his attention.

Meanwhile, Shelby walked up beside him, his hand on the butt of a pistol in his waistband. "Hurry up, Frank. We need to see a man about a reward."

Evie looked in the wagon bed and realized her pistol was missing from where she'd put it that morning.

"Pascoe!" The man with the silver buttons lining his black pants called out, his voice ringing.

Evie noted that he might have been the same age as Frank, but he was thinner and maybe a little taller. He had a scruffy beard that almost hid a long scar that ran from his left ear to his chin. As he approached, his eyes were slits and the smile on his face held no humor.

Frank moved away from the wagon, his hands up. "I'm not armed, J.J."

"Just how we like it, eh boys?" The two men with him stepped to either side of him, their hands low, close to the butts of their pistols.

"Now see here!" Peters interrupted. "You can't come gunnin' in here!"

One of the men, the thinner of the two, circled around and pushed him back toward the stable.

"I don't know who you men are," Shelby stated, "But this man is my prisoner!" He stepped back to show that he held a pistol on Frank.

J.J. grinned. "Between a rock and a hard place, Frank?" He laughed. "What did you do to upset the cub?" His gaze was hard as it raked Shelby. "Looks enough like you to be your son, don't he boys?"

Frank glanced at Shelby. "If you say so. I never rightly knew."

Aware that everyone is looking at him, Shelby exclaimed, "I'm not his son!" Silence greeted his assertion. Then, he took Frank's arm, as if to bring him away. "That doesn't mean a thing! I'm still takin' you in!"

"Takin' you in?" J.J. asked, interested. "For what?"

"The reward!"

"What reward?" The leader asked.

"A man back in Ohio let him think there was a reward on me," Frank explained.

"Ohio, eh?" J.J.'s teeth glinted in a tight smile. "Ain't that where you're from?"

Frank shrugged.

"J.J.?" One of his men asked, a warning note in his voice.

The leader looked around, noting that people were starting to gather at the corner. "We've jawed long enough. Get in the wagon."

Frank motioned for Nancy to step forward so that he could help her out of the wagon.

"Nope," J.J. told him. "She stays."

"There's no need," Frank told him. "They can stay here. I'll take you where you want to go."

"You went against me oncet, Pascoe. I wouldn't do it again." J.J. looked around. The liveryman and his son had disappeared into the barn. "Everyone into the wagon. Even the cub." With his pistol, he motioned that Frank should take the driver's seat. Then, he leaned in the back of the wagon and grinned at Nancy. "I wanna know how long it takes a family man to give up his secrets."

"You're takin' all of 'em?" The thin man asked.

"What is this, Slim?" J.J. demanded, suddenly angry. "Who's the boss of this outfit?"

"You've just changed the play is all," Slim stepped up beside Shelby and motioned for the pistol.

For a moment it seemed that the young man would resist. Evie held her breath. Then, he slowly gave it up and Slim motioned that he should get in the wagon.

Another man brought four saddled horses around the corner and into the livery yard. Nancy looked at him with some surprise, then brought her daughters closer. The outlaws mounted their horses then surrounded the wagon as if in escort.

As she looked out the back of the wagon, Evie saw the liveryman and his boy come out of the barn and watch as they left. The door to the office opened and out stepped the man with the big black moustache. Something prompted her to motion to him, as if encouraging him to follow them, to help them. Instead, he turned and walked back into the office and she sank against her mother in keen disappointment.

It seemed that they were on their own again.

"What's gonna happen, Mama?" Stella asked.

"I don't know," said Nancy. "This is something to do with Frank, I'm sure of it."

"And us," Evie reminded her.

"I'm glad they didn't search the wagon." Leaning over, Nancy flipped the edge of the quilt over the rifle that lay along the side of the wagon. Then, she opened the carpetbag and drew out the derringer along with a little deerskin pouch. It was smaller than the other that held bullets for the rifles and pistols. As her daughters watched, she put two bullets in it.

"You're loading that?" Evie asked. "I thought you said it might explode in your hand."

"It hasn't been fired in a long time," her mother admitted. "And, I don't know how it might act. But, I think we're gonna need to know it's loaded."

"Wonder what Mr. Sinclair would have said if he'd found he was holding a gun with no bullets."

"It's just as well that he didn't," was the reply. "Sometimes a good bluff works best."

There was the sound of a horse coming close to the wagon and they were silent. Then, a curtain was pushed aside.

"Your man ever tell you he was an outlaw?" J.J. asked them.

"No," said Nancy.

"He was." J.J. looked at Frank, then back at her. "Biggest and baddest." He laughed. "Good friend of Sam Bass."

Evie looked at her mother, her eyes wide. She couldn't believe it. She wouldn't believe it.

"You ever hear of Sam Bass?" He asked Evie.

"Yes sir."

"He robbed the Union Pacific of sixty thousand dollars!" J.J. laughed raucously. "It was a bodacious plan. Bold. Daring. And no one thought of doing it until Mr. Pascoe here suggested it."

"It was Joel's plan," Frank reminded him from the front of the wagon.

"I was there when you-all were discussing it. Sam wanted me in on it, too."

"Like hell," was Frank's reply.

J.J. spurred his horse forward and brought the barrel of his pistol down on Frank's head. He would have done it again, but the man held up an arm and deflected it.

Then, it took a moment for J.J. to get his horse under control because the animal had not liked getting pulled back so quickly after being spurred.

"I remember that," Nancy said. "I remember the gang was shot and killed and the money recovered."

J.J. laughed. "That's what they want you to think. They don't like to admit failure!"

Glancing at Frank, Evie saw him put an arm up to the side of his head and the sleeve come away bloody.

"You wanna know what happened?" The outlaw grinned and leaned toward the wagon. "The law got three of 'em, almost right off. And, in July the next year, they got Sam. One of his men betrayed him and the law got him."

Evie and Stella stared at the man with big blue eyes, but when he grinned, revealing dark and missing teeth, they looked away.

"But you know what? Sam had most of the money. The others had given it to him for safe keeping."

Nancy looked at Frank and noticed blood trickling down the side of his face. Taking the edge of her petticoat, she tore a strip and handed it to Shelby. Since he was sitting beside the man, it was easier for him to bandage him than for Nancy to try to do it from the back.

"Where is it?" Stella asked. "Where is the money?"

Because of the road, J.J. had to ride away from the wagon, but when he could, he was back at the open curtain.

"Nobody knows," he said. "Nobody but one man."

"Who?" Even Shelby was caught up in the story.

"Remember the train robbery and how some of the gang was shot and killed? Well, one man escaped scot free with nary a scratch."

"Jack Davis," Shelby put in.

"Very good!" J.J. was surprised to hear that he knew the story.

"He'd done such a good job of blendin' in with the populace; he took up his old trade of drivin' stage coaches."

"Jack never drove a stage in his life. He was a cattle drover." Frank cut in.

But, J.J. didn't miss a beat. "Like he done in Deadwood," the leader said, pointedly. "Only down here in Texas." He looked at the wide eyes of the girls. "Then, he decided he wanted to start a new life and all that. But," he held up a finger.

"He didn't have his share of the money," Shelby put in again.

"That's right!" J.J. slapped his leg in high humor, which made his horse startle. "Sam had it and Davis come back for it." He laughed at the thought.

"What happened?" Evie's eyes were wide.

"I told you, the Rangers shot Sam down in Round Rock, but he got away." It was clear J.J. was relishing the telling of the story. "Yet, he was hard hit and only made it as far as a farm outside of town. Here come Mr. Pascoe, otherwise known as Jack Davis, a drivin' the stage. He stopped to see if he could give assistance to a man lyin' in the shade of a tree, not knowin' who the man was. But, when he was face to face, he recognized him."

Evie noticed that the two riders near the back of the wagon had come closer, to listen as well.

"Sam begged him and begged him to take him away in the stage, but Pascoe wouldn't do it."

"He was too far gone and wouldn't let me help him," Frank said in quiet rebuttal.

"But, you know what he did do?" J.J. asked the girls.

Evie shook her head.

"Sam told Pascoe where the money was hidden. Forty five thousand dollars in gold coins."

All eyes went to Frank.

"That part is true," he admitted. "But, it's more like thirty five thousand. Sam liked treating everyone to drinks and he paid off the debts of a few men he thought were friends, like J.J. here."

"You lie!" J.J. jabbed spurs into his horse once more, but this time, his pistol was pointed at Frank's body.

"You want to know where the gold is?" Frank asked calmly. He pulled the team to a stop. "This is the turnoff."

J.J. stood in his stirrups and looked around. "We searched every inch of this area, years ago." His eyes were slits as they slid to Frank. "Are you sure?"

"I'm sure."

But, J.J. was not convinced. He backed his horse up until his pistol was pointed into the wagon. "Should we use the Truth Test?" His voice rang out, a challenge. "Which one goes first?"

Nancy brought her girls closer to her.

"I'm tellin' the truth," Frank said, tiredly. "This is the turnoff."

J.J. released the hammer of his pistol and rode up beside Frank. "Well, let's turn off, then."

"You're low down!" Shelby leaned forward. "You'd murder an innocent woman and her children to get him to talk?"

"Boy, that money's been lyin' out there a long time. And, there's a lot of it," he said with satisfaction. "An' I'll pay any price to get it."

"You may pay with your life, when the law comes after you!"

"What law?" J.J. scoffed. "What law there is has left and gone to the fort!"

"For now," Shelby settled back in his seat.

J.J. laughed. "That boy of yours needs an eddication! Law is where you find it, ain't that right, Pascoe? And, I think I just found it!" He raised his pistol and laughed, his men joining in.

"I'm not his boy," Shelby said, sullenly.

"I wouldn't claim him for a Pa, either, boy." He leaned over his horse to look at Shelby. "How'd you ketch him, son? The outlaw, Frank Pascoe, otherwise known as Jack Davis?"

The young man sat back, his arms crossed over his chest and his lips pressed together.

"Talk to me, boy. How'd it come about? Brace him on the street? Straight up, man to man?" He laughed derisively.

Shelby continued to look straight ahead, silent.

"You want me to tell you how it was?" J.J. leaned forward, his pistol pointed negligently in the direction of the wagon seat. "He was dead drunk for you to take him or you'd a been dead." Something in his voice brooked no argument. "Wasn't that it?"

Shelby cleared his throat. "Liquor was involved."

Beside him, Frank cast a glance his way, but kept driving.

"I knew it! I knew it!" J.J. was jubilant. "Wa'nt no man quicker with a pistol than Frank Pascoe, back in the day. That's why Sam wanted him along for the robbery!" He looked at him. "How are you now, Frank? Lost any speed?"

"That was ten years ago. We've all lost something."

Beside him, Shelby looked at him with new eyes.

"Now, he's a philos- a-feezer!" J.J. laughed loudly again.

"I reckon there's still Indians about, boss," Slim put in, quietly.

"You sayin' I'm too loud?" The leader was suddenly angry. "Why, this wagon's loud enough to wake the hull Indian nation!"

It was true. Between the squeaking of the wagon, the sound of the horses and leather, they were fairly noisy.

As they progressed, the track they were following grew rougher, with stone outcroppings tipping the wagon first one way, then the other. At times, Nancy and her daughters were hard put to stay in place. But, she managed to keep the rifle from sliding about. The sound of metal scraping on the wagon boards would have alerted the outlaws to it.

"You sure this is the road, Pascoe?" The other man that J.J. called Hack spoke up. "Sure is hell on the wagon."

"I don't think Sam brought a wagon out this way," was the reply.

"What I cain't figger," J.J. rode up beside the wagon. "Is why you didn't take the money and run when Sam told you."

Frank glanced at him. "I didn't have much chance. Someone told 'em I was Jack Davis and that put an end to my wanderin' for a while."

"Well, what about now? I mean, there was some time between when you got out and now."

"I had some business to tend to."

"In Ohio?" J.J. said, with meaning.

Frank nodded. "In Ohio." He glanced around them at the lowering sun. "We're going to need to camp soon. It's getting' dark. We'll miss the trail."

In the back of the wagon, Evie turned to face the rear, noticing the way the sky was growing darker. One of the riders came close to the wagon and leaned in. Even in the shadows, she knew who it was.

"Mama?" She said, quietly.

Nancy had been tending to Stella and had not noticed anything else.

"Uncle Albert."

Yet, the man had pulled away before her mother looked up. Nancy pulled the strap that released the curtain and it fell down, blocking them from view. Outside, she could hear his horse grunt from the violence of his legs and spurs as he rode away, answering J.J.'s call to make camp.

In the wagon, Nancy smiled at Evie, then gave a pat to the pocket in her skirt with the derringer in it.

Chapter THIRTEEN

"THIS IS REAL HOMEY LIKE, AIN'T IT," J.J. stood to one side of the camp, surveying the group.

Nancy was at the fire frying side meat, while Slim and Hack sat to one side, eating. Both Frank and Shelby were tied to a wagon wheel with the promise of being untied long enough to eat when the meal was ready.

"I could get used to having a woman around," he went on.

Frank looked up, but Nancy was ignoring the man.

At the horses, Albert stood guard, a rifle in his hand, but his eyes were on the camp.

In the wagon, Evie played with Stella, waiting their turn for food as well. When she heard the words, her eyes went to the long wrinkle in the quilt where the rifle was hidden.

J.J. walked to the fire and held out his plate.

Nancy filled it, then opened the Dutch oven and gave him some biscuits as well.

"Thank ya, Miz Pascoe," the man said with a grin.

For a moment, it seemed that Nancy might correct him. Frank

cleared his throat and she gave a little smile. "You are most certainly welcome." Her eyes went to the wagon. "Girls. Dinner."

Evie and Stella ate from the same plate, then the older girl cleaned all the plates so that Albert and the prisoners could eat. On the one hand, Nancy was concerned with the amount of food being consumed, but on the other, realized it might not matter.

When night came, it seemed darker than before, with no moon to brighten the sky. Camp was quiet in the dark, hushed as if knowing that sound might attract attention. In the bed of the wagon, her daughters slept on either side of their mother. Though it made it hotter, the curtains were down. Outside, Frank and Shelby rested as best they could, still tied to the wagon wheels.

The wagon moved and Nancy's eyes opened, then almost immediately shut. A man was starting to crawl in the back over the tailgate. Her hand closed over the derringer. Then, he gave a grunt and fell backward. There was the sound of more blows and grunting.

Slowly, she opened her eyes to see that the curtain was pulled wide and J.J. stood silhouetted against the stars.

"Sorry to disturb you, ma'am."

She gripped the derringer.

J.J. looked down at the fallen man. "He knew better than to do that."

Nancy nodded, but said nothing.

"Good night, Miz Pascoe." The curtain closed and the wagon was once more in darkness.

Outside, she could hear Frank let out his breath and she lay there a long time, staring at the canvas roof.

Breakfast was over quickly, probably because J.J. was eager to get to the money. At the picket line, men saddled horses and Frank and Shelby harnessed the team.

Nancy walked up to J.J. who kicked sand on the fire. "I wanted to thank you for what you did last night."

"Wa'nt nuthin'," was the reply. His eyes went to Albert's back as he saddled his horse. "He's a new man to me. I allus keep an eye on the new men." He grinned at her. "Don't wanna be like Sam. Get betrayed."

He looked at Frank. "My old gang wouldn't harm a woman." His voice rang out. "Ain't that right, Pascoe?"

"Thank you anyway," Nancy went on. She glanced at Frank, then at J.J. "And, my name is not Mrs. Pascoe. It's Cyrus. Mrs. Oliver Cyrus."

J.J. smiled. "Yes, ma'am. I knew that, too. The new man, Albert. He told me."

She frowned a little. "Then, why?"

"I like the truth, Miz Cyrus. And, I throw little bits of bait out there, to see who takes it."

Nancy straightened. "You're a strange man, Mr. Wilson. If you knew my true name, why did you take me and my children from the safety of the town?"

The outlaw leader rocked back on his heels. "I'll tell you, Miz Cyrus. It's because friend Albert didn't tell me til we was well on the road."

She nodded, then glanced at Albert who had turned toward the camp at the same time. Inadvertently, she shuddered.

"He's a mess, ain't he?" J.J. grinned. "Horse kicked him in the face. That's why he didn't come make hisself welcome in the daylight." The man laughed. "Ain't that right, Albert?"

Frank looked up and watched him walk by.

"He needs to get that looked after." Though Nancy cared not for the man, he was as she admitted to herself, still family. And, one of God's creatures.

"That's what I told him, too. But, he's insistin' on goin' with us." The man said, mockingly. "What with the Indians out and about, I couldn't say no."

His gaze traveled to Albert. "I've got an idee that he's playin' his own game." His words were soft and musing. Then, J.J. looked at her and smiled. "But, don't you worry. You won't come to no harm from him!" His tone dropped as he added, "I don't hold with harmin' women."

It was strange to think that she had an outlaw to thank for saving her from a relative, but the West was a different place and she reasoned that God would use the tools at hand to keep her and the girls safe.

With her chin up, Nancy climbed into the back of the wagon with her girls while Shelby took his place on the seat. Frank clucked to the horses, slapped the reins on their rumps and they were off. If Evie missed having Gypsy to ride, she did not say, since both the mare and the white gelding had been left in Denton. Nancy had to admit that she was glad to have her close by rather than on horseback.

The cavalcade of horses and wagon had not gone far when Frank halted the team and stood up to look around.

"You ain't lost, are you?" J.J. rode up beside the wagon. "Thought you said that was the turnoff." He jerked his head back the way they'd come.

Frank looked at him. "Things change in ten years."

The outlaw's eyes narrowed. "Thought you said you didn't come out when Sam told you."

A slight smile was on Frank's lips. "Well then," he said, "Things change in two years."

Slim had ridden up beside J.J. and he looked from one to the other.

"Sam give you the secret ten years ago and you never come lookin' for it?"

"Hard thing to do when you're in prison for eight years," Frank reminded him, sat down, then called to the team. The wagon started with a jerk.

"He went to prison?" Slim had not heard this part of the story. "For what?"

"For Jack Davis," the outlaw leader grinned with satisfaction.

"Jack? Jack's been gone these many years."

"I know it and you know it, but the Law didn't know it."

"They thought Frank was Jack?" Slim shook his head. "So. He went to prison." He turned in his saddle to look at his leader. "Eight years." The man frowned. "Eight years out of ten."

"I see where you're headed with that. They's somethin' missin'," J.J. agreed. "Somethin' he's not tellin' us."

The wagon tilted sharply as it went over a shelf of rock. Stella went sliding across the floor with a squeal and grinned when she stopped against the side.

"And, I think I know how to make him tell."

Slim followed his leader's gaze. "Them's no relation to him."

Just then, Frank called behind him to see if everyone was alright. Stella assured him she was fine with a little laugh.

"Maybe not by blood." J.J. urged his horse forward.

"You said you'd not harm women," Slim reminded him.

"They's more than women on this trip."

Slim followed his leader's gaze to where Shelby sat on the wagon seat beside Frank.

At their nooning, Slim brought Frank a cup of coffee as he sat by the wagon wheel, tethered to it by a rope around his feet. "I understand you went to prison."

Frank took the coffee and biscuit the man brought him.

"For what?"

The man on the ground ignored him.

"I asked you a question!" Slim kicked the sole of Frank's boot.

But, when Frank looked up, his gaze went to J.J.

"I'd like to know, too," the outlaw said with a humorless smile.

"Train robbery."

"You lie!" J.J. sprang to his feet. "No one has been tried for that robbery and you know it!"

Frank regarded him calmly. "I'm talking the Flat Gap holdup." His eyes were cold. "The other holdup Jack Davis is supposed to have taken part in."

As usual, after certain duties were taken care of, Stella would go back to the wagon and eat her meals there. Evie would join her and after the men had their food, Nancy would as well.

The girls kept their voices quiet, half-listening to what the men were saying, but their mother paid more attention. Her ears were attuned to the conversation outside when Evie took her wrist and wiggled it.

"Rider, Mama!"

Nancy looked up just in time to see a horse and rider disappear off the trail. "I seen him."

Outside, Frank continued the conversation with J.J. and Slim. Off to the side, Hack sat eating his meal, head down, but listening. Over by the horses, Albert sat, unabashedly eavesdropping.

"Jack was so cocky after the UP holdup that he decided to do it again." Frank's gaze met J.J.'s. "With you."

"You got that backwards," Slim corrected him. "Boss talked Jack into that job."

Frank ignored him. "I was a hundred miles away when you held up that train. But, I went to prison for it."

"I didn't know, Frank," J.J. was contrite. "I swear, I didn't know."

It was such a change from his usual bravado that everyone took note.

"They kept it quiet cause they wanted to get the rest of the gang."

Everyone in the camp looked from Frank to the outlaw who paced before him.

"So. That's why you went to prison."

"Yep. The law don't like it when an expressman and a conductor get killed during a robbery," Frank's voice was wry. "They think someone oughta pay."

"I give that expressman a warning, but he went for his gun anyway." J.J. smiled. "Some people don't care to live oncet they been robbed."

"What about the conductor?" Shelby asked, lured into the conversation.

J.J. made an impatient gesture. "He come up behind us with no warning. He deserved what he got."

"Some people just like to shoot unarmed men," was Frank's observation.

"You preach it, Pascoe." The smile was gone and the man's temper flared. "When the time comes, you'll have a gun in your hand."

"Loaded?"

"Yes, damn you!" J.J. flung out the words and spun on his heel as if to leave. Instead, he tugged at the bottom of his short jacket and walked around, his chin up. "I ain't afraid of you, Pascoe. Never was. Never will be."

Frank lifted an eyebrow but said nothing.

"Who cares who is afraid of who?" Shelby scoffed. "You've got the advantage!"

"And you'd best remember it," J.J. grinned at him and patted his holster. "I hold all the cards."

During the afternoon, clouds came and covered most of the sky, but it was still hot. The wagon creaked and protested as it crossed the rough country of stone and scrub. Evie and her mother walked along beside it, both for the coolness and to save the horses. Inside, Stella alternately played with her doll and dozed.

Since Nancy walked near the wagon, Frank began talking to her quietly.

"If I hadn't broke jail, this wouldn't have happened." His tone was soft but terse.

"That's right!" Shelby broke in, but neither paid attention to him.

Nancy nodded her head, slowly. "Yes. But, if you hadn't come along in Lester's Landing, I wouldn't have my little girls. If you hadn't been on the boat on the river, I wouldn't be here walking this earth."

A slight smile crossed her lips. "And, it is likely, I wouldn't be here, either. In Texas. The West."

"You're a strange woman, Miss Nancy," he said, softly, then called to the team. "Git up there, Tommy!"

She looked at him, her head tilted. "God uses us where we are." Then, her vision went inward, to a memory. "I'm glad you were there when Cecil was born."

"You did most of that on your own," he shook his head.

"You were there," was her quiet reply.

Her eyes went to the horizon where a gold band separated land and sky. "If I hadn't been so deadset on coming west, none of this would have happened." Her voice was husky as her gaze came back to him. "And though I loathe the fact that you broke the law, that you broke jail, I wouldn't have it any other way."

"Mama! Mama!" Stella reached out her hands to be taken from the wagon. Me, too!"

"Not now, Leelee," Nancy smiled at her. "We need your foot to get better."

But, after that little conversation, she and Evie walked a little behind where Frank sat and no other words were spoken between them.

When the wagon halted on a rise, J.J. rode up to it, demanding to know why Frank had stopped.

"Getting my bearings."

"Damn your bearings!" J.J's patience was thinning. "I thought you knew where this place was!"

"I told you," Came the quiet reply. "A lot has changed."

At the back of the wagon, Evie looked at the country behind them. Her hand reached for her mother's.

"I see him," her mother said, softly.

"Who is he?" Evie asked.

Nancy shook her head. "I don't know."

After another glance, the girl turned away so as not to draw attention to him. If only he would raise his head a little and get his face out of shadow, she thought, and then she would know if he was the man with the thick black moustache.

That evening, they camped at the bottom of a rocky outcropping. At its base, a small stream ran along it while overhanging trees shaded it.

"How far, Frank?" J.J.'s pistol clicked as the hammer was pulled back.

Frank looked up to see the pistol pointed at Shelby. If he was surprised, he didn't show it.

"Not far," was the reply. "I got turned around a bit this afternoon."

"It's good country to do that in," Slim agreed wholeheartedly. "All this rock and no big landmarks!"

"Shut up, Slim," J.J. growled. He waggled the pistol. "Show me."

Frank walked out of the camp, Slim and Hack following with Shelby pushed in front of J.J.'s pistol. On the other side of the creek, they climbed a large earthen mound with shrubs about its crown. He had just reached the height when he suddenly lay down. Everyone followed suit.

"What is it?" J.J. asked, softly.

"Indians."

The outlaw crawled up beside Frank and followed his gaze down to a wash on the other side. "I don't see 'em."

"In that group of trees," Frank nodded toward a grove of live oak trees.

"I see 'em," Slim spoke up.

And they all stared at the group of trees, waiting for a group of Indians to come out.

Behind them at the creek, Evie and Stella were playing in the water. It was shallow, but because of the trees and shade from the rocky cliff, the creek was cool. Downstream of them, Albert watered the horses, his eyes never leaving the children.

When it seemed that the girls were getting too loud in their splashing of one another, Nancy motioned for them to come out. They grabbed hands and skipped up the bank to their mother. She was glad to see that Stella was favoring her foot less and less.

It wasn't long after that, Nancy looked around, noticing the lack of activity. The camp was quiet, with the men down at the creek or on the hill. Her girls were under the wagon, playing dolls and getting visibly sleepy. She would have liked to give in to that as well. But, first, perhaps she could have some time to herself.

The shadowed pools of water in the creekbed called to her and she walked to it, further upstream from where her daughters had been. The creek was intermittent, depending on rain and snow for its water supply. But, trees lined its course and the undercut banks offered plenty of shade.

Most of the creek bed was dry, but every little bit, where it was shaded most of the day, there were shallow pools. Yet, under a slanted cliff where the creek undercut it, she found a deep pool. A large flat rock hung out over the clear green water, and she knelt down to touch it. The coolness prompted her to sit down and take off her boots.

Her shoulders sagged as her body relaxed with the effect of the water. Birds called in the little glade and a soft breeze caressed her cheeks. She put a hand in the creek and trickled water on the back of her neck. It was cooling, soothing.

Something caught her attention and she opened her eyes to see a deer crossing the creek before her. It halted and looked her way, eyes wide and ears up. In another moment, it flicked its tail and bounded up the bank.

Nancy started to turn to see what had startled it just as a rough hand covered her mouth. Another arm wrapped around her, strong, like an iron band. Yet, she struggled and used the back of her head to smash her assailant in the face.

He yelled out and for a moment, relaxed his grip. Nancy sprang to her feet to run, but he grabbed her again. She fought him and beat at him with her fists. She didn't need to see his face to know who it was.

"Let me go, Albert!"

But, he held onto her, dodging the knee she brought up to his groin and avoiding the elbows to his already swollen and bruised face. Seen up close and in daylight, Nancy could see that his jaw was misshapen and his mouth drooled because he couldn't close it.

He grabbed her by the hair on the back of her head and leaning forward, pushed her down to the ground. Nancy scratched his face with one hand, while the other searched in her skirt pocket.

She was able to wriggle free one leg and kneed him. He hesitated, then put an elbow across her chest, holding her down, while he sought her other hand with his own. Nancy struggled and tried to push him off. But, only using one hand made the task almost impossible.

Was there a shout? She couldn't tell because she was so focused on her assailant. His loud breathing shut out any other sound. She kept her right hand away from his grasp and pushed upward with her body, trying to throw him off. But, he pressed down all the harder. Her fingers found the pocket of her skirt and slipped inside.

A gunshot rang out. Albert stiffened, his eyes opened wide in surprise. "Dammit woman!"

Nancy tried to push him away, but he was heavy and sagged onto her before rocking back on his knees. "Don't make me shoot you again!"

Albert stared at her then looked down. Blood covered the front of his shirt. "You shot me!" He looked at her accusingly.

"You. You give me no choice!" She rolled away and stood up,

breathing hard. "I swear to God!"

He put a hand to his midsection, as if marveling at the fact that he was shot and she had done it. He tried to get to his feet but fell back.

From downstream came voices, one of which was Evie's crying out, "Mama! Mama!"

Nancy waved her away, but she didn't see the motion, her wide eyes on Albert.

"What happened, Mama?

"Go back to Stella." Nancy's voice was firm. "Don't you leave her again."

Obediently, the girl turned away, even as she asked, "Are you alright, Mama?"

"Yes. Do as I tell you." Her tone brooked no disobedience.

With a glance over her shoulder, the girl disappeared around the bend.

"Ain't you gonna help me?" Albert asked, put out that he was shot.

Nancy got to her feet and shook her head. "You don't deserve help. You took advantage of a grievin' widow." She knew she was shaking, but couldn't help it. "You took what wasn't yourn."

"I allus did like you, you know that."

"You got a strange way of showin' it."

Albert grimaced. "You got in my haid. I couldn't get you out." His face twisted as pain took hold. "The baby. What about the baby?" He tried to grin. "Our baby."

She crossed her arms across her chest. "Daid. Born daid."

"You lie!" Albert tried to shout, but groaned instead. "You killed it. Like you done to me!"

Nancy stared at him. Was it true? Had she killed him, when she knew it was a sin to kill? No! Surely she only meant to stop him.

He groaned again.

"No." She didn't believe she'd killed him, then shook her head to his question. "It was born daid," her voice was soft and sad. "The most perfect little baby you ever saw, but with the spark of life missin'."

Albert turned his head to watch J.J., Frank and Slim come running up. They took in the scene in a glance and when Frank would have gone to Nancy, J.J. stopped him.

"Up to yore old tricks agin', Al?" He looked at Nancy appraisingly. "An' she done for you?"

"Am I?" Albert raised up, beseechingly, as if the outlaw's words made it true. "Am I done for?" He looked down at himself. "I ain't that bad hurt, am I?"

"Sure looks bad, hit low like that," J.J. came forward and knelt beside him.

Albert moved his hands from his wound so that the man could see.

J.J. nodded. "I seen it afore. It will take you awhile, but you'll die." There was no doubt in his voice. "Nuthin' we can do."

"What about her?" Albert pointed at Nancy. "She can heal anythin', at least that's what's said at the Forks."

J. J. looked at him. "What about her husband?" He stood up and hooked his thumbs in his gunbelt. "She didn't heal him, did she?"

On the ground, Albert fretted from side to side. "I'm a' hurtin'. Got any whisky?"

Slim grunted with disgust. "I didn't hold with bringin' him on, anyway." He spat with contempt. "Any man who would mistreat a woman!"

"With the Indians about, we needed all the guns we could get." J.J. looked at Frank. "What about that, Pascoe? You said you saw Indians." He looked about them. "But, I don't see any."

Regardless of J.J. trying to block him from getting to Nancy, Frank now stood beside her, close but not touching. She still held the derringer in her hand, but he made no attempt to take it.

"Light caliber weapon." He looked around. "Wind blowing toward us. Their horses splashing in the water. Might not have heard it."

"Speakin' of weapons," Slim spoke up. "She's still got it."

"And, she'll keep it," J.J. scanned the area around them. "If there are Indians around, she may need it." He looked at Frank. "Get your bearings up there?"

"Good enough."

"Well, let's go." J.J. motioned that they should go back to camp.

"Go?" Albert's voice rose. "And leave me here?"

The outlaw leader stood over him. "I sure didn't mean to leave here with less men than I come with. But, you stepped into the hornet's nest. Guess you'll have to pay the price."

"No!" The fallen man held out a beseeching, blood covered hand. "Don't leave me here!"

J.J. knelt down beside him. "Hush now! Else them Indians will give you somethin' to holler about." He glanced up at Slim and nodded. "Slim will stay with you while I go make a place for you in the wagon."

"Thankee, boss!" Albert sank back gratefully. Because of his swollen mouth, he hissed the word, 'boss.' "Thankee!"

At the wagon, Nancy gripped the front wheel and pulled on it, shaking her head from side to side. "I've killed a man!" She trembled, then put a hand over her stomach. "I've killed Ollie's brother!"

"No!" Frank walked up behind her. "You defended yourself." He put his hands on her shoulders and tried to turn her to face him.

"I've killed the last of the Cyrus's!" She put an arm over her face, as if to blot out the sight.

Her body turned this way and that, as if to somehow escape the thought of her act. "God made woman to bring life into this world. Not to take it."

This time, Frank was able to turn her around and bring her into his arms. Taking a shuddering breath, she quieted.

"No. You didn't kill him." The word was said quietly and she looked up into his eyes. He was looking toward the creek.

Nancy followed his gaze. Down by the water's edge, where the ground was soft, Slim was plunging a knife blade into the dirt, to cleanse it of blood.

"I believe he has killed a man."

Chapter
FOURTEEN

Though she passed out biscuits and leftover side meat from breakfast, Nancy did not feel like eating and her girls barely nibbled on their portions. They had not witnessed Albert's death, but they knew something had happened and stayed close to her.

Frank finished hitching the horses to the wagon and started to climb onto the seat when J.J. stretched out an arm and wheeled him around.

"Where is it, Pascoe?" The outlaw said, loudly. "The old gang already went over this area." He backhanded Frank across the face. "Lost your way?" This time, he punched him in the face. "Or did you drink it out of your memory?" His other fist doubled the man over with the blow.

J. J. stepped back and pulled his pistol, pointing it at Shelby who sat on the seat, watching. "Shoot the cub?"

Nancy gathered her girls behind her, trying to hide their faces. Was the young man going to be killed in front of them?"

"Shoot your lady friend?" The outlaw asked, lazily bringing the pistol around to aim at her.

"I'll tell you!" It was a struggle, but Frank stood upright.

J.J. hit him in the stomach again, doubling him over.

"I'll show you!"

"Where is it?"

"Not far!"

"You better be tellin' the truth!" J.J. clubbed Frank with the pistol and he dropped to the ground.

Regardless of how close or far the gold was did not matter, for they'd barely gone half a mile when the left front wheel of the wagon fell off and broke two spokes on a rock. Tommy snorted and lunged, threatening to bolt with the sudden change of weight, but Frank soothed him into standing still beside Tony.

"Help them," he told Shelby, nodding to the back of the wagon. He kept hold of the reins, even as he stepped down to the ground.

Quietly, the young man helped Nancy and her girls out of the wagon and ushered them to the side of the trail.

J.J. rode up and looked at the wheel then at Frank. "You did that."

"Tell me how and when," was the reply. Though his face was bruised, his gaze remained steady as he returned J.J.'s accusing stare.

For answer, the outlaw kicked his horse into a lope and rode to the next rise. He spun the animal around, surveying the land about them. Then, he charged back down the slope, to pull up to a sliding stop in front of them.

He looked over the faces turned to him. "What to do? What to do? That wagon is sure slowin' us down." Of course, that meant that the passengers were slowing him down as well.

"Leave you here?" J.J. grinned at Nancy.

"We have Albert's horse," Slim reminded him.

"That's right," the outlaw agreed. "Ain't much of a horse, but Frank can ride it. Frank can ride anything."

"I'm not leavin' them."

"I'm not askin' your opinion," J.J. reined his horse to bump into him. Frank pushed back at him, then stepped aside when the outlaw continued to urge the animal into him.

"Why don't we put 'em all on horses?" Slim asked.

"That one rides," Frank nodded to Tony, the off horse. "This one doesn't." He gave Tommy a pat on the rump.

"We could leave him behind," Slim's chin indicated Shelby.

"No," Frank cut in. "We all go."

"Wal, that makes it a problem, don't it?" J.J. looked up at the sky, as if considering the time of day. Then, he narrowed his eyes at Frank. "Well, Mr. Pascoe, looks like you have bought yourself some more time." He leaned on his saddle horn. "Fix it."

Frank looked at him.

J.J.'s eyes narrowed. "Where'd you do your time?"

"Montana."

"Well then, I'm sure you know about fixing wagon wheels." He looked about them. "There's plenty trees about. Fix it."

It was as J.J. had said. Frank knew about fixing wagon wheels. Nancy had bought the wagon in the East, where there was more humidity and moisture. Now that they were in Texas where the air was drier, the wheels had dried out and their metal tires threatened to come off. The left front wheel had lost its tire only a little ways before coming off, so it was easily found and replaced.

Devising a jack from some dead trees, Frank took off each wheel in turn and soaked it in the creek. Before soaking the right front wheel, he eased one of the spokes out and put it in the left front wheel.

"I think they'll be alright, just missing one spoke," he told Nancy.

"But, you're gonna have to walk some."

"We can manage that," was her reply.

"Stella can ride," he quickly put in. "Beside me."

Nancy knew that he meant if it came to a wreck, he would grab the little girl and jump. If she remained in the wagon bed, it might turn over and throw her out.

"Thank you," Nancy was grateful for his consideration, but at the moment, it was hard to feel anything. Whether he deserved it or not, Albert was dead and she'd had a hand in it. Back at the Forks, the women would nod their heads and say he got what was coming to him, but the men? What would the men say? She certainly would not be on their list of eligible women to marry. The thought made her almost laugh. It was one of the reasons she had gone west. If she decided to marry again, there weren't that many men around the Forks that she would consider eligible.

The sky darkened early that afternoon, threatening a storm, so they did not move on even after the wheels were fixed.

"I wish I could promise you protection," Frank spoke, his voice soft. "But, I can't." His hands were bound behind him as he sat tied once more to the front wagon wheel.

Nancy moved around the campfire making supper, but her ears were attuned to his voice.

"Maybe not," she replied, then looked to the sky above. "But, He can."

Frank made an impatient sound, but she smiled.

The camp was deserted for the moment. J.J. was riding to the top of the rise yet again, as if at some point, he would be able to see what he desired. Slim had gone with him, Hack was watering the team and her girls were playing in the back of the wagon. Frank thought it wouldn't harm the wagon any since it was stopped.

At the back wheel Shelby was tied, but his attention was on the voices of the girls inside the wagon.

Frank tried again. "I apologize."

Nancy startled a little, not expecting him to speak. "For what?"

"For getting you and your girls into this." He leaned this way and that, straining at his bonds.

Nancy stopped and looked at him. "This?"

"My bad choices." He shook his head in frustration and cursed under his breath.

Nancy glanced up the slope to where J.J. and Slim sat their horses, then knelt down close to the fire. "I believe God has a hand in everything." She turned a little so that her eyes met his. "And, regardless of how this turns out, we were meant to be here."

Frank looked at her, his chest heaving from his exertion, and his eyes held a question. "Everything?"

She held a quietness about her that brooked no question. "Everything."

There came the sound of the riders approaching the camp and she stood up to finish the cooking.

"If there's any way to keep you safe," Frank called to her, just enough so that she could hear. "I will do it."

Though her back was to him, she nodded to show that she had heard.

"Like hell," Shelby muttered and he gave Frank a hard look. It was certain that he did not believe him.

J.J. rode up to the camp and dismounted with a flourish, throwing the reins to Slim who walked off to take care of their horses.

"What's for supper?" His mouth stretched in a grin as his eyes went from Nancy to Frank. Walking over to the prisoner, he kicked his boot. "Can you feel it? Getting' closer all the time, aren't we?"

When Evie and Stella came around from the back of the wagon, J.J's eyes lit up. "Hullo girlies!" He glanced at the man at the wagon wheel. "Makes you long for hearth and home, don't it, Frank?"

Nancy walked over to them, looking each one in the face. "No playin' in the creek. Get washed up and hurry on back up here." Her hand slipped into the pocket of her skirt, then into Evie's.

"Yes, ma'am," Evie felt the weight of the derringer in her pocket, but made no sign it was there. "Come on, Stella."

"You won't get away with this," Shelby spoke up.

"What?" J.J. seemed surprised. "The cub speaks?"

"This," Shelby went on, indicating the camp with his head. "Murdering the lot of us."

"I have no thought of murderin' anyone!" He looked at Slim who came into the firelight.

Clouds covered the horizon, blocking the light of the sinking sun and bringing the dark of evening more quickly. An occasional flash of lightning heralded a coming storm.

"I bet it was the Indians that did it!" J.J. went on and laughed at his own humor.

"I'm sure of it," Slim agreed. "Massacreed the whole bunch of 'em!"

Both men laughed at their humor, but only Shelby seemed effected by it. He tugged at his bonds, seeking a weakness, but they held and he sank back, discouraged.

Down at the creek, Evie and Stella dutifully washed their faces and hands. If they kicked at the water to make it bounce into waves, no one knew but them. Or so they thought. There was a noise in the bushes beyond and Evie stopped, her hand going to the derringer in her pocket.

The man with the black moustache emerged from his hiding place, a finger to his lips. In his other hand, he held something round and silver that gleamed in the dim light. He beckoned to them and smiled encouragingly.

Still, Evie stood on the opposite bank, considering. Stella tugged at her hand, trying to reach a stone in the creek.

The man tipped his hat to Evie and that decided her. With her hand on the derringer, she walked closer to him.

At the camp, Nancy lifted the lid of the Dutch oven to see that the biscuits were almost ready. She would have made johnny cakes, but she'd used up all of the cornmeal feeding the Indians.

Off to the side, J.J. strode back and forth, which told of nervous tension.

A bright flash of lightning made him jerk, and with the resulting roll of thunder, he laughed. "Never could stand lightning," he spoke. "Not since that stampede at the Red River.

Remember that, Frank?"

"It's not something you forget," was the calm reply.

"Balls of lightning, bouncing off the horns of the cattle." J.J. stared into the darkness. "Lightnin' right on top of us. I was close enough to one to get my arm singed!"

"And how many men lost in the stampede?" Frank asked softly.

"Too many. Billy Powell was one of 'em."

"Your partner."

J.J. shook his head. "Some things stay with you all your life." He glanced at Frank.

"Findin' his hand here and his boots and spurs over there," Frank went on.

The outlaw gave an involuntary shudder. "Had a dream about him just last night."

"Aw, you act like you care!" Shelby leaned forward, his face screwed with fury. "You'd kill women and children like it was nothing!" He spat. "You're the dregs of humanity!"

J.J. stood stock still as if shocked into immobility. "The cub speaks." Then he turned and indicated the young man. "Shut him up."

Slim held a pistol and nonchalantly backhanded him. With the blow, Shelby sank to the side, stunned.

From the deepening shadows around the camp, Hack walked forward.

"I've done yer biddin' fer quite a few years now, boss," said the big man, slowly. "But, I don't hold with harmin' no chillern."

J.J. looked from him to Slim then back again, his tone and attitude contemptuous. "What do I have here? A bunch of yeller bellies? Slim don't want no woman harmed and you don't want no children hurt?" He put his hands on his hips, indignant. "I'm the boss around here! If I say someone dies, they die. And, if I say a child or two gets sold to the Comancheros, they get sold."

"Boss!" Hack stared at him for a moment, his face a mixture of hurt and disbelief at betrayal.

As if realizing he had said too much, J.J. looked around, noticing that Nancy had stopped moving, frozen to the spot. Behind her, Frank and Shelby gazed at him. It was worth noting that the young man stared incredulously while Frank gauged him.

"But, my mind could be changed at any moment." He added with a shrug.

Behind him, Hack came forward, fixated on his leader. "You'd sell chillern to the Comancheros?"

"We're in this for the money, ain't we?" J.J. asked as the man came up to him. It was almost comical to see the big burly man tower over the outlaw yet be subservient to him.

"Not the chillern," Hack's voice was growing firm as if he had decided something.

"Aw hell, Hack," Slim spoke up. "You took the money we got at Fort Stockton."

Hack stared at J.J. "You sold the chillern? The chillern we found after their Ma and Pa had been killed?"

J.J. shrugged. "We couldn't take 'em with us!"

With a yell, Hack lunged forward, his hands going for J.J.'s throat. But, in the next moment, he stiffened and staggered forward, Slim's big knife in his back.

J.J. looked around the camp, his eyes landing on Shelby. "Anyone got anything else to say?"

At the wagon wheel, the young man's eyes seemed about to pop out of his head. It was his first time seeing a man killed.

It took both J.J. and Slim to drag Hack out of the camp and roll him into a nearby ditch. They threw a few stones onto the body with the thought that it would do for now.

While they were busy with that morbid duty, Evie and Stella returned. Unobtrusively, the older girl passed the derringer back to her mother. Nancy gave them each a biscuit and sent them to the wagon. Behind them, Slim walked into the camp, the big knife in his hand. He turned it this way and that in the dim light to make sure the blade was clean.

"You keep killin' and you'll be doin' the diggin' yourself, J.J.," was Frank's comment.

The outlaw whirled on him, his face alight. "I was right! He did bury it!"

"I buried it."

J.J. stared at him. "You?"

"After Sam told me where he had cached it, I found it and buried it."

"That's why we couldn't find it!" He looked at Slim. "He always was a sharp one, was Frank Pascoe! You couldn't get anythin' by him!"

"I thought you said you got arrested right away?" Slim asked, slowly.

Frank looked at him. "I said I got arrested. I didn't say when."

As they were speaking, Evie and Stella came from the wagon with something in their hands. Stella walked up to Frank, while Evie went up to Shelby.

"What is that?" J.J. asked sharply. "What have they got?" His right hand dropped to the butt of his pistol.

Nancy was puzzled at first, then realized what they were. "Plague bags."

"What? The plague?"

"It's a medicine bag. To keep away harmful spirits."

Frank bent forward to help Stella get the neck string over his head.

"Superstitious, eh?" J.J. gave a short laugh. "I've heard of you hill people, speakin' of haints and such."

"Some say it's superstition," Nancy said softly. "Others say it is true."

They watched as Stella kissed Frank's cheek. At the other wagon wheel, Evie dropped the necklace with the little burlap pouch around Shelby's neck.

"Don't I get a kiss, too?" He asked with a lopsided grin. Already his face swelled from Slim's blow.

Evie straightened and looked into his eyes. "I only kiss when it matters."

"Only when it matters, cub!" J.J. laughed derisively. "Remember that!"

The girls turned and went to the back of the wagon while their mother followed. Outside, the men could hear low murmuring as Nancy prayed with her children and then, the wagon moved as she got out of it.

Taking up the dishes and cooking utensils, she walked down to the creek. It wasn't that far and her head bobbed in and out of view in the flickering firelight.

The wind was picking up, sometimes blowing one direction, then changing. It swirled and sparks from the fire leapt into the air in a rush. Horses stamped, then blew.

"Just the storm," Slim said to no one in particular.

But, J.J. stood up and looked anxiously in their direction. A picket line had been strung between two trees near the creek and the horses were tethered to it. Suddenly, there was the sound of scrambling, snorting and whinnying. A horse reared up and they could hear the rope snap. Jumping to his feet, Slim ran to them, J.J. following.

"Two of the horses are gone!" He held up the broken end of a rope. "Albert's and Hack's!"

"Wal, that's two we won't have to worry with."

Slim looked at the man. "You're just naturally sunny, aren't you?"

J.J. held up the end of the rope. "Broke, not cut."

When the other man did not seem to catch his drift, he went on. "Not Indians."

"A silver linin'," was Slim's ironic reply.

"If it had been Indians, they'd a taken all the horses," his leader added.

"And we'd be dead," was the other man's summation. "And not be worryin' about no women, chillern or gold," was said under his breath.

They went through the picket line, making sure the horses were tied and calming them with word and touch. When they walked back to the camp, they were met by Nancy who came around the back of the wagon, her eyes wide and staring, her hair disheveled.

"They're gone!"

J.J. looked around them, noting that Frank and Shelby remained tied to the wagon wheels. "Who?"

Nancy stepped to the wagon and drew aside a canvas curtain. "They're gone! My babies!"

He walked forward and looked around the wagon bed. Though clouds hurried over the sliver of moon, it was easy to see it was empty. "Where'd they go?"

"They took 'em!" She motioned beyond the wagon with her arm. "They took 'em!"

"Who?" Slim stood beside J.J. Both men had their hands on the butts of their pistols. "Who took 'em?"

"The haints," her eyes were wide as she pronounced the words. "I come up from the crick, just in time to see 'em. I chased 'em, grabbed for my girls, but they was too fast!"

The men stared at her.

"Naw, they've just run off," J.J. assured her, but his voice wasn't steady. He looked about the camp as the wind swirled.

Nancy's shoulders sagged as if her body was deflated. "I come West for a new life. I done the best I could." She looked up at the sky. "Lost the baby. Now, I've lost the girls." She shook her head, defeated. "I cain't do this no more."

The outlaw leader looked around uneasily. "Where did they take 'em?"

She pointed to the sky. "Up."

They all followed her gesture.

"I couldn't ketch 'em." Her gaze went to Slim and she held up her hands imploringly. "You'll help me, won't you? Help me find my girls?"

"Sure, lady. They can't have gone far." The thin man stepped forward.

"This way, this way!" Nancy beckoned him to follow her into the darkness beyond the firelight.

At the picket line, the horses began thrashing about.

"Go see to the horses!" J.J. commanded.

Slim hesitated, torn between Nancy's imploring and his boss's order.

As if to emphasize his words, J.J.'s hand slipped down to his gun.

From where he was tied to a wagon wheel, Frank said, "Looks like you're gonna be doin' your own diggin' tomorrow."

"Boss . . ." Slim looked at the man in disbelief.

"The horses!" J.J.'s voice was loud, as if volume made the command stronger.

It was with an effort that Slim looked away from Nancy. "I'm sorry, ma'am."

"Oh please!" Nancy's cry was heartbroken. "Please help me!"

Slim kept walking toward the picket line.

"Oh my girls!" Nancy called out. "My babies! Where are you?" She tugged at her hair, then wrapped her arms about her middle, as if torn between grief and fear.

"Shut up!" J.J. growled.

Nancy moved about the camp, looking here and there, distraught yet fearful of venturing into the darkness. She went up to J.J., her eyes and voice pleading. "Will you help me, sir? Will you help me get my girls?"

The man spun on his heel. "I don't know where they are." He put some distance between himself and Nancy.

But, she'd already turned away and run to where Frank sat. Dropping to her knees beside him, she held out her hands in supplication. "Oh Mister! You'll help me get my girls, won't you?"

Frank nodded. "Yes." He scanned her face as if seeking an answer to a question. "Sure I will."

"Oh thankee! Thankee kind sir!" Nancy thrust herself forward onto his chest in a hug and in the next moment leaned back. "You believe me, don't you?"

"Yes. I believe you." He gave another nod, then realized that she had slipped something under his jacket. It was heavy; heavy enough to be a pistol.

Nancy leaned forward in another quick hug. "Oh thankee, mister! Thankee!"

"Keep the faith, little lady," he assured her. "Everything will be alright."

But it was as if Nancy had forgotten what had just been agreed on. She put her hands to her head and looked at the night sky. "O my girls! Where are my girls?"

Her eyes searched the faces around her, but she wasn't seeing them.

When she took a step toward J.J., he took several steps back.

"You!" She pointed a finger at him. "You won't help, eh? You'll be callin' for help ere another day is through!" Her voice held the firmness of prophecy.

J.J. stared at her, but Nancy had already turned away.

"My girls!" She cried as she walked behind the wagon. "Where are my girls?" Her voice came back to them, an eerie echo on the night wind.

"Good riddance," Slim had returned from looking after the horses.

"What do you think she meant by that?" The outlaw pondered aloud. "Cryin' for help?"

"She's out of her head, boss."

J.J. thought for a moment. "That's too bad. Such a nice lookin' woman, too." He looked up at the sky. "You got the first watch, Slim? I'm turnin' in."

"Ain't too much night left."

"You're not gonna go look for those little girls?" Frank asked, contempt in his voice. "All alone in a strange land. At night?"

"They won't go far," J.J. assured him as he sought his blankets. "We'll find 'em in the morning."

Chapter
FIFTEEN

THE FIRE WAS LOW and the horses had quieted when a low moan came on the fitful night breeze. J.J. lay on the creek side of the fire, but did not stir. Sitting on a rock near the horses with a tree trunk as a back rest, Slim's head lay to the side, lost in slumber. Shelby's head was tilted back against a spoke, his eyes closed. Only Frank was awake and he looked about for the source of the sound.

The moan came louder.

J.J. sat up abruptly, his pistol in his hand. "What the hell is that?"

"I heard it before," Slim replied, his eyes blinking away sleep. "I think it's that woman."

"What?"

"It's comin' from the wagon."

The moan grew in volume and lasted longer.

"Shut her up," J.J. growled and lay back down, his pistol beside him.

"How?" Slim asked. "I ain't hurtin' no woman. She's grieving and got every right to it."

J.J. shuddered.

When the moan came again, he got up and went to the wagon. Lifting a curtain, he looked in. "She ain't here!"

"Of course not," was Slim's matter of fact reply, though he'd just stated the woman was in the wagon. "She's out lookin' for her chillern."

The sun had not yet appeared over the horizon when Slim released Frank's bonds.

"You say we're not far?" J.J. asked. He looked as if he hadn't slept much and the cup of coffee he'd had for breakfast had not helped his irritability.

"You can almost see it from here," Frank replied.

"Well, let's go." J.J. considered Shelby and his hand was on the butt of his pistol. "Could get rid of the excess baggage."

Frank noticed the young man had not been released and stood beside him. When he turned to face J.J., it was noticeable that he placed his body in front of him. "We all go."

Before J.J. could answer, Nancy walked around from the back of the wagon, her hair even more of a mess than before and her skirt was dirty with tears in it.

"O mister!" She walked up to Frank and tugged on his arm. "Can you help me find my girls?"

"Sure," his face and tone softened as he looked at her. "Sure I will."

"Oh thankee!" Her eyes lit up. "Thankee!" Then, she pulled him after her. "This way! This way!"

"Not now," J.J. put a hand on the butt of his pistol.

"This way! This way!" Nancy tugged the harder.

Frank tried to gently extricate himself from her grip, but it was hard. She kept trying to pull him away. Finally, he took her by both arms and looked into her eyes. "Not now!"

Nancy searched his eyes then her body slackened. "You lie. You won't help me find my girls." She sank to the ground and put her hands over her face, sobbing.

The men stared at her and J.J. shook his head.

"I hate it when they cry." The outlaw leader looked about the camp. "I wasn't gonna take the wagon, but now that she's here . ." He motioned to Frank. "Harness the team."

He was obeyed, yet, when Frank stepped up to the wagon seat, Nancy ran to him once more. "Don't go! Don't go!" She cried out. "I have a bad feelin' about this!"

Out of patience, J.J. spun her around and slapped her across the face. As she fell to the ground, he whirled to face Slim who had a hand on his pistol. "I had to do it, Slim. It was this way or daid."

For a long moment, the two men stared at one another. Then, Slim let his hand drop away from his gun.

It was up to Frank to get down, pick Nancy up in his arms and put her in the back of the wagon. His eyes went to the red mark on the side of her face and as he stood there, his jaw clenched along with his fists.

"Let's go!" J.J. motioned that he should get back in the wagon.

In a rocky land full of boulders and fitful areas of grass, with unseen washes and every rise and fall looking like the rest, it was with some surprise when the cabin came into view. The board and batten siding was dark and weathered, blending in well with the landscape. Frank's steady urging of the team over the boulders and grades brought them before it by mid-morning.

"You'd not know it was here!" J.J. remarked at the way it was built almost into a live oak tree that shaded the porch.

"It's a sweet place," was Slim's observation. He rode about the cabin and noted that it was well built and not that long ago. "Who does it belong to?"

"Me," was Frank's reply. "I built it."

J.J. and Slim looked from him to the cabin and back again.

"You had to haul a long way for all that wood," Slim commented, respect in his voice.

Frank looked at the building. "It was built for a dream I had."

"What was that?" Shelby asked from beside him. His voice no longer held a sarcastic note. Even he seemed to realize that this was the end of the road.

Light blue eyes met his. "The dream of a family."

The young man looked away.

"Quite the romantic, ain't he?" J.J. asked, jeeringly. "Where's the gold?"

"You're looking at it."

The outlaw was incredulous. "You spent thousands of dollars on that?"

Frank shook his head. "Didn't spend it."

"You buried it," J.J. remembered a previous conversation.

"I did." Frank got the rein weight out and clipped it onto Tony's bridle. "I buried it and built the cabin on top of it."

From the back of the wagon, Nancy looked at him, but it was hard to tell what she was thinking.

"Why'd you do that?" Slim asked as he dismounted.

"I got this fool idea that I'd build a cabin. Go back east and get my wife."

"Your wife?" J.J. raised his eyebrows in surprise.

"Yeah," Frank replied. "People get married." His eyes slid to Shelby. "Sometimes for the wrong reasons."

The young man shifted uncomfortably.

"I'd get my wife," Frank repeated, "and I'd bring her out here."

"That's why you went to Ohio," J.J. put in.

Frank went on, "I'd see how she liked the west and how she did in this little house. A place I built with my own hands."

Under his breath, so low that only Frank could hear it, Shelby said, "She would have hated it."

"And, if she took to it, you'd dig up the money," Slim finished for him.

"Something like that."

There was a moment of silence and quiet, as if paying respect to a man's dream that had died.

As they walked up the steps to the porch of the cabin, it was easy to see why it was situated on the rise. There was a commanding view and since it faced south, one could enjoy both sunrise and sunset from it.

Behind the cabin was a small barn and corrals. It was clear that the corrals had been kept in good repair by others using them.

"Build those, too?" Slim asked.

Frank nodded.

They followed him into the cabin.

"And the fireplace?" The thin man walked over to it and put a hand on the mantel.

Another nod from Frank.

Nancy looked down at the ashes of long dead fires, then at the smoke blackened walls of the chimney. "Draws good." It was a simple response to what she saw before her, but Frank stood a little taller.

"You went East," Slim said, slowly. "To get your family. Your wife. What happened?"

Frank shrugged. "I had been gone too long. She thought I was dead. Married another."

J.J. came in from looking at the two bedrooms and laughed loudly. "You get all the breaks, don't you, Frank?"

At the sink, there was a pump handle. Slim worked it a few times and water came out. "All the comforts of home."

The next moment, Nancy exclaimed, "Oh no!" She stared at the corner of the room nearest the fireplace. "Haints!"

"What?" At her first cry, Slim had put a hand on his gun.

"Haints!" Nancy wheeled about, motioning with her hand. "This place is full of haints!" And she ran from the cabin.

J.J. followed her to the door and watched her run down the slope and past the wagon, to disappear into the trees lining the creek. Then, he turned to Frank and drew his pistol. "I don't see no trap door."

"There isn't one."

"What?" Slim looked around them at the floor. "No trap door? How do you get to the money?"

"I don't," was the mild reply. "I built the place over it. Didn't want to be tempted to get it. Use it."

J.J. frowned at him then suddenly grinned. "You're a strange bird, Frank. An outlaw suddenly goin' straight."

Frank shrugged. "It's been done before."

"Slim!" J.J. called out. "Go out to the barn. Find a shovel." The barrel of his pistol moved to cover Shelby. "Give it to the cub."

When the shovel was retrieved, and Frank figured it was a miracle it was still there, Shelby was sent under the cabin to dig. The other men stood around, watching the proceedings.

"Where is it?" J.J.'s pistol pointed at Frank's midsection hinted there should be a reply.

"Toward the back, about in the middle."

When Shelby went to the spot indicated, there was little room for him, let alone space for any digging.

The outlaw leader looked the place over. "Burn it," he said, simply.

Slim stared at him, then at Frank.

"Burn it," the outlaw leader said again.

"The Indians," Slim reminded him. "They'll see the smoke for miles."

J.J. cocked his pistol. "Burn it."

Slim ran to do his bidding, then the pistol wandered over to Frank. "Pascoe! Kindlin'!"

But, Frank was helping Shelby out from under the cabin. When he crawled out, the whole front of his shirt and pants were stained with dirt and sweat.

J.J. fired a warning shot. "I said, kindlin'!"

Frank turned to face him. There was a look on his face, as if he'd had enough, but the outlaw wasn't looking in his direction.

"Cub!" J.J. called to Shelby, changing the aim of his pistol. "You're not needed no more!"

And then, he pulled the trigger.

Yet, even as he spoke and fired, Frank said, "Get down," and stepped in front of the young man.

Shelby dropped to the ground as the older man half turned with the impact of the bullet. Yet, rather than falling, Frank turned once more to face J.J., this time with a pistol in his hand.

The outlaw stared; surprised at this turn of events and the fact that Frank Pascoe now had a gun. His mouth moved as if to speak, then he brought his pistol to bear and fired again, but his shot went wild. Seeing that it had no effect, he spun about to run down the slope just as Frank fired. Whether the shot was a hit or miss, the outlaw kept running.

At the cabin, Slim appeared on the porch, a pistol in his hand, surprised to see J.J. on the run. He drew his pistol and aimed at Frank who had gone down to one knee. Before either could shoot, a shot rang out and the thin man fell, face down.

"Bullet." Frank held out his hand to Shelby.

"What?" The young man stared at him.

"Plague bag."

Shelby jerked it from his neck, opened the pouch, found the bullet and handed it to him.

Though his chest heaved as if it was hard to breathe, Frank opened the cartridge door, flipped out the one shell and loaded the pistol again.

Shelby got to his feet, staring, shocked at the turn of events.

And then slowly, so slowly, Frank began to crumple, at first seeming to bow to the pain and then to roll to his side, his face to the sky.

"Don't!" It was the first thing that came to the young man's lips. "Don't go!" For without the thickset man's presence, it seemed that the world was going to be a very empty place.

Nancy got there as soon as she could, followed by a man with a thick black moustache carrying a rifle. When she came up to Frank, she dropped to her knees, her eyes going to the wound in his abdomen.

"Burn it," he said. His hand motioned to the cabin.

"All your hard work?" Nancy smoothed back his hair from his face.

"Burn it."

The man with the black moustache stood beside him, his shadow giving Frank some shade. "I stayed out of it, til I seen how it would go."

"You get Slim?"

"Yeah."

"J.J.?"

"You got him."

"Thought I might have missed," Frank grimaced.

"Slick piece of shootin'," said the man. "You got him as he turned. Here," and he pointed to his left side. "He was dead right then, but didn't know it."

Frank relaxed, seemingly satisfied.

"I'm sure sorry it had to end this way," there seemed to be genuine regret in the man's voice.

"Not over yet. Burn it."

"He wants us to burn the cabin," Nancy explained.

Shelby had come closer. "You can't get to the gold any other way."

The man with the black moustache turned to the young man. "I'm Tom Burnett, Texas Ranger."

"Shelby," the young man replied. "Shelby Sinclair. Deputy, Clark

County." He looked down at Frank. "I meant to bring him in. For the train robbery."

Burnett looked him up and down. "Looks like there's no need, now."

"He's that bad?" Shelby asked cautiously.

"He made a deal with the Rangers. Give up the money. Clear his name." He looked at Frank. "Jack's name. Whoever."

"No reward?" The young man sounded disappointed.

"There's one on him," Burnett said, curtly, nodding toward Slim. He had no patience for bounty hunters.

On the ground, Frank shook his head from side to side. "Don't." He took a breath. "We all have to . . . learn."

Burnett nodded and knelt down beside him to check the wound.

"Burn it," Frank repeated. The words were said with effort.

"What about the Indians?" Nancy asked. "Won't they see the smoke?"

Burnett looked at the cabin, then all around them. "They'll just figure someone else got to it before they did. They like using the corrals for their stolen horses and cattle. Won't miss the cabin."

Shelby brought hay up from the barn and scattered it around the cabin while Nancy dumped the last of the lamp oil on it and the walls. When they both left the building Burnett lit a match and tossed it onto the hay.

"How does it feel to see your past go up in smoke, Frank?" The Ranger asked, when he was once again outside and standing beside the prostrate man.

Nancy held Frank's head in her lap, while Evie and Stella sat on either side of him, each holding one of his hands. Shelby stood to the side; all eyes on the burning building.

"It feels good," Frank smiled at Stella, then looked at the empty plague bag and winked "It feels real good." His eyes met Nancy's. "Gettin' rid of the past." Slowly his eyes closed and the smile left his face.

"Wait!" Shelby hit his knees beside him. "I didn't tell him thanks!" His eyes met Nancy's. "For saving my life!"

She smoothed Frank's hair away from his face. "He knows."

Chapter
SIXTEEN

Since it was a Saturday and regardless of the command to vacate it, the streets of Denton were busy. Wagons rolled up and down the main street, while riders moved in and out, impatient of their slowness.

"Wait for me, Mama!" Stella called out, a peppermint stick in her hand. Already it was melting in her warm fist and smeared on her face. It was a glad day for her because her mother had relented and let her put away her crutch for the day.

Evie held her other hand while she considered the peppermint stick in her own fist. Would it be too child-like to eat it? What did young women do? Her eyes scanned the crowded boardwalk as they followed their mother.

They'd just gone up the steps at the hotel, when Nancy abruptly stopped and the girls walked up on either side of her. Shelby stood before them, saddlebags in hand.

"So. You're ready to go?" She asked the young man.

"Yes," he smiled. "Back to Ohio."

"You could always stay here. We'll need a good hand on the ranch."

Evie looked at him, hard, willing him to change his mind.

"I appreciate the offer," Shelby said. "But, there's some things I want to set right."

"Are you gonna kill Wynn Tucker?" Stella asked. "For trickin' you into chasin' Mr. Frank?"

Shelby laughed. "That's not done in the east. Maybe I'll run for office against him."

"Or turn in your badge," Evie put in. "So you can come West. For a fresh start." She grinned and tried to make it sound like she was joking, but she wasn't.

He walked down to where his horse stood tied to the hitch rail. Evie expressed concern that Angel was again a blinding white, while Stella stated that she wanted to ride behind him to the edge of town.

Nancy watched the byplay, noticing that Evie's eyes were telling more than her lips.

Behind her, two men came out of the hotel, one helping to support the other. He led the weaker man to a rocking chair.

"Excuse me, ma'am," a man, dressed in his best, stopped in front of Nancy.

She turned to face him as he pulled off his hat.

"My name is Horace Whittaker. I own the W Bar W. I've heard your story and well, I know this is sudden, but my wife passed away three months ago, leavin' me with two little ones. And, I was wonderin' if you'd do me the honor," he hesitated, then rushed on, "to be my wife."

For a moment, it seemed that the whole world had gone quiet. Then, Nancy spoke up.

"Mr. Whittaker, I am honored by your proposal, but I am sorry. I cannot accept it."

"I know it's sudden ma'am, but if you're gonna be in the area, perhaps you will reconsider." His eyes were kind and hopeful.

Nancy smiled. "You've done me a great honor and I appreciate it. However, the answer is still no."

Yet, as the man put his hat on and walked away, he did not seem the least bit downcast by her refusal. Instead, he smiled and seemed pleased with himself.

At the end of the porch, the man sitting in the rocker watched the byplay.

"I've often thought of doing the same thing."

"What?" Nancy looked at him in surprise.

"What he did," he nodded toward Whittaker's back as he strode down the street. "What the other men have done all along the way."

Nancy walked closer to him. "What's that?"

"Propose to you." Frank's eyes never left hers.

"Why didn't you?" There was a smile on her face.

Frank shook his head. "I never felt like I had the right." He looked at Shelby. "Not with the cub breathin' down my neck." His voice grew husky. "And, with other things to atone for."

"What about now?" She asked lightly. "Still feel that way?"

Frank smiled a little and shook his head. "Nope. I feel like a free man."

"How free?"

"Free enough to ask you to marry me."

Behind her, Evie and Stella bounced up and down, their hands clapping silently.

"What do you say?"

"I wouldn't be here without you," she said, slowly.

"You saved her life," Evie reminded him.

"I'd say that goes both ways."

"And I wouldn't have my girls without you."

Frank was silent, waiting.

"You broke jail," Nancy said, considering the facts.

"I did. But, it was for a good cause."

"You don't have a good record."

Evie stared at her mother.

"Not anymore," Tom Burnett spoke up. "Besides, he went to prison as Jack Davis, not as Frank Pascoe."

"He saved my life!" Shelby put in from where he sat his horse in the street.

It seemed that everyone on the porch was caught up in the drama going on before them. No one spoke and even the passing traffic seemed to grow quieter.

"I admit, I haven't been the most upright of men," Frank told her, his eyes never leaving hers. "I've run with a tough crowd and I've roughhoused with the best of 'em." He got to his feet and it was plain to see that he was still weak. "You'll just have to take my word for it that I have put aside those ways."

They looked at each other, and she tilted her head, gauging him.

"Well?" Evie asked her mother.

"A girl," she said, then corrected herself, "a woman, likes to hear somethin' more."

Frank nodded in agreement. "Something like, I love you?" His eyes met hers and it was as if they were the only ones in Texas. "I love you, Miss Nancy," he said simply. " And, if you say no to marryin' me, I'll wish that bullet had done a little more harm."

Evie looked from one to the other of them.

"You don't have to wish it," she admitted. "I love you will do," Nancy smiled but suddenly felt shy, though she was a grown woman.

He put a finger under her chin and lifted her face, but she held herself apart from him.

"There's one more thing."

"What's that?"

"You said God never did you any favors."

Frank nodded. "I did say that. But, I was wrong." He looked at Evie and Stella.

When she did not speak, he went on. "All I know is that God kept putting you and the girls in my way. In that store and in the river." He glanced at Evie and Stella, then back to their mother. "Then, of all barns for me to take refuge in, it was the one where you were camped out!" He shook his head, but he was smiling. "What were the chances? And then for you to decide it would be best for us to go west together; God had to have a hand in it."

"Whither you goest, go I also!" Evie put in her version of the Bible verse.

"Yes," said Frank. "Just like that."

But Nancy tilted her head down so that he could not see her face. "Can I trust you?" She whispered so that only he could hear.

"Yes," was the simple reply. "I will be kind to you. And gentle. And, I will listen when you want to talk and I will talk when you want to listen."

But still Nancy hesitated, resisting the pull of his nearness and the comfort of his presence. "I'm scared."

"Me, too," he said. "I don't know how all this will work, me bein' who I am. But, I know I will work hard for you and the girls. I will do all that I know to do to make you happy."

It seemed that the world quieted and everyone on the porch held their breath, their eyes on the couple at the end of the porch.

"Well then," she smiled at him. "What are we waiting for?"

Frank shook his head, but he was grinning. "I'm waitin' for a girl from the hills to stop talkin' so I can kiss her."

Nancy was silent and watched as he took off his hat. Then, he brought her close and kissed her, but the girls couldn't see because the way he held his hat blocked their view.

Behind her, Evie and Stella began bouncing up and down again. Then, the older girl took Frank's hand, Stella took her mother's and they put them together.

"We're home now, Stella!" Evie told her little sister.

"Home! Home!"

Nancy moved away from Frank, but kept his hand in hers. "We've come a long way, but we're home."

"Well folks, I wish you happiness," Shelby sat his horse, having watched the whole scene. "And I bid you adieu."

"The offer still stands," Nancy reminded him. "Come back out. You've always got a home with us."

Shelby looked at Frank.

"What she says goes," he smiled, then added, 'Cub."

Shelby threw him a glance then reined his horse around.

"You'll be back," Evie announced and pointed to her heart. "I know it."

Tom Burnett looked from Evie to Shelby. "Lord save you from a girl what's set her cap for you."

Whether the young man heard him or not, he waved to them, then kicked his horse to a trot and rode down the street.

"He'll be back," Evie stated. "He's just got to find the long way home."

At the railing, Frank drew Nancy to him. "Like me," he said. "I found the long way home."

Thank you for reading *The Long Way Home.*

Discover other titles by Langdon Pierce
available on Kindle, and in paperback on Amazon.com:

Heaven Bend Down

Pillars of Heaven

Hope of Heaven

Moultrie

The Salt Horses

The Benteen Brand

Weapon of Choice

Mrs. Dennison

Sam Dollar and the Santa Rita Rose

Connect with Langdon Pierce on Facebook
And on Twitter @langdonpierce12.

CPSIA information can be obtained
at www.ICGtesting.com
Printed in the USA
LVHW031059261122
734043LV00001B/9